THE POSSESSION OF URIEL

THE POSSESSION OF URIEL

SHIRLEY BASSETT

Copyright © 2021 by Shirley Bassett.

All rights reserved. No part of this book may be reproduced in any form or by any electronic or mechanical means, including information storage and retrieval systems, without permission in writing from the publisher, except by reviewers, who may quote brief passages in a review.

ISBN: 978-1-63821-644-5 (Paperback Edition)
ISBN: 978-1-63821-645-2 (Hardcover Edition)
ISBN: 978-1-63821-643-8 (E-book Edition)

Some characters and events in this book are fictitious. Any similarity to the real persons, living or dead, is coincidental and not intended by the author.

Book Ordering Information

Phone Number: 315 288-7939 ext. 1000 or 347-901-4920
Email: info@globalsummithouse.com
Global Summit House
www.globalsummithouse.com

Printed in the United State of America

THE POSSESSION OF URIEL

Our story starts with a small boy named Uriel. He grew up in Rawlins, Wyoming. He lived with his family, his mother Madison, his father Ethan and his little sister Destiny. Uriel was the older of the two siblings he was ten years old, and his little sister was eight. They grew up in a small but very old house on West Davis Street. The house itself was built well back in 1800's; it had three bedrooms, and one bathroom. Down the hall was the kitchen, a reading room and medium size living room. There was a basement but it was not finished, they just used it for laundry, and storing odd things that did not fit in the upstairs rooms. They did not have much furniture but what they had was in itself old. Ethan worked as a guard in the nearby Wyoming Frontier Prison which was located on West Walnut Street, not far away from their home.

Madison however did not work, she was a stay at home mother who looked after her two children, and seen to it that they went to school every day and that they had food to eat. Everyday Uriel and his sister Destiny would walk to school which was about three blocks away from their house, Madison was fine with the fact that they walked to school and from every day knowing they were safe.

One day at the age of twelve years old Uriel became very different, and withdrawn. He was not acting himself, and his family noticed it, this is his story of what happened to him as he got older.

CHAPTER 1

At the age of twelve Uriel became a different young man. He had a separate bedroom from his parents and his sister which was located at the end of the hallway, his sister's room was next door to his, then the bathroom and then their parents' bedroom. One night Uriel went to bed early, he did not want any dinner that day only to go to bed and be by himself. His mother begged him to eat something but all he did was yell at her in a very loud voice. Ethan just stared at him and pointing to his room he said go you just go to your room young man and stay there. Uriel almost ran to his room, and slammed the door behind him. The rest of the family sat in the kitchen and had their usual meal. Today Madison had made chicken, with vegetables and rice, and for dessert they had apple pie, which both Uriel and Destiny and Ethan loved. Destiny always wanted whipped cream on hers. Madison replied ok but you are going to get fat one day, then you won't be able to have any pie, she smiled at Destiny as she handed her a small plate with some pie and whipped cream on top. Ethan just took a regular slice of pie and smiled back at Madison, thank you was all he said to her. The family sat there in the kitchen and finished their meal. When dinner was over Destiny helped her mother to clean up the kitchen and wash the dishes and put them away. Since it was a school night Destiny had to go to bed early because it was hard for her to get up in the mornings to go to school, ok it is

8:00pm time for you to go to bed now Destiny Madison told her. Ok mother she said and off she went. Ethan and Madison sat in the front room area and listened to some radio news, they would always listen to the news before they went to bed. It was very late now when Madison looked up at the clock on the wall noticing it was after 10:00pm. Ok I am going to bed now she told Ethan, are you coming she asked him with a smile on her face? Yes I will be right behind you he told her, as he got to his feet and turning the radio off, and the lights off he turned and headed towards their bedroom.

Madison went into the bathroom to wash her face, brush her teeth and comb her hair, and then she went into their bedroom where she found Ethan waiting for his turn in the bathroom. As soon as he left the room Madison got underneath bed covers and waited for his return. Soon afterwards Ethan came into the bedroom and he got under the bed covers on his side of the bed and turned the lights out. He rolled over and kissed Madison good night on her forehead, and they fell off to sleep. The next morning Madison woke up first as she normally does at 7:00am and went about the house waking everyone else up. Ethan always got himself up and was in the shower by the time the children were up and dressed. By the time he was finished the children were still getting ready for school. Ethan swallowed a cup of coffee and grabbed some toast for his breakfast along with his lunch bucket, which Madison had prepared for him the night before and out the door he went kissing Madison good bye as he left the house. Madison was already dressed and helping the children to get ready for school. As they sat at the table having their breakfast Madison made sure she had made their lunches for them, which always or normally consisted of peanut butter and jelly sandwiches, along with some biscuits and always a piece of fruit, usually an apple or banana. Soon it was time for the children to leave for school so Madison made sure they were wearing their proper clothing and had their lunch buckets, and school books, leading them out the door and walking towards the school area just down the road from their house. After the children had left for school Madison sat down to have her coffee in silence at the table, just thinking about the day ahead. She also needed some breakfast so she took some cereal from one of the cereal boxes, poured it into a bowl, added some sugar and a little milk and sat down to eat it. When she was finished she got up and walked over to the sink and started washing the morning dishes, and cleaning up after breakfast. Today she thought she had a busy day doing some laundry and cleaning the house. After the kitchen area was cleaned up to her satisfaction, she went into the children's bedrooms to gather up their dirty clothes for the wash and of course picking up after them.

She entered Destiny's room first, and looking around seen everything thrown all over the room, she went about gathering up what she thought was the dirty clothes and putting them into a laundry basket she had brought with her, then started to tidy up her room, putting everything back where they should have been. She then cleaned her room, and upon leaving she took up her laundry basket leaving the room behind her, closing the door as she left. Next room down the hall was Uriel's room. As she entered she got this smell of something very stale lingering in the air, she did not recognize it but she went in anyways. She dropped the laundry basket on the floor and started gathering up Uriel's dirty clothes. She then started to clean up his room, even though his room was much messier than his sister's Madison knew that boys would be boys no matter what you told them. With this disgusted look upon her face she left his room a little cleaner than it was, taking the laundry basket with her, shutting the door behind her.

She then headed for the bathroom where she gathered up all the dirty towels and face clothes and dirty clothes that were lying on the floor and put them into the laundry basket. She started to clean the bathroom, toilet sink and bath tub, boy this room is always the dirtiest room in the house, no one knows how to keep it clean she thought to herself. When she was finished in the bathroom, she headed down the hallway to the master bedroom. She gathered up all the dirty clothes, and she even stripped the bed of the linens and threw them into the laundry basket, then she turned around and said to herself, wow I think this basket could not get any fuller, it is over flowing and it shall take me all day to do this laundry. She cleaned her room and leaving everything in its place left the room closing the door behind her.

As she was about to head to the kitchen area to gather up dirty laundry passing Uriel's room she thought she could hear this very strange noise or sounds like someone talking in a strange language. She put the laundry basket on the floor and walked over and opened the door to his room, once inside she saw nothing out of place and no one inside. This is strange she thought to herself and left his room closing the door behind her. She walked towards the laundry basket and picking it up, headed for the basement and towards the laundry machines. Once down in the dungeon as she called it, she turned the lights on, and started separating the clothes, when done she opened the washing machine and loaded in the white clothes and linens first, then she added some laundry soap and a little bleach, just a little extra cleaning power she thought, once done she closed the lid down and started up the machine. Madison then headed upstairs to the kitchen where she put some water into the tea kettle, and turning on one big burner, she sat down at the kitchen table to wait for the kettle to boil she needed a good hot cup of tea now. About ten minutes later the kettle was just whistling away, she got to her feet walked over to one of the cupboard and took out a big mug, and placing one tea bag into the cup she then added some of the boiling hot water from the tea kettle. She stirred the tea for a while until she was happy with the color of the tea, then she added a little milk. She then took up the mug and walked over to the kitchen table and sat down to sip on her tea while waiting for the laundry downstairs to finish.

Madison waited for about forty minutes then returned to the basement to find the first load of laundry was done, she took the wet clothes out of the machine and put them into the dryer, she walked back to the washing machine and put in the next load of clothes, adding a little soap, then closing down the lid and starting up the machine, each load takes about forty minutes to complete. She started up the dryer and timed it for about one hour, there she said out loud to herself, I shall return in about one hour. She then turned and went back upstairs to the kitchen and to the table where her tea was still quit hot, sitting there waiting for her. She sat down, resting and sipping on her tea until the one hour had come along. Oh my guess I must return to the basement and to my laundry, with that said she got up from the table and headed towards the basement where she went downstairs and over to the laundry area. She took the dried clothes out of the dryer and laid them into the basket, then turned and taking the wet clothes out of the washing machine, placed them into the dryer, closed the door and turned it on for about one hour she thought. She then put in to the machine the next load of clothes, this time only putting in some soap no bleach on coloured clothes she thought. She closed the lid down and started up the washing machine, wiping her hands off on her apron she then headed back upstairs to the kitchen where she sat down one again at the table. Madison looking up at the clock on the wall said to herself, oh my the children will be home from school soon, she sat there sipping her tea.

About fifteen minutes later the front door opened, Destiny was the first one in running towards the kitchen. Hi mom what can I have to eat I am really hungry she said looking into the refrigerator. Three seconds later Uriel came in Hi he said, then grabbed some fruit that was on the kitchen counter in a blue bowl and went off into his room as he usually did, not smiling or saying anything else. What a unusual child she said to herself. I wonder what is going on with him lately he has been acting very strange to say the least. Mean while Destiny grabbed some fruit from the bowl on the counter as well, looking at her mother said I am going to my room to do my home work. Ok Madison replied make sure you finish it all because I want to see it when you are done smiling at her daughter as she left the kitchen. About thirty minutes later Madison decided to go down into the basement and see to her laundry. When she reach the laundry machines she found that both had stopped, then she knew they were done their cycle. She then took all the dried clothes out of the dryer and put them into the laundry basket, then took all the wet clothes out of the washing machine and put them into the dryer, closing the lid and starting it up. There she said to herself, they will be finished within the hour then I can start supper. As she walked up the stairs she thought to herself, mm wonder what we shall have for supper today. When she reached the top, she then headed for her daughters room, and upon opening the door she said, here is your clean clothes, you can put them away please smiling at Destiny as she put the clothes on her bed. When she was finished she walked into her own bedroom then started to put you own clothes and Ethan's clothes away. When she was finished she then turned and headed for Uriel's room. As she approached she knocked on the door. Uriel its mom dear can I come in I have your clean clothes here. Come in was all he said, she opened the door to find Uriel sitting on his bed reading a book. She could not make out the title of the book so she started to put his clothes away. As she reached to open the closet door she thought she could smell something awful again and as the door opened it smelt like someone or something had died in there, she held her nose and said Uriel what is in this closet, it smells really bad.

She turned to look at her son whom didn't even answer her. Uriel she said only this time she spoke louder. He only looked up at her and said I don't know. Well you had better come and clean this up or I will get your father in here. Madison quickly turned and left his room closing the door behind her. Well, she said to herself there is definitely something wrong with that boy. She then headed to the kitchen where she decided to make a shepherds pie for supper. She started cooking and dinner was then put into the oven has it had to bake for about thirty minutes or so, she headed down to the basement to collect the rest of her laundry. When she reached the dryer she took out all the remaining clothes putting them into the laundry basket. She then left the basement turning off the lights as she headed upstairs. Once there she put the basket on the floor and went to check on supper. All was good she thought so she continued on to put the rest of the laundry away, which this time was mostly linens and towels, so she put them all away and went back to the kitchen. No sooner did she sit at the kitchen table when Ethan came home from work. Yelling out he said I am home Madison what's for supper? He headed for the kitchen where he found her at the table. Shepherds pie she replied it will be ready in half an hour. Ok Ethan replied placing his lunch bucket on the counter and heading for the living room where he turned on the television set and sat down. All of a sudden there was this very loud bang, it came from Uriel's room, Ethan ran to the door and pushed it open to find nothing wrong, his son was sitting on his bed with a book in his hands, he then stopped and looking up at his father said, what, what's wrong? What was that loud banging noise I heard he said looking very surprised? What noise Uriel replied I heard no noise. Ethan stood there scratching his head, he then turned and walked out of his room closing the door behind him. He then walked into the kitchen where he found Madison standing there at the table looking at him, well, she said what was the loud bang? Nothing apparently Ethan replied, I went into Uriel's room and there was nothing there.

Maybe we are hearing things that are not really there he said looking very surprised and awkward. Mmm Madison replied. Supper is almost ready I will set the table you go and wash your hands and call the children. Ok he replied then turned and left the room. Five minutes later Ethan and Destiny came into the kitchen and sat at the table for their supper. Where is Uriel Madison asked? I will go and get him Ethan replied getting up from the table and leaving the room. A few seconds later both Ethan and Uriel came into the kitchen where they both sat down and started eating their supper. All accept for Uriel, he just starred down at this plate pushed some beans around with his fork, then stood up and said, with his head to the floor I'm not hungry, then he turned and went back to his room where he slammed the door shut. I wonder what is wrong with that boy Ethan said. Yes Destiny replied he has been acting very strange at school to. Well in what way Madison replied? Well Destiny said he goes to class but then he's kicked out of the class because he throws things at his teacher he is sent to the office almost all of the time. MM Madison said I will have to call the school tomorrow and see what I can find out, why is he acting this way. I don't know replied Ethan but he had better straighten up and quick. The family finished supper, then Madison and Destiny cleared up the dishes. Destiny went to her room and said I am going to bed after I read for a while. Ok. Ok replied Madison. Madison went into the living room area and watched some Television with Ethan before they went off to bed.

CHAPTER TWO

It was 3:00am when Madison heard this terrible crying and moaning sound it startled her enough she sat up in bed and listened again. The sound was gone for a few seconds then it returned like someone turning a radio on and off. She sat there and looked towards her husband Ethan just lying there sleeping like a baby, mm she thought he didn't even wake up, he must really be tired, or maybe I was the only one who heard that sound. She sat there for a few more minutes listening. Then all of a sudden there was this very loud bang. She jumped out of bed waking her husband. He sat up what., what is going on he asked? I heard this very loud bang and and before that I heard this moaning sound she told him. Ethan just looked at her scratching his head. Are you having a bad dream or something because I don't heard anything he said. Madison starred back at him said, no I did not I Know I heard this strange sound and then this very loud bang. Ethan replied do you want me to go and have a look around the house? Yes, yes please I know I heard something. Ethan slowly got out of bed, Madison followed closely behind him and they looked everywhere about the house. Slowing peering into Destiny's room where they found her sleeping peacefully, and then Uriel's room, where the only thing they found was this very bad odour coming from under his bed. They slowly closed the door thinking oh, it's only his dirty clothes lying on the floor. Madison whispered I will have to talk to that boy in the morning about leaving his dirty clothes lying about. They continued throughout the house but found nothing, they went back to bed closing their door behind them. Well Ethan said, there is no one here, we checked everywhere, now go to sleep please. With that said they both got underneath the bed covers and feel off to sleep. The next morning Madison woke first, got out of bed, and headed for the kitchen where she put on the morning coffee, and started to make the lunch's for the children. Soon afterwards Ethan got up and came into the kitchen. I hope you're not having bad dreams or something he said and grinned at her pouring him a cup of coffee. No I am not and I know I heard strange noises last night. She picked up her coffee cups and headed towards the table, where she sat down and asked Ethan what he wanted for breakfast. Eggs and toast he replied. Ok she replied and walked over to the stove to prepare his breakfast. Just as he was about to enjoy his breakfast, Destiny came into the kitchen.

Morning she said what's for breakfast? What would you like Madison asked her? Mmm I'll just have cereal today mother because I have to get to school early today, I have to prepare for a test this afternoon. Ok Madison replied handing her the cereal box with the milk carton. Destiny poured herself some cereal and ate her breakfast. While at the table Madison asked her, Destiny did you hear any strange noises last night? No mom why do you ask? Oh no reason Madison replied, just asking. No mother, with that Destiny got up from the table, gathered up her school books and said, dad can you take me to school today please? She looked at her father and waited for a reply. Ok come on then. I have to run Ethan said to Madison, grabbing his lunch bucket and kissing Madison on the cheek as he walked past her, see you tonight have a good day. Destiny also kissed her mother on the cheek as she past good bye mother I'll see you after school. Ok good luck today Destiny I hope you pass your test. Madison smiled at both of them as they walked out the door towards Ethan's truck. Just after they left Uriel came into the kitchen. Good morning Madison asked him, how are you this morning she asked him? Uriel did not reply, did not even raise his head to look at her. I'll just have toast this morning he said. He walked over to the toaster placed some bread into the toaster and pushed it down and waited for it to pop back up again. When it did he buttered his toast, grabbed his school backpack, and went out the door not saying one word to his mother. Well bye Uriel have a nice day she said to herself. Madison grabbed herself another cup of coffee and sat down at the kitchen table. Looking outside into the morning sunshine while sipping her coffee, she thought to herself. I know I heard sounds and noises last night I just know I'm not going crazy. She pondered on that thought for quite some time, she soon found herself very hungry so she started to make herself some breakfast. Today she thought she would have some boiled eggs and toast, it is quick and very nourishing. After her breakfast was ready to eat she sat down at the table and started eating. When she was done eating she got up form the table and was about to go over to the kitchen sink to wash up the morning dishes when once again she heard this very loud bang. She stopped in her tracks. A few seconds later the loud bang came again over and over about four times before it finally stopped. By this time Madison had her hands covering her ears, she slowly let go and heard nothing, no more banging sounds. She lowered her arms and took in a deep breathe she was afraid to go about the house looking for something that was not there. She then continued on washing up the morning dishes. When she was finished she made herself a nice hot cup of tea and sat down at the kitchen table. Looking up at the clock on the wall she noticed it was about 11:00 am.

Well she said to herself guess I should do some cleaning and some house work, there is no one else around here to help me she giggled to herself and walked over to the broom closet beside the back door and took out a cleaning bucket, with mop and broom. She started to clean starting in the master bedroom, dusting down cobwebs and making her bed, putting away dirty and clean clothes that lie on the hamper. She then swept the floor and gave it a good mopping. When she was happy with her job, she continued on to Destiny's room. As she began picking up Destiny's clothes and papers from the floor area she said to herself, boy these children soon have to look after their own rooms I am getting tired of doing it for them, I can just imagine what Uriel's room looks like I might even be afraid to go into that room. Madison started to clean and tidy up Destiny's room, also dusting down cobwebs, and dusting off the furniture. Then she swept and washed the floor. When she was happy with the job, she walked down the hallway towards Uriel's room. She hesitated before opening the door to his room, with her shaking hand on the door knob she slowly opened the door. Once inside she could smell that awful odour again only this time it seemed to be getting worse. Once inside she started to pick up school books, papers. One in particular she noticed Uriel had drawn this awful looking person or thing, she could not make out which one it was, it was a tall dark black image of some thing or someone pointing a long finger at the door to his clothes closet and at the end of it's finger was this red-ish, orange colour it looked like fire. Madison dropped it to the floor and started cleaning up his room. She did not dust or take down cobwebs in here as she did in the other rooms, no she said to herself, Uriel can do that for himself. She then swept the floor area then moped it over and left his room closing the door behind her.

She then headed for the bathroom which was about halfway down the hall. This house only has one bathroom, good thing she thought to herself as she entered the bathroom, she looked around at the mess everyone else had left. This room was where she spent most of her time cleaning. As she scrubbed and scrubbed the bathtub, all of a sudden she thought, she could feel this hand laid on her right shoulder. Madison froze in her spot not wanting to move one inch. She could feel the fingers as they moved about her shoulder, she closed here eyes and waited. About what seemed to be forever in time the hand disappeared. Madison slowly got to her feet and quickly turned about, nope, no one was there, as if she was expecting to see someone standing behind her. By this time Madison was shaking in her boots, trembling with fear. She finished cleaning, yes in spite of what happened, and she left the bathroom,sparkling clean as always. She headed for the kitchen putting away the cleaning supplies. She made herself another cup of hot tea and sat down at the table. All the time thinking whatever should I do, should I call someone because Ethan does not believe me, Destiny does not believe either. She sat there for a while thinking it over and over in her mind. Finally she decided to call on her friend who lives just down the road. Her name was Agatha she might help me understand what is going. She walked to the telephone and dialed her number. It rang about fifteen times no reply, so Madison left a message for her to call Madison back when she returned home. Madison returned to the kitchen table where she sat down and waited. Looking up at the clock Madison found it to be 3:00pm oh the children will be home from school soon. I have not heard any more sounds coming from Uriel's room so maybe it is ok now, maybe it was just my imagination, yes that is what it was.

   Madison went into the bathroom to freshen up and comb her hair. As she was leaving the bathroom she thought she could hear this growling sound, like a dog was behind her and was about to attack, again Madison froze, she waited until she could no longer hear the sound and quickly left the bathroom on her way to the kitchen. Ok that's it she thought now I know I am hearing things. She sat at the kitchen table waiting for the children to return from school. About twenty minutes later Destiny came running through the door, Hi mom yes I past my test, going to my room now ok. Oh yes ok Madison replied and good work keep it up please Madison smiled at her daughter as she fled past her heading for her room. Shortly thereafter Uriel came in through the door, still with his head low looking towards the floor he said Hi mom as he past her and kept going and went straight to his room slamming the door behind him. Well, Madison thought, isn't he a pleasant one I wanna know what is going on with him, how do I find out she asked herself. Madison sat at the kitchen table reading the morning mail which just came through the slot in the front door. Boy even the mail man is late today. As she looked through the mail she came across two bills, one was for electricity, oh my she said, so expensive, this one is for $25.00, and the other one was the heating bill, this one was $9.95 this one was ok she thought. Madison put them aside and looked through the rest of the mail which was only junk, like magazines and such. After finding nothing interesting to her she put all the "junk mail" into the trash bin and made herself another cup of hot tea. She sat at the table when Destiny came into the kitchen, hey mom what can I snack on until supper? Well we have some fruit over there on the counter she said try some it's good for your health then she smiled at Destiny. Destiny took a apple and some grapes I think this will do she said and went back into her room.

Tomorrow Madison thought I will do some baking for the children, make some cookies and cakes I know they are hungry when they get home from school. Madison decided to make some fried chicken, with rice and vegetables for dinner today. She took some chicken out of the freezer and started thawing them out ready for cooking. Shortly thereafter Ethan came through the door. Hi sweetheart how was your day he asked Madison? Well she started to tell him what happened but then she stopped. Oh no you are hearing voices again he said and smiled at her as he past her and walked over to the refrigerator, looking for a nice cool beer to have before dinner. Madison smiled back at him and said.. oh no I thought I heard something but it was nothing, nothing at all. Well alright then Ethan said and went into the living room, sat down in the big comfy chair and turned on the television to the news channel. He sat there until dinner was ready, this was his normal thing to do once he got home from work. Madison knew he had long hard working days so she just let him. I will let you know when dinner is ready she said to him. Ethan just raised his arm and waved back at her as if to say ok dear. Madison was busy in the kitchen cutting up the chicken into pieces and preparing the vegetables. She coated the chicken which she cut into slices with first some seasoning, then dipped them into an egg mixture, then coated them in this bread crumbs. She then placed into a large pan with oil covered bottom, then turning on the oven she covered the chicken pieces with foil and closed the oven door. She thought to herself this will take about one hour to cook, just to be sure the chicken is cooked all the way through.

She then started to cook the vegetables and then the rice. When that was all done and was cooking on the stove top, she took out some salad vegetables from the refrigerator and made a big bowl of garden fresh salad. Family loves salads she thought. Madison put four kinds of lettuce in the bowl all washed and ripped apart, she then cut up some peppers of three different co lours, green, red and yellow, all sweet of course, then she cut up some cucumbers, then washed and cut up some tomatoes and after tossing everything in the bowl she placed the bowl in the refrigerator, to keep cool until dinner was ready. About forty five minutes later the timer on the stove went ding ding telling her that the chicken was cooked. She took the chicken out of the oven and turned the oven off, resting the pot of chicken on the stove top to keep it nice and hot. She checked the vegetables and the rice and all seemed to be cooked and ready for eating. She had already set the table so she took a big platter from one of the cupboards and placed the chicken on it and arranged all the vegetables around it, then in another bowl she placed the rice. She set all of the dinner on the table and returned to the refrigerator to take out the salad which she placed on the table as well. After arranging everything she called everyone to dinner. Ethan came in from the living room, Destiny came in from her room, but there was no sign of Uriel. Uriel she called again and again. Ethan stood up and went to his room and opened the door, having a whiff of this terrible odour. Uriel come for dinner right now he demanded. Uriel came out of his room and walked past his father into the kitchen where he just ignored everyone. Madison had everyone sit down and take what they wanted, in the mean time she looked straight at Uriel noticing that all around his eyes it seemed to dark in colour, like he hadn't slept for years. Uriel what is wrong with you, Madison grabbed his arm and shook him. Uriel snapped his arm back and said nothing is wrong leave me alone. Just leave me alone. He grabbed some food and took his plate back to room where he slammed the door shut again, this time shaking the whole house. What is wrong with that boy Madison Ethan asked her? I don't know Ethan he has been acting strange for the past few weeks now and still fighting at school too Destiny added.

I will have to have a talk with him after we have our meal Ethan replied. The rest of the family sat and finished their meal. Destiny got up and took her dishes over to the sink and as she past her mother she said, thank you mother that was a very good meal. Thank you dear Madison replied. When everyone else was finished Ethan went back to the living room, he waited for a few minutes then decided to go in and visit his son and see what he could find out while Madison cleared and washed the dishes and put everything away. She then walked into the living room where she sat down. She waited for Ethan to return, he finally came in from Uriel's room with this disgusted look upon his face. Well Madison asked, what did you find out she asked? Nothing he replied, the boy is just… what can I say, out to lunch !!! The parents sat there for a while watching some television then decided to go off to bed. Ethan walked around the house making sure all the doors and windows were locked and secured and turning off all the lights as he went, both Ethan and Madison headed towards their room. Ethan went off towards the bathroom first and then when he was done, Madison took her turn. Once the both of them were in their pajamas and under the bed coverings they laid there for a while just thinking about the day. I thought you were going to find out what is up with Uriel after diner Madison said. Oh well I can not talk with him, tomorrow I will try again he said, now go to sleep I have a very busy day tomorrow he replied, then kissed his wife good night and turned off the lights. Again it was 3:00am exactly when Madison was waken by this strange sound. It was the sound of a group of people talking all together yet their sound was muffled like they were miles away but yet they were not. Madison slowly sat up in her bed listening and wondering, should I get up and have a look or should I not??? Then there was this loud bang and knocking. And with that Ethan jolted up what, what is that he asked? He looked around even though he was half awake and half asleep rubbing his eyes to see better. Madison replied, do you believe me now when I say I am hearing things she asked? Ethan did not reply, they both sat there listening intensely, soon the banging and sounds stopped. They both sat there for a while and when nothing else was heard they both went back to sleep.

CHAPTER THREE

The next morning Madison woke first as usual and after getting dressed she headed for the kitchen to make breakfast and lunches for everyone. She made sandwiches for everyone, today it was ham and cheese on white bread. She also packed some candy and some fruit for everyone, then packed up the lunches leaving them on the kitchen counter by the door so they could grab them easily when they went out the door. About fifteen minutes later Destiny came into the kitchen, what's for breakfast she asked looking at Madison, how about some boiled eggs and toast with some juice. Madison looked at Destiny whom agreed. Madison placed breakfast down in front of Destiny, and waited for the rest of the family to come into the kitchen. Ethan came in next ok I'll have what she's having looking right at Destiny, good morning daughter how are you this morning he asked? Destiny replied I am fine dad going to school soon she replied. Oh good Ethan said, Madison placed his breakfast down in front of him, along with a cup of hot coffee. Then she poured herself a cup of coffee and sat down at the table waiting for the arrival of Uriel. About fifteen minutes later he showed his face in the kitchen. He looked at everyone and said good morning. Everyone looked at him with a very surprised look upon their faces. Uriel looking back said, what, what is wrong with everyone can't a guy say good morning to his family? He looked very perturbed, ate his breakfast, got up and said bye gotta go to school and he left. Well said Ethan at least he's talking to us, yes in deed replied Madison. Well Destiny said, off to school for me, after kissing her mother on the cheek she left. Ethan got up from the table, grabbing his lunch bucket, kissed his wife good bye and he left. Madison was left all alone once again, sitting at the kitchen table sipping her coffee. She finally got up from the table and started cleaning up the breakfast dishes and mess.

After putting everything away in it's place, she decided to put the kettle on and make herself a cup of nice hot tea. She sat at the table waiting for the kettle, when it was boiling, she walked over to the stove, turned it off and made herself a cup of hot tea. Madison sat down at the table, about twenty minutes later the telephone rang, Madison walked over to the phone and picked up the receiver, Hello she said, oh hello this is Agatha I am returning your call she said. Oh hello my dear friend how are you doing Madison asked her? Oh I am not too bad and how are you and everyone over there? Well, Madison replied, we have run into a small I think, problem. You know my son Uriel, well he has been acting very strange lately, and getting into trouble at school, throwing things at the teachers, getting fights. At night here the rest of us are starting to hear strange noises coming from his room. This all happens at exactly 3:00am every night. I thought maybe you might have some idea of what is going on with him Madison asked. Well replied Agatha, maybe I should come over for dinner one day, sit with you and the family and see what I can find out, if anything she told Madison. If I find something wrong I can not do anything about it but I think I might have a friend who can help. Oh ok replied Madison when can you come over? How about tomorrow, what time is dinner at your house Agatha asked? How about 5:00pm Madison replied, we'd love to have you for dinner it's been a while hey. Yes Agatha replied, I shall see you tomorrow then. Ok replied Madison until then you take care good bye for now and with that Madison hung up the telephone. Well Madison thought to herself maybe we can figure this out and stop all this nonsense. She then turned around and sat back down at the table sipping on her very hot tea. Today Madison thought she would tend to her garden outside in the backyard. Madison had always loved gardening especially with flowers not vegetables. She got up from the table and went into her bedroom to change into something she called gardening clothes, which consisted of old blue jeans and an old t-shirt. She then headed outside to the backyard. In the backyard there was a small wooden shed, just outside from the back door about three feet to the left, she walked over to the door opened it and went inside where all the gardening tools and shovels were kept. She picked up a small hand tool it looked like a claw, it was made of medal so it would not bend too easily. The ground here was very very hard for digging, so she would need this small hand tool. She grabbed this tool and a pad to kneel on while digging in the dirt. She turned and walked out to the flower bed. She had several on the go, one which was along the back of the house and one along the right side of the house. She was about half way through weeding the flowers at the back of the house, she stood up to straighten out her legs and have a stretch, She walked to the far back of the yard, which was about fifteen feet, and all fenced in, looking around she turned to walk back to the house, looking up at the house she thought she could see a figure standing in the window of Uriel's room. His bedroom window faced the back yard, while the rest of the rooms faced west. She stood there for a moment, shut her eyes and opened them again, nothing she could see nothing this time, wow she thought I must be going crazy now I am seeing things that are not there. She shook her head and headed for her garden to continuing the weeding. Madison had finished weeding this garden, so she got to her feet and headed for the flower bed at the side of the house. When she reached the other side she noticed that some kinda of animal had dug up some of her flowers, as she approached she said to herself, well, I wonder what did this. Upon inspecting it further she noticed it was small holes. Oh she said to herself, it is only squirrels they are starting to bury their nuts for winter already, but do they have to pick on my flower bed? MM what can I use to stop them from digging up my flowers she thought, standing up she scratched her head giving it some thought. Well I have no idea she said to herself.

She finished her weeding, and returned the tools to the small shed. She headed in doors to wash up before everyone got home, and change her clothes. She got inside and headed for her room where she changed her clothes, and walked back into the kitchen. Looking up at the clock noticed it was 4:00pm, well children should be home soon, if not they are late today. She made herself a cup of hot tea and sat at the table wondering what to make for supper today. She decided pork, beans, and soup. She took the pork out of the freezer and starting thawing it out. She headed for the pantry looking for some beans to have with the pork, and find some soup. Today she did not have time to cook her own home made beans, or home made soup, because usually she would work all day long making her own home made beans and soup. She spent too much time outside today doing the gardening. She found a large can of beans with molasses and a big can of cream of potato soup. She took both cans over to the stove where she opened them into pots. By this time the pork had thawed out,so she took out a large frying pan, placed some cooking oil inside and the pork and started cooking. As the pork was cooking she sat at the kitchen table waiting for everyone to arrive home. Shortly after she heard strange noises coming from Uriel's room, she thought she would be brave today and go and have a look. Without hesitation she walked over to Uriel's room and opened the door. Nothing she looked around and saw nothing, nothing out of place and nothing strange., but the odour was still there. I will get to the bottom of this strange happenings I swear she thought and left Uriel's room closing the door behind her and went back into the kitchen and checked on dinner which was still cooking on low heat on the stove. About twenty minutes later Destiny came in through the door Hi mom, I will do some homework until dinner is ready. She smiled at Madison as she walked past her heading for her room. Ok replied Madison.

Madison attended to dinner which was still cooking, she turned the heat on for the beans and the soup and waited. Ten minutes later Ethan came home. Hi love what's for dinner today it smells good whatever it is, when will it be ready he asked? Oh about forty-five minutes she replied as Ethan walked past her and went into the bedroom to change his clothes. He then headed for the TV room and turned it on to watch the news of the day. Uriel also came home and of course headed straight for this room slamming the door behind. Uriel yelled out Ethan what is wrong with you, Uriel, but no reply. Ten minutes later, as Madison was setting the table, she called out dinner is ready. She then started pouring out the soup first into the bowls she placed at the table, also was the bread she had cut up and placed in the middle of the table, as she was just finishing up pouring out the soup and placing the pot on the counter, she turned to find everyone had come to the table for dinner even Uriel. She then placed out the pork and the beans on each plate. When she was finished she sat down at the table herself, where everyone started eating. Ethan was the first to speak up, well he said how was everyone's day? Destiny replied first, well I past my test today got "A" plus. Well that is good news Ethan replied. Uriel how about you. He just looked up at his father and said it was ok I did not get into trouble today, well that is also very good. Madison he looked over her way how about you, how was your day? Madison replied, same as usual nothing out of the ordinary she said looking up at Ethan with a funny look on her face like I'll tell you later. Oh ok good. When everyone was done eating, Ethan headed for the TV room to watch some TV, Uriel went off to his room while Destiny as always helped her mother in the kitchen to clean up after dinner and putting the dishes away. When they had finished in the kitchen, Destiny went off to her room while Madison headed for the TV room to sit beside Ethan. What was that look for at dinner he asked her? Well I called a friend of mine today who is coming over for dinner tomorrow, maybe she can help us figure this out, also she hesitated, I was outside doing some gardening, I stopped for a minute, stood up to straighten out my legs, walked to the far back fence, and when I turned about to head back to my garden I looked up and thought I saw a figure, standing in the window of Uriel's room. Ethan replied, what, what did this figure look like he asked? Well Madison replied, I don't know exactly, he just looked like a dark tall figure of a person, I could not make out a face or anything, I looked away for a moment then looked back and it was gone, so I thought I was just seeing things that aren't there she said smiling at Ethan. Well Ethan replied that is strange, we both know that there is no one else living in this house, I hope your friend can help us out tomorrow or at least suggest something we can do hey he replied. What is her name again he asked Madison? Her name is Agatha, she said if she can not help us she knows of someone who can, we shall see tomorrow Madison said. Well Ethan said, I am very tired let's go to bed I have a early day tomorrow, ok Madison replied. They both got up Madison heading for the bathroom before Ethan got there, while Ethan went about the house making sure all was locked up and secure and shutting off the lights.

When he was finished he headed for the bathroom, where Madison had finished and gone to their room. Ethan got finished in the bathroom and laid down beside Madison, hugging her and giving her a kiss, good night lets sleep well tonight ok hopefully no noises shall wake us this time. He smiled at Madison and turned over going to sleep instantly as Madison turned the lights off and fell asleep as well. Sure enough it was 3:00am again when Madison was awaken by a strange noise coming from Uriel's room, even before she got up out of bed she knew it would be coming from Uriel's room, as she was about to get out of bed she heard this crying sound like a child crying for its mother, it got louder and louder. Madison placed her feet out of bed and onto the floor, moving slowly she walked out towards Uriel's room, with every foot step the hairs on the back of her neck stood straight up, as did the hairs of her arms as she started rubbing her arms to keep warm. Hugging herself she drew closer and closer to Uriel's room. Before knocking on the door she noticed this bright reddish/white light coming from under the door, she hesitated should I go in or should I go back. She hesitated and was about to back away when the door suddenly flew open and Madison saw the room had been filled with a heavy smoke like cloud. She turned around quickly and ran back to her own room awaking Ethan. Ethan she said Ethan wake up as she shook him. What he said what is wrong? Come Madison said come and look for yourself. Madison pulled Ethan out of bed and in his bare feet she dragged him to Uriel's room, where five feet from the door he could see the heavy cloud of thick smoke. Rubbing his eyes he said, what

, what is going on. He started to go inside Uriel's room when all of a sudden the door to his room slammed shut. Both Ethan and Madison stood there dumb founded. Let's go back to bed Ethan said they both turned around and headed back to their room, once inside Ethan closed the door they both got back into bed pulling the covers up, hanging onto one and other. As time past they both fell off to sleep. Nothing else happened during the night the house remained silent. The next morning Madison woke as usual, getting up out of bed, went into the bathroom, washing up and combing her hair. She then headed into the kitchen to put on the kettle and make breakfast. She never thought any more about what happened last night, the thoughts just disappeared. For the lunches today she thought she make everyone ham and cheese again because everyone seemed to like them, along with some candy and fruit.

Today she would do some baking she thought. Just as she was about to start on breakfast Destiny came into the kitchen, what is for breakfast she asked? I don't really know Madison replied looking at Destiny she asked, what would you like? Mmm how about some pancakes they are nourishing and very good Destiny replied smiling at her mother. Ok Madison replied pancakes it is, coming right up. As the pancakes was cooking, Madison asked Destiny did you hear anything last night, did anything wake you up? No Destiny replied, no why do you ask? Oh I was just wondering Madison replied, then placed the stack of pancakes on Destiny's plate, here you go enjoy she said. Thanks mom. As Destiny was enjoying her breakfast, Ethan came into the kitchen good morning everyone he said smiling at both Destiny and Madison. Good morning dad Destiny replied. Madison asked him, pancakes for breakfast? Why yes he replied then I must go, got to be at work early today we are just loaded with work, we might even have to work late today hope you don't mind, I will call if we are working late he said to Madison. Oh ok she replied placing the stack of pancakes on a plate in front of him, here eat your breakfast, also placing a cup of coffee beside his plate. When both Destiny and Ethan had finished their breakfast placing their dirty dishes in the sink, Ethan then grabbed his lunch bucket, kissed Madison and said good bye see you later. Good bye replied Madison remember Agatha is coming for dinner today, if you are late I will just explain it to her not to worry Madison said as Ethan was leaving. Destiny had yet another twenty minutes before she had to leave for school, sitting at the kitchen table drinking her orange juice reading a book. Just then Uriel came into the kitchen, do you want some pancakes Madison asked him? No got no time he replied got to go, he grabbed his lunch and left. Your brother has been very very strange this past few weeks Madison said looking at Destiny, yea I know Destiny replied don't know what's up with him. Well I must go now Destiny said picking up her lunch and heading out the door good bye mom see you later. Good bye Destiny have a good day Madison replied. Once again Madison found herself alone in the kitchen left to clean up. After cleaning up the dishes, Madison put the kettle on to make herself a cup of hot tea. Once the kettle had boiled Madison made her tea and sat at the table. Well she thought to herself what should I make for dinner today with Agatha coming. She thought for a while then decided on a good beef roast, with roasted potatoes, vegetables and salad, yes that is what we shall have. With that thought she walked over to the freezer and took out a good size roast of beef, placing it on the kitchen counter to thaw out. Let me see Madison said to herself, I shall put that roast on about 3:00pm and we shall have dinner early like 6:00pm. In the mean time think I will do some cleaning around here just so Agatha doesn't think I don't clean, after all it is quite dusty around here. When Madison had finished her tea, she went about cleaning the house, dusting down all the cob webs she could find, dusty off the furniture, and even cleaning the bathroom again just to be sure. Then she vacuumed all the carpets and swept and mopped all the floors, I just want this house to be clean when Agatha gets here she said to herself.

Looking up at the clock on the wall she noticed it was time to put the roast on for dinner. She took out the roasting pan, placed some cooking oil in the bottom and placed the roast itself on top, and placed the lid on top of that, then placed it in the oven, where the oven had reached it's proper temperature of 375 degrees, there she said closing the oven door, it should be ready at 6:00pm. With that done and dinner cooking she decided to make herself some lunch. She decided on soup with biscuits. When the soup was heated she placed some in a bowl, and placed it on the table along the biscuits. She then sat down and had her lunch. Mmm she thought to herself I've been home all morning and nothing has happened, wow maybe it has stopped already she thought. She sat and had her lunch and sipped her tea she had made for herself. Sitting there Madison decided to do some baking tomorrow she would have more time then. Well think I am ready for Agatha's company, everything is clean, and dinner is in the oven cooking, yes I will be ready she said to herself with a smile on her face. Madison had heard nothing today coming from Uriel's room, nothing at all, but she was going to tell Agatha all about what was happening and see what Agatha had to say about this situation. Well 5:30pm came along so Madison decided to get the vegetables ready, and as she was washing and peeling them, there came a knock to the front door. Oh she thought that must be Agatha wiping her hands on her apron, Madison went to answer the front door. Upon opening the door there stood her best friend, so nicely dressed Madison thought, oh hello Agatha, please, please come in and make yourself to home. How are you Madison asked her? Oh I am fine and how are things over here Agatha asked? Well still the same Madison replied, come into the kitchen sit down here and I'll make us some tea. Agatha and Madison made they way towards the kitchen where Agatha sat down at the table while Madison prepared some tea.

Nice and hot Madison handed Agatha a nice hot cup of tea here you are my friend, but be careful it is quite hot Madison said smiling at Agatha. Ok Agatha replied. Dinner shall be ready for 6:00pm hope that is ok with you Madison asked her? Oh yes that will be fine. Soon my children will be home from school Madison said, but Ethan might be a little late said he had to work late today they are very busy at work. Oh I am sorry if I have to miss him Agatha said, I was looking forward to seeing him again too she said. Ten minutes later Destiny came in, oh hello Mrs. Downing how are you doing, I am fine, glad to have you over for a change, we don't get much company Destiny said. Oh I am fine thank you Destiny, oh how big you got since last time I saw you, Agatha smiled at Destiny. Madison said, they don't stay small forever smiling at Agatha. About five minutes later Uriel came in the door. He stopped in his tracks when he saw Agatha, oh Hi he said who are you he asked? Madison piped up this is Agatha my best friend she will be staying for dinner. Oh Uriel replied and went straight to his room slamming the door behind him. Well he seems like a normal child Agatha said looking at Madison with a surprised look on her face. Really, Madison said, really?? Agatha just looked at her. I have to finish making dinner here Madison said you just make yourself to home until it is ready ok. Ok replied Agatha, do you mind if I look around a bit I haven't been here for a long time. Oh yes go ahead and I will let you know when dinner is ready replied Madison. With that said Madison went back to her vegetables and placed them on the stove to cook while Agatha had a look around the house. About thirty minutes later, the roast was cooked so Madison took it out of the oven and was preparing the gravy when Agatha walked into the kitchen, oh may I help here she said to Madison. Oh no you just rest there you are company and company does not help cook dinner, Madison smiled at Agatha. Madison went about finishing dinner, she made the gravy, placed it in a bowl, and sit it aside, She started to cut up the roast and place it on a platter. She then placed the cooked vegetables out and in a bowl and placed everything on the table. Agatha you can set the table how about that Madison smiled at Agatha, ok she replied. Madison pointed to the cupboards, plates and glasses over there, cutlery in that second drawer Madison told her. When the table was set and the food set out Madison called everyone to dinner. While they sat having their meal, no one said anything. Destiny looked up and said nice job mom dinner tastes very good, no lumpy gravy either she smiled at her mother. Hey hey Madison said I never make lumpy gravy, with that everyone laughed , except Uriel who just went on eating his food got up from the table and went straight to his room. Well said Madison that was really rude. No no don't worry about that he is fine Agatha replied let him go. All three girls sat there for a while just talking, all of a sudden Destiny got up and said, ok I am off to my room I have home work I got to finish. It was nice to see you again Mrs. Downing and she smiled as she left the room. Ok good bye Destiny I shall be leaving soon to go home.

    After Destiny had left and the two woman sat there Madison asked her, what do you think, is there anything strange in this house ? Agatha hesitated for a while then said, well I do feel something terrible is happening here, I don't know what it is. But to be sure maybe I should bring a friend of mine over, she is very helpful in these situations, she is a clairvoyant, she can help, I shall call her when I return home. Guess I should get going it is getting late Agatha said. Well ok Agatha, it was very nice of you to come for dinner, hopefully your friend can help us out, you will call and ask her? Yes I will Agatha replied I will call you when I get her on the phone and bring her over. Ok replied Madison. Ok I will, with that Agatha headed for the front door, the two women hugged and said good bye, I shall call you Madison, don't worry about it, things will turn out just fine Agatha said, then walked out the door. Madison waved at her as she left the house and walked down the street. Madison walked back into the kitchen, she cleaned up whatever mess was left, as she was just finishing up Ethan walked into the house. Hi sorry I was so late he said guess I missed dinner hey? Yes you did Madison replied, but I prepared a plate for you I will warm it up for you, go wash up and I'll put it out for you. Ethan walked off, cleaned up, changed and came back into the kitchen where Madison had prepared a warm plate of dinner for him. As he sat down to eat it, so did Madison. Well what did you friend Agatha have to say today he asked her? Well, she said that she could feel something terrible here so she is going to ask another friend of hers to come over and help us out. I just have to await to hear back from her Madison replied. Oh ok Ethan said as he finished his meal. It was already getting pretty late so Madison headed for the bathroom as Ethan went about locking all the doors, securing the house and shutting off all the lights. When he was done he headed for the bathroom as Madison had finished and gone to bed. When he was finished he came into the bedroom changed into his pj's and slid under the covers. Well that was a very long day indeed he said to Madison, and tomorrow I believe will be yet another one, I'm afraid I won't be home again until late much like today. That is ok Ethan I'm sure I'll survive without you, as she giggled and nestled in beside him. Soon afterwards they both fell asleep.

It was 3:00am once again when Madison was awoken by this strange unnerving sound, coming from down the hallway. This time it started to hurt her ears as she listened intensely. Not standing it any longer she got up out of bed, slipped into her slippers and started down the hall, but before she got six feet from Uriel's door, she felt like the floor under her feet was sinking, like she was in quick sand, she tried pulling herself out but was unsuccessful, she tried calling out to Ethan screaming his name, over and over. He finally made an appearance and saw Madison knee deep into the wooden floor, he could not believe his eyes, thought he was dreaming, he slowly walked towards Madison who was still screaming and holding out her arms trying to grab Ethan, slowly he approached her and laying on his belly on the floor caught Madison's arms and started pulling her out of the floor. The harder he pulled, the deeper Madison seem to sink, he pulled harder and harder almost pulling his arm out of its socket, the floor gave way and let go of Madison, like it didn't want her any more. Ethan slowly pulled her towards him, once she was out he hugged her like she was dying or something, but soon let go, and they got to their feet. Arm in arm they went back to their bedroom, not really knowing what had just happened. Ethan spoke first, what, what is God's name was that all about? Madison replied, with a nervous voice, I, I don't know but I don't want to do that again, if anything like this happens tomorrow night I will definitely stay in bed with you, I will NOT leave my bedroom. Come on Ethan replied lets go back to bed. They got into their room closing the door behind them where they got under the covers, holding each other finally fell asleep. The next morning Madison woke up first as usual, she went into the bathroom, washed her face, brushed her teeth, combed her hair, and leaving the bathroom headed for the kitchen. She immediately put the kettle on to make the morning coffee. When the kettle had boiled she made the coffee and thought, what should we have for breakfast. Just then Destiny came into the kitchen good morning she said, what's for breakfast ? What would you like this morning Madison asked? Mmm maybe just cereal and juice Destiny replied. So she went to the cupboard took out a bowl and poured herself some cereal. Madison spoke up did you hear anything last night she asked? Well no why did something happen Destiny asked with a smile on her face?

No oh no I was just asking Madison replied. Just then Ethan came into the kitchen poured himself a cup of coffee and asked the same question, what can we have for breakfast this morning smiling at Madison? We are just having cereal today Madison replied, what kind would you like she asked him? Maybe I'll have oatmeal, can you whip me up some quickly he asked as he sat and sipped his coffee. Madison quickly made some oatmeal enough for two, she thought she would join him. About three minutes later she poured some out into a bowl and handed it to Ethan, here you are Madison said with a smile on her face. Ethan sat and ate his breakfast as did Destiny and just as they were finishing up, Uriel came running into the kitchen, all he said morning everyone, grabbed his lunch and left the house. He does not even take the time to sit and have breakfast with us anymore Ethan said to Madison, yes I know she replied. Destiny had finished up, set her dishes into the kitchen sink and said, well good bye folks off to school for me I'll see you later she smiled as she left the house. I hope your friend Agatha can help us out, this is just getting ridiculous Ethan said as he walked towards the door picking up his lunch as he did so. Good bye Madison he said as he kissed her on the cheek I'll be home regular time tonight I hope, with that he waved his hand and left the house. Madison was left there sitting at the kitchen table alone once again. Madison must have sat there for a good three hours when all of a sudden she heard the telephone ring. She walked over to the phone and picking it up said Hello.

A few seconds later Agatha said hello my dear friend how are you this morning she asked? Well a bit shaken from last night but we are all fine. Agatha replied, tell me what happened? Madison started telling her of the events from last night. We just could not believe what we saw, even Ethan was stunned. What should we do Agatha Madison asked? Well my friend can not come by until tomorrow her name is Madam Ashley of Blairsdale. It is a three hour drive for her to get here. She will come by about 1:00pm tomorrow afternoon and I will meet her at your house. Will this be suitable for you Agatha asked? Oh my yes Madison replied that sounds great, I can't wait to meet her and oh thank you ever so much my dear friend hopefully she can help us because I am my wits end now I have no idea of what will happen tonight, it seems every night about 3:00am something always happens. What is it about 3:00am Madison asked? Well I believe they call it the witching hour, with that Agatha started giggling. Most people believe that the ghosts and deviled people come out at that particular time to haunt people whom they think are being a bother to them and want them out of their way. Oh my Madison replied, I am really getting concerned now, is there anything I can do to help prevent anyone from getting hurt at that time? Well no not exactly Agatha replied, all you can do until my friend and I get there, is just stay in your room, no matter what you hear or think you hear. Just stay way from Uriel's room, ok. Well ok replied

Madison but I feel like I should be doing something. No replied Agatha just sit tight no matter what you hear, also tell Ethan the same, do not go into Uriel's room again, especially at that time. Ok replied Madison, until tomorrow then and the two women hung up the telephone. Madison went and made herself another nice hot cup of tea and sat down at the kitchen table. Oh my Agatha has me very scared now she said to herself. Well I shall just do as she asked now for. With that thought she decided to make herself some lunch as she was getting hungry now.

She decided on some soup and a sandwich. Cream of potato soup which she poured from a can into a pot on the stove and heated it up. mmm what kinda sandwich shall I have today she thought. Grilled cheese, yes that is it. Madison went to the refrigerator and took out some cheese, walked over to the far counter and took out a few slices of bread and also took out a small frying pan, and put in some oil. Turning on the heat she buttered the both sides of the bread and placed some cheese in between them and started cooking her sandwich until it turned golden brown. When it was cooked she took it out of the frying pan and placed it on a small plate, then she poured herself out a small bowl of nice hot soup. Madison sat down at the kitchen table to have her lunch. Just as she was about to touch the tip of the sandwich to her lips, she heard this very loud bang, like glass breaking and falling onto the floor. She almost jumped out of her chair. But she stopped and listened intensely expecting more sounds and loud bangs, a few seconds later yet another very loud bang and this time she thought she could hear people talking. Madison dropped her sandwich and stood up very quickly not knowing quite what to do. She decided to walk slowly over to Uriel's room and place her ear up against the door. As she did so, the door shook like there was a earth quake, she backed away from the door and ran back to her chair at the kitchen table, and sat down to wait. Wait for what she thought to herself. She sat there for quite some time before she decided to finish her lunch and clean up the dishes.

Oh I am just be silly now she said to herself. I shall go about and do some more cleaning, yes I shall do that and keep myself busy until the rest of the family comes home. Madison set about cleaning up the house, she went from room to room, dusting, vacuuming and mopping the floors. The bathroom always took her longer as this was the messiest room in the whole house, everyone uses it she thought to herself. It took Madison about forty five minutes just to clean the bathroom alone, and in doing so she tried to keep her mind clear and not on what happened a few hours earlier. Soon Madison had finished cleaning the bathroom and as she mopped the floor she backed out of it closing the door behind her. Madison stood up and looked towards Uriel's room, no I shall not enter that room until Agatha and her friend does something to help us so I will just bypass his room. Madison then headed towards the living, dusting and taking down cobwebs, straightened everything out, then vacuumed the room. She then cleaned the hallway dusting the pictures on the walls, then vacuuming the carpet. She then headed for the kitchen. I think I will need a cup of tea now, that little bit of work made me tired she said to herself. She walked over to the kettle, filled it with water and placed it on the stove to boil. When it had boiled she made herself a single cup of hot tea and sat down at the kitchen table. Looking up at the clock on the wall she noticed it almost dinner time. What shall we have for today's supper she thought to herself. Madison decided to bake some cookies today for the children and then, make some shepherds pie. She went about the kitchen putting together all the ingredients, frying up the meat, then placing everything in a pan, piled it high with smashed potatoes. Then she made the cookies, and placed them on a cookie sheet to bake them for about 10 mintes then placed it in the oven at 350 degrees. After the cookies were made she then placed the pie in the oven and closed the door. There she said that should take about one and a half hours, by that time everyone will be home. Soon Destiny came through the back door, Hi mother how was your day she asked Madison with a smile on her face? Oh just fine thank you dear, and how was your day? Just hunky dory Destiny replied. I will be in my room until dinner ok.

Ok replied Madison I will call you when dinner is ready. Destiny went off to her room as Madison sat in the kitchen at the table waiting on dinner to cook. About thirty minutes later Ethan came through the door. Hi how was your day he asked as he walked up to Madison and gave her a kiss on the cheek? Just fine she replied and how was your day? Oh it was just ok, just a normal day he replied. He placed his lunch bucket on the kitchen counter then went into the bathroom to freshen up before dinner as he always did, then he went changed his clothes and walked into the living room and turned on the TV to watch the news. I will call you for dinner Madison yelled out to him. Ok was his reply. Soon dinner was ready and as Madison was placing it out on the table she called out dinner is ready everyone and as she did so Uriel came running into the house, hi mom I'll be in my room was all he said and went running to his room. Hey are you hungry for dinner it is ready would you like some she asked him? But Madison got no reply. As Destiny and Ethan came into the kitchen they sat down at the table, and started to eat There was a plate of shepherds pie, with a serving of salad beside it. There was also some cut up bread slices for anyone whom wants some. As the three family members sat and had their meal, there was no sign of Uriel. What no Uriel again Ethan spoke up looking up at

Madison? No I guess he is not hungry replied Madison, he just came in and ran into his room I asked him if he was hungry but he said no. With that Madison raised and lowered her shoulders smiling at Ethan. No reply from either Destiny or Ethan today, they just sat there eating their meal. When they were finished Ethan got up first and went into the living room to watch some TV until bed time while Destiny helped her mother clear up the supper dishes, wash them and put them away. Are you finished with your homework Madison asked Destiny? Yes mother I am I will watch some television with father until bed time she replied then went into the living and sat down on the couch and put her feet up. Soon afterwards Madison came into the living room and sat down beside her husband. A few hours later Destiny started yawning, ok she said I am going to bed, good night folks she said and smiled at her parents as she went to her room. Good night replied Madison. Soon after that Ethan got up and said well that's it for me bed time I think, as he went about the house locking all the doors and windows and shutting off the lights Madison headed for the bathroom as she always did before going to bed. When Ethan was finished it was his turn in the bathroom, soon he joined his wife in their big comfy bed, as he kissed her good night he said, I hope there won't be any disturbances to night. I hope not too, Agatha is bringing her friend here tomorrow to do something and maybe get rid of whatever is in our house Madison told him, oh ok that sounds good, with that he drifted off to sleep, but Madison lay there thinking and was ready for any type of noise that came along tonight, soon she fell off to sleep. Again she awoke at exactly 3:00am to the sounds of a lot of people partying down the hall, yes it was in Uriel's room again. She was about to get out of bed, when she thought, no no I shall just say here and ignore the noise, it will go away I just know it, she said to herself covering her head with blankets. She closed her eyes tightly and tried very hard not to listen but she could not ignore the noise.

It must have continued on well into the night as now the sun was just coming up. The noise subsided as Madison got herself out of bed and looked at the clock, it was a few minutes before the alarm would go off, so she canceled the alarm and got up out of bed and went into the bathroom. She then headed for the kitchen to put on the kettle for morning coffee, as she past Uriel's room she tried to listen but could hear nothing. In the kitchen the kettle had boiled so she made the coffee and with the smell of coffee in the room, soon Ethan got up out of bed and went into the bathroom, he got dressed and went into the kitchen where he found Madison sitting at the table sipping her coffee. Good morning, how did you sleep last night he asked her? Well I woke up at 3:00am again to the sound of people having a party in Uriel's room, I did not get out of bed I just laid there and finally fell off to sleep again. Well I certainly hope that this Madam Ashley can help us out here Ethan replied, I am getting pretty tired of all of this and angry he replied. Me too Ethan we will know something today hopefully she told him. Soon Destiny came into the kitchen good morning all, I will just have cereal this morning for breakfast she told her mother. She went over to one of the cupboards took out a box of cereal, then a bowl from another cupboard and poured herself some cereal, added some sugar and added some milk from the refrigerator, sat at the table and had her breakfast, while Ethan had his coffee and toast was all he wanted this morning. Soon Destiny stood up and said well, I'm off to school, she kissed her mother on the cheek and grabbing her lunch bag from the counter said good bye everyone see you later and she smiled as she left the house closing the door behind her. Well we have trained her right Ethan pipes up smiling at Madison. Yes we have I am not too sure about Uriel though, Madison smiled at Ethan. He stood up and walked over to the counter grabbing his lunch bucket, he kissed his wife and said well I'm off too, have a good day and find out something please, I hope to hear some good news when In get home today he said to Madison. Me too Madison replied I will tell you everything she said. With that Ethan left the house as Madison made herself some toast and poured another cup of coffee. She just sat down at the table when Uriel came running through the kitchen, he didn't even look at his mother or say anything, he just grabbed his lunch and went out the door.

Well Madison said to herself there has to be something wrong with that boy I just know it she told herself. Madison sat there for a short time before getting up and cleaning up the kitchen she had to get ready for Madam Ashley and Agatha. Madison had finished cleaning up the kitchen and had just finished mopping the kitchen floor when all of a sudden the whole room started to shake, the whole HOUSE started shaking. Madison braced herself like it was a earth quake, she stood there in that same spot with her arms out stretched, ready for anything. All of a sudden she heard this loud deep masculine voice telling her to get, get out of this place. Madison stood in disbelief, what was going on now she thought, what is God's name is going on. She shut her eyes tightly and held her breathe. All of a sudden the voice and the shaking stopped, like it never started, the room was normal as she opened her eyes. OMG she said to herself now I know there is something going on in this house, I just know it. After a few minutes she decided to move, this is complete craziness she thought. She bravely made herself a nice not cup of tea and sat down at the kitchen table. Madison stayed there at the table until she heard the ringing of the front door bell. Oh that must be Agatha and Madam Ashley she said to herself. Madison got up and slowly walked towards the front door. She grabbed the door knob and turning it to open she saw Agatha standing there, today she wore blue jeans, and nice top, also an overcoat as the air was getting chilly out this time of year. Beside her was this rather short woman, with long black hair, very blue eyes and her skin was rather wrinkled or so Madison thought standing there looking at her. Oh my please come in. Madison smiled at both of the women as they entered her house. Madam Ashley looked around with this odd look upon her face, as Madison closed the door behind them. Please come into the kitchen and I will make us some nice hot tea, Madison gestured the way to the kitchen both women followed her and taking off their coats they sat down at the kitchen table. Madison made some tea and placed it before each one and she sat down. Madam Ashley ran her hands along the table and stared right down the hallway towards Uriel's room. After a few minutes of silence Madam Ashley said, I feel a terrible presences in this place. She stood up slowly and walked towards Uriel's room. She stopped when she reached the door to Uriel's room. She circled her hands at the door then walked back to the kitchen.

May I have a further look around your house Madison. Why yes please do go right ahead Madison replied. With that in mind Madam Ashley removed her scarf she was wearing, and took out of her bag a long thin stick, it had a bright light on the end of it, which turned green when she went near Uriel's room. As for the rest of the house the end was orange in colour. As she went about her business Madison asked Agatha, what is she doing? What do the colors mean if anything? After a few seconds Agatha replied, I think she is feeling around for the presence of an apparition, ghost like figure or any evil being. When the light turns green that means that there is an apparition near, when it turns orange there is nothing. When it turns red that means that the apparition is coming towards you, meaning you bodily harm. Madison's eyes opened widely and stared at Agatha, really, was all that came out of her mouth. Yes replied Agatha. Madam Ashley will explain further when she returns. Oh my Madison said, and stared in the direction that Madam Ashley went, waiting for her return. After a few minutes Madam Ashley returned her stick in hand. She placed the stick back in her bag, and sat down at the table. Madison waited...well Madison asked what did you find? Madam Ashley looked at her and said. There is definitely an evil being in your house. We can try and get rid of it ourselves with your permission. Madison shook her head yes, yes please it seems to be getting worse and worse every day and I am getting scared being here alone every day. I can see why Madison, you must be afraid for your life and that of your families Madam Ashley replied. Madison just shook her head looking right at Agatha, how soon can you start? Well first I must ask a few questions Madam Ashley said. Oh yes what is it Madison asked, what ?

Well replied Madam Ashley, when were you in Uriel's room last and what did you see when you were in there? Well I guess it has been just about one week now. When I was in there I saw nothing out of the ordinary Madison said. Madam Ashley asked. Did you happen to see a "Ouija" board she asked? A what Madison asked? A Ouija board, its a small board, could be made of wood and on it across the middle there would be letters of the alphabet. Then below that would be a row of numbers. At the top on the left above the letters would be a word "Yes" and on the other side would be the word "No". Then there would be a small tear drop size palette with a hole in the center of it, that you would use on the board. Have you seen anything that resembled that Madam Ashley asked? Madison thought for a moment then shook her head again no not that I remember seeing she replied. This would be an instrument in which the subject, being your son Uriel, would conjure up an spirit or apparition. If he used it alone which I believe he did, we could not tell which spirit or apparition he conjured up or talked to, and the longer he has talked to it, the more the spirit will get stronger and try to take over his body, which your son Uriel could not have any way of getting rid of by himself. He would not probably have any idea that it has even happened, he would just seem to be himself. Could you please just check around, looking under his bed and in the closet, if you dare go into his room and see if you come across one Madam Ashley asked. Oh oh no no way Madison replied I could not possibly do that I am afraid for my life even being in this house. Could maybe you do this Madison asked Madam Ashley? Madam Ashley hesitate for a while then replied, ok but you must come with me followed by Agatha here, just in case she is needed. Oh ok that is fine by me, Agatha? Oh yes, I am fine with that. All three women stood up and headed for Uriel's room. Madam Ashley was the first one to reach for the door knob, and slowly open the door. The women entered his room, it seemed to be a normal kids bedroom with the smell of dirty clothes laying around. Well Madam Ashley said waving her hand in front of her face. This is a normal room, so we will act quickly. Look around for what I described to you please, and see if there is anything out of the ordinary in here. Ok replied Madison. All three women were looking around the room, lifting dirty clothes from the floor with a big stick, and anything else that was on the floor. Madam Ashley looked under the bed, nothing there except dirt and dust she thought, then She headed for the closet. She opened the door turning on the light looked around, saw nothing wrong then left closing the door behind her. The other ladies had finished looking and they found nothing also. Standing up Madam Ashley said, ok lets go, as the women were leaving the room, there was this very fowl smell, and as the last lady left, just one foot out the door, it slammed shut quickly behind them, like someone in there did not want them in that room again. MM replied Madam Ashley, as they walked back to the kitchen, Madison made some more hot tea, and Madam Ashley and Agatha sat at the table whispering. Well what do you think Madison asked? Well I will have to go home and do some research, a lot of research and if and when I find out anything, anything at all I will call and explain it to you. Oh ok replied Madison passing out the hot tea to the ladies. All three women sat there for a few more minutes, then Madam Ashley stood up and said, I must go and gather some information that is needed. Wait, wait a minute Madison said, what, what should I do in the mean time, until you return?

What can I do to protect my family from... from whatever is in that room Madison asked with a doubtful look upon her face. Madam Ashley looked in her bag and pulled out another bag, it was much smaller and was tied at the top. Madam Ashley waved her hand above the object muttering some words in Latin that Madison did not understand. She paused and handed it over to Madison. Here she said, place this above the door to Uriel's room, some place where your son can not find it so easily. I shall return with all the information that is required, along with some of my closest friends to help me out. I should return within one to two weeks she said to Madison. In the mean time if you hear any more sounds in the witching hour or any other time, please try to ignore it, it will go away eventually. With that which I gave you, you should be safe until we return. Oh ok Madison replied looking straight at her, thank you for this help we really appreciate anything you can do, as we are getting desperate. Madison smiled at the two women as they were leaving her house, she waved at them as they walked down the street to Agatha's house. When they got far even away, Madam Ashley said to Agatha, I could spell this odour, like wet dog or fried wings of a bird floating in the air in her son's room, could you smell it as well she asked Agatha? Why yes, now that you mentioned it Agatha replied. The women got to Madam Ashley's car which was parked along the road in front of Agatha's house and got in. She rolled down the window and said I will definitely check this out and get back to you before I say anything to Madison ok she said looking up at Agatha, ok Agatha replied I hope to talk with you again very soon, I know Madison and her family are very worried about this incident and want it gone as soon as possible. They fear for their son I know it Agatha said to Madam Ashley placing her hand on Madam Ashley's shoulder, then lifting it out. I will keep in touch and get back to you as soon as I can Madam Ashley replied rolling up her window and waving good bye. Agatha stood there for a minute waving back at her until her car was out of sight, then walked into her house. Agatha walked back to her house and went inside. Once inside she prepared herself some to eat (it consisted of a bowl of hot chicken noodle soup and a grilled cheese sandwich) and sat at the kitchen table deep in thought.

CHAPTER FOUR

Looking up at the clock on the kitchen wall Madison noticed it was getting close to dinner time. What should we have today she asked herself. She decided on stew so she went about preparing the stew meat and vegetables and placing them in a slow cooker and turned it. There she said that should take about three hours just in time for dinner. She made herself a hot cup of tea and sat down at the kitchen table thinking about what Madam Ashley and Agatha had told her, sipping on her tea she wondered about the outcome. Today however, there were no sounds or shaking of the house everything seemed quite normal for a change. Madison sat there for quite some time deep in thought. Madison went to get up from the kitchen table and noticed this weird smell coming from somewhere. As she stood up straight and looking around she noticed the door to Uriel's room was ajar. As she walked towards the door the terrible odour overwhelmed her almost knocking her off her feet. Madison held one hand over her nose, stumbled and quickly closed the door to Uriel's room . She stood there for a few seconds and as she did so looking down at the floor she noticed there was this bright red glow coming from inside his room. Madison reached out to grab the door knob to open it, but caught herself, and instead turned around and went back into the kitchen and sat down at the table. Oh no she thought to herself this is not happening again, not now.

She sat there trembling for a few seconds then started to relax. I certainly hope that Madam Ashley and Agatha can help us, because I am getting tired of this nonsense it has to end and end soon she muttered to herself. In the kitchen Madison went to work making the family dinner, and this time she was preparing to make some homemade tea biscuits to go with the stew that was simmering in the pot. She made real good tea biscuits, and as she stood at the kitchen counter measuring out the ingredients she was also thinking about the two women and what possible solution they could come up with to solve the mystery. She rolled out the dough which she had prepared and floured the counter surface, then cut the dough in two inch roll circles, then placed them onto a cookie sheet which lay beside the dough. Once all the dough was cut and placed on the cooking sheet she turned around then turned the oven to the stove on and set the temperature to 350 degrees then waited for the oven to warm up. Once it was the proper temperature she placed the cooking sheet into the oven and closed the door.

There she said to herself, they should take about twenty minutes, she then checked on the stew simmering in the pot and gave it a quick stir then placed the lid back down. She then put the kettle on and made herself a nice hot cup of tea, while everything was cooking and sat down at the table. Looking up at the clock on the wall she noticed it was soon time for everyone to be coming home so she sat and waited. About thirty minutes later Destiny came running in through the door, hi mom how was your day she asked smiling at her mother, oh just fine honey and how was your day? Just fine, oh by the way mother there is a school dance coming up next week can I go please she asked? Waiting for a reply from her mother Ethan came home and was standing in the doorway and placing his lunch bucket on the counter looked up at both the girls and asked, what is going on today? He smiled at Madison waiting for a reply. Well it seems Destiny here wants our permission to go to a school dance they are having next week, do you think we should let her go she asked Ethan smiling at him? MM he said scratching his head with his left hand, let me think about it and I will let you know, ok? Destiny looked at her father with the smile gone and said ok, please father can I go please she begged him? I will let you know after dinner he replied. Destiny turned and went into her room closing the door behind her. Ethan chuckled well maybe we could let her go yes he said looking at Madison. Yes I think it will be fine, I mean it can do no harm right she replied smiling at Ethan? Ethan walked past Madison and went into the bathroom to change and wash up for dinner, when he had finished he went into the living room and turned on television to watch some news while waiting. By this time Madison's biscuits had finished cooking so she took them out of the oven, and turning the oven off she placed the cooking sheet on the counter to let them cool down. Ethan yelled out from the living room, whatever you are cooking today sure smells real good, hope it tastes as good as it smells he said. Madison ignored his comments and said, I will let you know when dinner is ready. As the stew was just about finished Madison set the table for dinner. She placed a plate and a bowl on top of the plate along with a spoon and knife, beside each and another smaller plate beside the bigger plate. Soon the stew was finished, she turned the cooker off and went about spooning some stew into each of the bowls on the table. Dinner is ready she yelled out. She then placed a plate of tea biscuits on the table and sat down and waited for everyone to arrive, which they did. As everyone sat at the table eating their meal, of course Uriel was no where in sight yet, Ethan asked Madison about her day and asked if anything new had come up with Agatha and her friend who had come over today. What, what Destiny asked, what's going on she asked her mother? Well today I had Agatha and her friend come over to see what could be done about all this non sense going on in Uriel's, they will be working on it she told them and while we are waiting she gave me a small pouch filled with something I do not know what Madison said, which I had to put over the door to Uriel's room out of sight. Well what is it suppose to do Ethan asked. I am not sure they did not say, but they did say that it would help Madison replied. And what if Uriel finds it, then what Ethan asked? I don't really know Madam Ashley did not say, Madison replied but we will find out right!! About twenty minutes into eating their meal Uriel came in through the door, did not say one word but went straight for his room. When he got within reach of the door knob he stopped, he went to open the door to his room, when all of a sudden he stopped and lowered his arm. He tried the second time, same thing happened. He returned to the kitchen where everyone was having their dinner, and said. What, what is going on I felt really weird when I tried to go into my room, like something is trying to stop me. Madison looked at him and said, why don't you sit down here and have some dinner with us, then maybe that feeling will go away she told him.

No he yelled I want to go into my room. Ethan stood up from the table and stared at him....Uriel you will do as your mother wants and do it right now he told him very firmly. Uriel waiting for a few seconds then obeyed his father. He nibbled at his food, stirring it over and over again with his spoon. Eat Ethan demanded, eat. Uriel took another few spoonfuls, then all of a sudden he stopped, closed his eyes then fell off his chair. Ethan went around to him and noticed he was out cold like he had just fainted or something. Ethan picked him up off the floor and carried him to his room. Upon opening the door to Uriel's room nothing happened Ethan just walked in as normal. Ethan placed Uriel on his bed and covered him up with a blanket Ethan felt Uriel's forehead but he felt fine, so Ethan backed out of his room closing the door behind him and went back to the kitchen table where he finished his meal. Well Madison asked, what happened in there? Ethan looked at her and said, nothing happened I just walked into his room like a normal person, he was still out cold so I covered him with a blanket and left him, I am sure he will be fine, With that said, Ethan got up from the table after finishing his meal, great dinner today Madison, tasted real good and he walked back into the living room to watch some television. Both Destiny and Madison sat at the table looking at each other wondering, what in dam nation just happened. Well I don't Destiny, so Madison got up from the table and started to clear away the dishes, while Destiny helped her as usual. They cleared the table and washed up all the dishes then put them away. Well I'm going into my room to finish up my homework Destiny said smiling at her mother. Ok dear I am going to watch some television with your father for a while. Destiny went to her room while Madison walked into the living room and sat down beside Ethan.

About one and a half hours later Ethan started yawning so he got up and said well, I think I'm going to bed I am very very tired he said. Ok Madison replied, let me into the bathroom before you get there she smiled at him as he walked away. Ethan went about checking the house for security reasons and turning off all the lights as he went. By this time Madison had finished in the bathroom so it was free for Ethan's turn. Madison headed for their bedroom while Ethan went into the bathroom. Soon afterwards Ethan joined Madison under the bed covers and as they kissed each other good night they both fell deeply asleep.

Again at exactly 3:00am Madison was wakened by this strange sound. This time it sounded like a pack of wolves or some kind of animal gathering their flocks for something. The sound was so piercing that Madison had to cover her ears. About thirty seconds later the sound faded away, until complete silence over came the whole house. Madison lowered her hands from her ears, and looking over at Ethan noticed he had not awakened, it seems that sounds do not bother him Madison said to herself. She lay there for quite some time but heard nothing else, slowly she drifted off to sleep again. Shortly there after Madison awoke to the sound of the morning alarm going off. She got herself up out of bed and slipped into her warm slippers and went down the hallway to the bathroom where she freshened herself up, then walked into the kitchen where she put the kettle on for morning coffee. As she stood at the window overlooking her flower bed waiting for the kettle to boil, she noticed that something had up turned her flowers in the far left hand corner of the backyard. Well she said to herself, what has happened to my flowers, after breakfast I shall have to go out there and have a look. Soon the kettle had boiled and Madison was making the morning coffee. With the aroma of coffee in the air, soon Madison heard Ethan getting up and washing himself. Shortly thereafter he came into the kitchen, coffee sure smells good may I have some he asked Madison smiling at her,,,good morning was all he said. Madison poured him a cup and asked, what would you like for breakfast this morning smiling at him? Well how about some bacon and eggs with toast he said. I guess I could mustard that up for you she replied.

Soon Madison had gone about the kitchen taking out some bacon and eggs and placing the bread in the toaster she started cooking breakfast. With the smell of bacon in the air Destiny came into the kitchen, yawning as usual she said good morning everybody, may I have some too please? Oh my well I guess so Madison replied smiling at her. Are you awake now Madison asked Destiny looking at her? Mmm yes I am and I am starving she replied. When are you not ever starving Madison replied smiling at her. Soon the bacon and eggs were cooked and the toast had just popped up out of the toaster. Madison placed some bacon and eggs and two slices of toast on each plate and place it in front of Ethan and Destiny, there you are now eat Madison said. Would you like some orange juice with that Madison asked Destiny, holding the jug of juice in her hand? Yes please she said, and Madison poured some into her glass. Soon Destiny and Ethan had finished their breakfast, Destiny got up from the table and grabbing her lunch bag from the kitchen counter said, well off to school I am I will see you all later then she smiled at both her parents and went out the door. Bye Madison said as Destiny disappeared. Soon Ethan had finished his breakfast and was getting up from the kitchen table, then grabbing his lunch bucket from the counter, walked over to his wife kissed her on the cheek and said, good bye Madison I will see you later. I hope Uriel is feeling better, maybe he can stay home from school today. I will see have a good day at work then Ethan left.

Madison then sat down at the kitchen table sipping on her coffee and now having her breakfast. About ten minutes later Uriel appeared, morning he said, what's for breakfast he said? Bacon and eggs Madison replied, ok he replied and he sat down at the table. As he sat at the table eating his breakfast Madison asked, how are you feeling this morning? Uriel looked up at this mother and said fine mother I feel fine. Oh ok she replied and with that Uriel grabbed his lunch bag from the counter and left as well. Madison was left sitting there by herself sipping on her coffee. Shortly after Madison got up from the table and started clearing up the morning dishes and mess. When she was finished she decided to go outside and go look at her flower bed at the back.

When she got dressed and went outside she walked to the far back to look at her flowers. Yes sure enough the whole back bed of flowers was dug up, it looked like a long trench a dog had dug up looking for a bone or something. Madison knelt down on her knees and upon a closer look noticed that yes sure enough there were many bones laying about. She picked up one or two to have a closer look but she could not distinguish weather the bones were human or animal. mm she said to herself, I shall have to save a few and have Agatha or Madam Ashley have a look and tell me what kind of bones these are. Madison placed a few of the bones in a small plastic bag and closed it up tightly and put it in her coat pocket. She then went about trying to straighten out the mess that was left behind and make her garden look normal again. When she was happy the flower bed looked kind of normal again, she stood up, turned around and went back into the house, brushing the dirt off her clothes before going inside. She then put the kettle on for she really needed a nice hot cup of tea to warm her up. It was getting quite chilly outside now she thought to herself. Soon the kettle had boiled, she made herself a cup of tea and sat down at the kitchen table to warm herself up. That had better not happened again she said to herself, maybe it was just some animal digging up bones. Today she decided she had to do some laundry as there were no clean clothes left to wear. After she finished her tea, she went about the house gathering up the dirty laundry and putting them into the laundry basket, she headed down to the basement laundry room. She turned on the lights has it had got quite dark down there, she placed the first load of laundry into the washing machine, pour in some soap, closed the lid and turned the machine on. There I shall return in thirty minutes to start the next load she told herself. Madison then headed upstairs to the kitchen, where she once again sat down at the kitchen table. About forty minutes later she returned to the laundry room in the basement. She found the laundry had finished, so she took the wet clothes out of the machine and placed them into the dryer, and turned it on. She then turned and went back to the washing machine and placed the next load of laundry into the machine, threw in some laundry soap, closed the lid and turned it on. Wiping off her apron as she always does, there she said I will return in about one hour, to put in another load of laundry. Madison then went back upstairs to the kitchen where she made herself another cup of hot tea. About one hour and twenty minutes later she went back down to the basement laundry room, where took the dried clothes out of the dryer, placing them into the laundry basket, she took the next load of wet clothes out of the machine and placed them into the dryer, closed the door and turned it on.

She then went back to the washing machine where she put another load of dirty clothes into the machine, added some soap, closed the lid and turned it on. Just as she was about to turn and go upstairs, she felt a strange hand on her right hand shoulder, Madison did not know what to make of it, she stood there for a few seconds frozen in shock, dare she turn around and have a look, the hand on her shoulder did not seem to want to move, it just laid there. Soon Madison decided to move she raised her left hand to the spot where the hand was upon her shoulder and as she just reached her shoulder the hand had quickly disappeared, it was gone in like a instinct. Madison was still shaking but decided she should go back upstairs and finish her tea. oh it's just my imagination she thought. Madison quickly went upstairs and sat down at the table where she found herself still trembling.

CHAPTER FIVE

Madison sat there for a long time trying to compose herself with the thought, oh my God what was that, was it my imagination or was it real, I can not tell. She decided to make herself another cup of hot tea and continue on with her day. Oh well it will pass she thought to herself as she sat at the kitchen table sipping her tea. About forty minutes later she decided to go back downstairs to the laundry room and see to her laundry. The last load of laundry was complete so she took the wet clothes out of the machine, and took the dried clothes out of the dryer and put the wet ones in and turned the dryer on to dry them and placed the dried clothes into the laundry basket. She then headed back upstairs to finish her tea. One hour later she headed back downstairs to get the last load of laundry. She reached the dryer and took out the last load of laundry and placed them into the basket. She then turned off the lights and quickly headed back upstairs, turning the basement light off as she headed towards her bedroom with the laundry basket.

As she was dividing up the clothes, she placed Destiny's and Uriel's clothes into a special pile, then she put her clothes and Ethan's clothes away in their proper place, then headed to the linen closet to put the fresh towels and sheets away. She then headed towards Destiny's room where she laid Destiny's clothes on her bed not putting them away that was Destiny's job Madison thought to herself. Madison was approaching Uriel's room when she heard this growling sound and a loud piercing voice say........ stay away stay away Madison dropped the laundry basket with Uriel's clothes in it and backed away from his door. She headed back to the kitchen where she tried to call her friend Agatha. She walked over to the telephone and dialed Agatha's telephone number. It rang and rang, no answer, suddenly the answering machine came on and Madison left her a message…Agatha this is Madison could you please call me when you get home, thank you, then she hung up the receiver. She then walked slowly over to the table and sat down, like she waiting for the telephone to ring again, but it did not. Madison was getting hungry by this time so she made herself a hot bowl of soup, looking up at the clock on the wall she noticed it would soon be dinner time and that she would have to decide what to make for dinner today. As she sat and ate her soup she was deep in thought, I sincerely hope Agatha's friend can help us out, because now I am starting to be very afraid in my own home. Madison soon finished her lunch and decided to make pot roast for dinner. She walked over to the refrigerator and took out the roast she had waiting in there. She then walked over to the kitchen counter and took out the biggest pot she had from the cupboard. She then placed some water into the bottom of the pot and placed the roast inside and turned the stove on.

Soon it had started cooking and Madison turned the heat down to simmer for a few hours. Madison sat in the kitchen for a long time before deciding to go back and pick up the laundry that she dropped in front of Uriel's bedroom door. She reached Uriel's room and bent down the pick up the laundry when she saw a blue light coming from within his room, oh my what is going on in there I'd like to know she told herself, but I will not enter and do as Agatha told me until such time as they both return.

Madison sat in the kitchen for a while tending to the pot roast for dinner, she didn't want it to burn. All of a sudden the telephone rang,so she went over to answer the phone. Hello she said, hello. Hi Madison this is Agatha I got your message, how are things going with you she asked her? Well I called you for a reason I hope I am not bothering you too much Madison replied? Oh no no Agatha replied, what has happened? Well every now and then, it does not matter where I am in the house I always find someone or something touching me on my shoulder, I wait then touching my own shoulder then it disappears. A few hours ago I was putting away the laundry when I got close to Uriel's room I thought I could hear a voice telling me to stay away, it sounded very rough and used a rough raspy voice like I've never heard before it really scared me, what is going on here do you know yet? Have you asked Madam Ashley? If so what has she said ?

No replied Agatha I will call her right now and see what I can find out. Ok replied Madison, I will say good bye for now so you can call her. Good bye my friend replied Agatha and they hung up the phone. Madison sat at the kitchen table for a while then looked up at the clock on the wall and noticed it was getting near dinner time, so went over to the pantry and took out some vegetables which she cleaned and placed into the pot roast along with some spices. She then replaced the lid and let it simmer. Soon after the back door opened and it was Destiny arriving home from school, Hi mother she said, how was your day, mine was just fine she said as she smiled at her mother. Oh my day was just fine Madison replied.Destiny replied I'll be in my room as I have alot of homework to get done today. Ok replied Madison I'll let you know when dinner is ready. About thirty minutes later Ethan arrived home Hi dear how are things here at home today he asked her as he bent down to kiss her on the cheek? Nothing out of the ordinary she replied and I still have not heard from Agatha. Oh well, maybe she will call you soon, I am going to get cleaned up and change for dinner he said as he walked past Madison and went into the bathroom. Soon he came out and walked into the living room where he turned on the television as usual and sat down to watch some TV before dinner. While the pot roast was almost done, Madison made some salad to go with the meal then set the table. She placed the salad bowl on the table, along with some bread slices, then returned to the pot roast to finished it off making some very nice gravy. Then she placed the roast on a platter and set it on the table calling for Ethan to come and cut it. As he did so Destiny heard the goings on the kitchen so she came in and sat down at the table. Mmm she said that smells very good she sat there very impatiently waiting to eat. Soon all family members were sitting at the table having their meal. Looking over at Uriel's chair at the table Ethan asked where he was today. I have no idea Madison replied I have not seen him all day or heard from him, have you Destiny she asked? Have you seen him at school today she asked?

Mmm Destiny replied, come to think about it no I have not, usually I at least see him somewhere on school grounds but today I did not. They all just continued eating their meal and when they were done, Ethan went into the living room to watch some television while the ladies cleaned up the table and the dishes leaving a plate out for Uriel in case he should return home to eat. Soon Madison and Destiny joined Ethan in the living room to watch some television before going to bed. Soon Destiny stood up and said, well it's bed time for me good night folks and off she went to her room, good night Madison replied, sleep well. About thirty minutes later Ethan stood up and said he was getting pretty tired and that he was headed for bed also. Well what about Uriel

Madison asked him, should we wait for his return she asked him? No I am not waiting for him any longer he will return when he's ready he replied and went off to lock all the doors and shut off all the lights, leaving the porch light on in the backyard for Uriel in case he returns. While Ethan was doing that Madison was in the bathroom getting ready for bed and was soon in bed under the bed covers, waiting for her husband. Shortly there after Ethan arrived and closed their bedroom door behind him and got under the bed covers, rolled over to kiss his wife and fell off to sleep. Madison lay there for a while just thinking, soon she fell off to sleep leaving the bedside lamp on forgetting to turn it off. Again it was exactly 3:00am when Madison awoke to the shaking of the whole house, it was like a earth quake or something, even their bed was moving and shaking, Ethan jumped up and said what is going on what is it he asked looking at Madison. She shook her head in a no replied. Both just sat up in their bed holding onto the bed frame afraid to let go. All of a sudden it stopped and they could hear this voice saying get out of here, get out of here over and over again. Ethan got up out of bed, opened their bedroom door and looking down the hallway saw what he thought was a tall dark figure standing just in front of Uriel's bedroom , but inside the room looking out, apparently at Ethan.

It was the shape of a human but had no eyes or mouth with which to speak yet it did, he raised his arm out towards Ethan repeating get out of here, get out of here. Ethan looked down at the floor about to backup when he noticed this figure was not standing on the floor but he was floating two feet above the floor. Very nervously Ethan backed up and went back into his bedroom closing the door behind him and just sat on the edge of the bed. Madison reached out to touch his shoulder and found he was shaking all over like he saw a ghost or something. What, she said what did you see she asked him? ? Ethan could not replied right away, but after a few seconds he said, a very tall dark figure, floating off the floor standing in the doorway to Uriel's room, he he was pointing at me telling me to get out, I don't know what to make of this, if Agatha does not get back to us soon I will find have to find a priest or someone else to help us, and I mean right away he said. Come on now Madison said let's try and get some sleep, tomorrow I will call our priest and have him come over here to bless our house, maybe clear it of evil or whatever they do. With that thought both of them eventually fell off to sleep. The next morning Madison woke as usual, and getting out of bed put her slippers on and headed for the bathroom. When she had finished in there she went into the kitchen to put on the kettle to make the morning coffee. As she sat at the kitchen table waiting for the kettle her thoughts were of last night…what, what will happen next. Soon the kettle had boiled and she was making the morning coffee. Soon with the smell of coffee in the air Ethan got up, Madison could hear him in the bathroom getting ready for work, then heading towards the kitchen. He said nothing of last night but asked about breakfast. What would you like Madison asked him? How about pancakes this morning he said I just feel like pancakes. Well ok Madison replied pancakes it is. Madison went about making the pancakes for his breakfast as he sat at the kitchen table sipping his coffee. Soon the pancakes were ready and she served Ethan a full plate, stacking them very high, then placed the bottle of syrup in front of him. Enjoy she said and as she turned around she saw Destiny enter the kitchen, pancakes she asked her with a smile on her face. Why yes please she replied and sat down at the table. Soon Madison placed a plate of pancakes in front of Destiny along with a glass of orange juice. Ethan asked did Uriel come home last night he asked Madison looking straight at her? Why no not that I seen Madison replied. Did you hear anything strange last night he asked staring right at Madison, no. Soon Ethan had finished his breakfast, stood up, and walking over towards the kitchen counter took up his lunch bucket, walked back to Madison and kissing her on the cheek said, good bye everyone I am off to work, he smiled as he left the house. Destiny was the next one to finish her breakfast, and she did the same thing. I have to be in school early today she told her mother because I have a science test this morning. She ran over kissed her mother and said good bye mother. You had better pass that test this morning young lady, I hope you studied for it she said with a smile on her face. Yes mother I did and I will bye and with that she was out the door leaving Madison sitting at the table all alone once again. Madison decided to make herself some pancakes, then go about cleaning the house as it became awfully dusty the telephone rang. Madison walked over to the telephone and picking up the receiver said, Hello. Hi Madison this is Agatha, how are you doing my friend she asked? Oh dear Madison replied I was waiting for your call, have you found out anything to tell me yet she asked?

Well no, but Madam Ashley called me and she will be coming over here to talk with me today, maybe she will have some answers for us today, that is what I am hoping. Oh ok I hope so because every night now something is always happening here, and it's always at 3:00am. Ok don't worry as soon as I find out anything from Madam Ashley I will definitely call you ok Agatha told her. Ok thank you Agatha. I was thinking of having our family priest come over here today to bless our house, what do you think she asked her. Well that might be something to do, yes, definitely call and ask him if he will do that for you Agatha told her. I will, good bye Agatha said, when I find out anything from Madam Ashley I will call you, ok. Ok Madison replied good bye for now and she hung the phone. Madison went back to the table to finish her lunch, then she walked back to the telephone and called her family priest, the phone rang four times before someone answered. Hello it was the voice of a young woman. Hello this is Madison Appleby could I possibly talked with Father Anthony she asked. Well father Anthony is busy right now, but I will have him call you as soon as he is finished, what is your telephone number she asked. Madison replied 217-675-9004, ok I will leave the message, good day to you Madam then she hung up the phone. Madison went back to the table to sip on her hot tea and waited. About one and one half hours later the telephone rang. Madison walked over to the telephone and picked up the receiver. Hello she said, after a few seconds of silence Father Anthony replied Hello Mrs. Appleby this is Father Anthony how may I help you he asked? Well Father I was wondering if you were not too busy with your schedule could you possibly come by and bless our home, we have had strange things happening around here. Father Anthony asked her what kind of things and Madison told him of the strange sounds and things going on. Well he replied, let me see what I can do and possibly come by later today. Oh that would be so greatly appreciated she told him and thank you, thank you. Father Anthony could hear the emotion of fear in her voice. Good bye Mrs. Appleby he said and hung up the phone, Madison replied good bye Father.

Madison wondered if she should continue on with the household chores, that meant going into Uriel's room which she did not want to do as Agatha told her to stay out of there until she heard back from her. Madison stood there for a moment then decided to clean everywhere else except there. About one hour later she had finished cleaning the whole house, except for Uriel's room of course. She then put away all the cleaning supplies. Then sat down at the kitchen table to have yet another cup of hot tea while she waited, hopefully for news from someone she thought to herself. It was about 4:00pm when the telephone rang. Madison went over to answer it and found it to be Agatha. Hello she said, what did you find out Madison asked her very quickly? Well Madam Ashley told me, there is a very bad apparition, evil spirit if you will, in Uriel's room who wants to take over Uriel's body and the longer he is in there the better his chances are of taking over. She told me what to get together and that her and I will come by this evening to perform a ceremony that should get rid of it, will that be ok with you and your family Agatha asked her? Oh yes, yes please as it seems to be getting worse and worse around here, do you have any idea what time you could come by Madison asked her? Madam Ashley said around 7:00pm will that be ok Agatha asked? Oh yes, well ok we will see you then she said good bye for now then they hung up the phone. Just as she hung up the phone the front door bell rang. Madison went to answer it, and as she opened the door she found Father Anthony standing there. Well hello there I am Father Anthony. Hello please come in Madison told him, please. As Father Anthony entered the house, he held the bible in one of hands and muttered to himself some words Madison did not recognize.

Please Madison said to him go where ever you like and bless every room she told him. Father Anthony nodded his head, and went everywhere until he came to Uriel's door, then he stopped. He took a step back, lowered his head and started praying under his breathe. He slowly raised his left arm and without touching the door drew a small cross to the north, to the west, to the east and to the south. When he was finished he walked back to Madison who was waiting in the kitchen. I am surprised at the feelings I get from your son's room. I know there is something in there or someone whom does not want me here. I will need to talk with my parishioners and head of our cardinal priests and get back to you . He lowered his head and went to the front door. I shall take my leave now and get back to you as soon as I can he said. Oh ok Madison replied, I hope to hear from you real soon. Madison watched as Father Anthony left their house and walked to his car which was parked on the side of the road in front of their house, got in and drove off. Madison noticed it would soon be supper time and everyone would be home, she returned to the kitchen to finish making supper, as she was just about finished Destiny came in Hi mom when is supper she asked walking past her mother? In about one hour I will call you Madison replied. Destiny smiled and went straight to her room closing the door behind her. About twenty minutes later Ethan came home. Hi Madison how was your day he asked? Well it was shall I say...uneventful. Madison smiled at Ethan as he walked past her heading towards the bathroom. I'll just get cleaned up for supper he said. Ok I will call when supper is ready she told him. About twenty minutes later all was ready to serve out and eat. Madison placed supper on the table and called everyone. Ethan and Destiny came into the kitchen and sat down but still there was no Uriel. The family ate their and as they did so Madison explained that Father Anthony was in their house today and he blessed every room except Uriel's, he told me he had to consult someone else in the church and get back to me as soon as he could and left. Oh ok Ethan replied, anything else?

Well I was talking to Agatha today and she will be coming by with Madam Ashley about 7:00pm tonight to try something, after all she said something has to work, right!!! She smiled at Destiny and Ethan who smiled back. When everyone had finished Destiny helped her mother clear away the dishes and wash them so that the kitchen would be clean once again. Soon Ethan was in watching the television while Destiny was in her room doing her home

The Possession Of Uriel

work. About five minutes later there came a knock to the front door. Madison went to the front door and upon opening it found Agatha and Madam Ashley standing there. Hi ladies welcome, please, please come in she told them with a smile The two ladies came in and taking off their coats, Madison hung them up in the front hallway closet, the ladies walked into the kitchen where they sat down at the kitchen table. Madison sat down with them with this uncertain look upon her face. Well she asked them what can we do if anything right now, this matter has to be cleared up she asked? Madam Ashley took out of her bag a whole lot of strange looking stuff, and placed a bowl in the center of the kitchen table, she asked Madison ton place six white candles around the center of the table and light them. While Madison did that Madam Ashley placed some odd items into the bowl, first what seemed to be some small bones, then some dark brown looking dust, a feather of sorts and then she poured a small amount of liquid into the bowl. Madam Ashley chanted some Latin words which Madison did not understand, then lowered her head and said don't look up please look down at the table. As they women did so Madam Ashley tossed into the bowl a lit match which caused a puff of bluish gray smoke to appear. The whole room was in sudden darkness and silence. About ten minutes later Madam Ashley raised her head and said ok, you can look up now. Madam Ashley stood up from the table and headed towards Uriel's room. She recovered the small pouch about the door, took her necklace from under her coat, chanted some more Latin words over it, then entered Uriel's room, slowly opening the door. There was no sign of any trouble, no smoke, no sounds and definitely no voices telling her to get out like before. Madam Ashley slowly entered Uriel's room, and upon going inside, she slowly gazed around the room, all she saw was Uriel asleep on his bed, he did not move, or attempt to talk to her. While in Uriel's room Madam Ashley chanted more Latin words, waving her arm around the room and soon came back out again, closing the door behind her. She walked towards Agatha and Madison whom were still sitting at the table, with their eyes opened very widely just gazing at her. She commenced to put all of her belongings back into her bag and said, with a smile on her face Madison Agatha I do believe the evil spirit has finished, disappeared. I don't believe you will be bothered any more.

Oh my goodness replied Madison, I am so very very grateful. As the women walked out to the front, they stopped to get their coats, and turning towards Madison said, well good night my friend, I believe we are finished here, but if there is any more mishaps, please do not hesitate to call upon us. Both Madam Ashley and Agatha turned and left Madison's house and walked down the street to Agatha's house. Madison watched as Madam Ashley got into her car, waved good bye and left Agatha standing at the curb waving at her as she drove off down the road. Madison went about making dinner for her family as she knew they would be coming through the door any time now.

She started preparing some chicken, vegetables and rice. As the chicken was cooking, she decided to make some salad to go with the chicken. She was cooking the meal when Destiny was the first one to show up, Hi mom how was your day she asked her? Oh just fine, how was school today? mmm was ok Destiny replied with a smile on her face, I am going to my room to do some homework, I have a project I must get done for tomorrow, but I'm almost finished it she said as she walked past her mother who was cooking supper at the stove. Soon after that Ethan came in through the door, hi everyone I'm home, what's for supper today he asked as he walked towards Madison, giving her a kiss on the cheek. As you can see she replied chicken, it will be ready soon

Madison told him. Ok I'm going to wash up and get changed. As he left for the bathroom, Uriel came in through the door, without looking at his mother he walked past her and straight to his room. Hello Uriel Madison said as he went by her. She got no reply. Soon Ethan came into the living room area and turned on the television to watch some news before dinner as he always did. Soon Madison had set the table, placed the salad at one end and started putting out supper a little on each plate, supper is ready she called out They all came into the kitchen except Uriel, as they sat down to eat Ethan said where is Uriel today he asked Madison. He's here but in his room, and won't come out. We'll see about that Ethan replied, stood up and walked over to Uriel's room. He knocked very hard on the door and said Uriel come to supper and come right now. All of a sudden there was this loud howling sound, which threw Ethan on his but and tossed him half way down the hall. Ethan sat there with a very surprised look upon his face, then got to his feet, walked past Uriel's room and into the kitchen and sat down again. He stared at Madison and said, something has to be done about that boy. Madison looked at him and said. Father Anthony was here today and he told me there was something in Uriel's room and that he was going to come back and tend to the matter, also Agatha and Madam Ashley were coming by later this evening to perform a ceremony to try and rid us of this evil thing in Uriel's room. Agatha did not know and neither did Father Anthony kn ow what is happening in there but they will help us get rid of it. I have faith in Agatha, Madam Ashley and Father Anthony.

    They all sat there and had their meal without Uriel who did not wan t to join in. When everyone had finished their meal, Ethan went back into the living room while Destiny helped her mother clean up after supper, washed and put away the dishes. Thank you

Destiny for your help, Agatha and Madam Ashley will be here soon. Oh ok Destiny replied guess I will go directly to my room and stay there until further notice. She smiled at her mother and went to her room closing the door behind her. Madison stayed in the kitchen and made some hot tea for the ladies who were to arrive soon, and she set out a plate of biscuits. Thirty minutes later there was a knock at her front door. Madison went to open the door and found Agatha and Madam Ashley standing there ? Hello she said please come. Agatha and Madam Ashley walked into the house down the hallway to the kitchen where they sat down at the kitchen table. Ladies can I offer you some hot tea before we begin Madison asked? Why yes thank you Agatha replied, no not for me Madam Ashley replied and smiled at Madison. The ladies sat at the discussing the matter and what they were going to do, as Madison listened intensely. There was silence for a moment then Madam Ashley spoke up. Let me prepare for the spell I must cast to rid your house Madison. Ok relied Madison. Madison and Agatha sat at the table watching as Madam Ashley started preparing the items she had brought with her. She asked Madison to clear the kitchen table, place a white table cover upon it, then place the six white candles Madam Ashley had given her in a circle in the middle of the table. Madam Ashley then took out a small bag and upon opening it told the ladies what it consisted of. Here we have a handful of graveyard dirt, some salt, bones of a small animal, blood from a recently deceased demon, and some goofa dust. She then commenced to tie the small bag closed again. Madison listening with great intrigue and such a wondrous look upon her face, a face of disbelieve. Madam Ashley then placed the small bag of items in the center of the table and lit all the candles. May we have the lights off please Madam Ashley asked Madison. Madison got to her feet and walked over to shut off the kitchen lights. Destiny had gone to her room and Ethan had gone to his room so there were no other lights on the house, all Madison could see was the white glow of the lit candles. Please come and sit down Madam Ashley told her. Lower your heads, close your eyes and please don't move, leave your hands on the table palms down. After Agatha and Madison complied, Madam Ashley lowered her head and started praying out loud, Latin words that Madison could not recognize or even know what they meant. Then there was a moment of silences. Madam Ashley's head fell to the table like a rock, shaking it. Madison and Agatha dare not look up or open their eyes. After a few minutes, the whole house seem to shake like there was a earth quake, then the sound of a window smashing like someone had thrown a rock threw it, then there was this terrible howling sound, like a wolf calling for help or in pain. Then silence again for about forty five seconds.

All of a sudden the door to Uriel's room blew open like there was a sudden burst of explosives, followed by a red glowing light, more shaking of the house again, then nothing, complete silence. They waited for a few minutes, when Madam Ashley spoke up, Madison, you can please turn the lights back on, I believe we are done now. Madison slowly got to her feet and walked over to the light switch turning the lights back on. As she turned around to look at Madam Ashley and Agatha she noticed the small bag Madam Ashley had placed on the table was up in smoke, and e candles had gone out. What, what happened Madison asked Madam Ashley? I believe your evil spirit has gone, left the building she replied with a smile on her face. Agatha looking at her also smiled at Madison. Well I believe we have solved your problem Madam Ashley said. I will go and have a look into Uriel's room and see for myself she said. Madam Ashley got up from the table and slowly walked over to Uriel's room and slowly reached out with her right hand to open the door to his room. After a few seconds of silence Madam Ashley stated when she looked into Uriel's room she saw nothing out of the ordinary. Uriel was asleep on his bed, like a normal child. Madam Ashley slowly closed the door behind her and went into the kitchen. She started gathering up her belongings and when she was finished her looked at Agatha and said well we must go now, I have things I have to do. Agatha agreed and both the ladies walked towards the front door, turned and said good night Madison your home should be back to normal now, then they smiled at Madison as they outside towards Agatha's car and got in and rove away. Madison stood at the door still waving goodbye to them as they disappeared down the road. Madison closed the front door, returned to the kitchen where she cleared things up and went off to her bedroom to join Ethan.

Ethan lay there looking up at her…..well..what is going on now he said? Well I think the ladies have solved our problem Madison replied, I am sure we can sleep good tonight there should be no more problems. With that said, Madison changed into her pj's and got into bed beside Ethan. Ethan kissed her good night as they both drifted off to sleep.

CHAPTER SIX

It was quiet for two days after the ritual with Madam Ashley and Agatha. Nothing woke Madison during the night so she slept like a baby for a change. The next morning Madison awoke as usual and went into the kitchen to make the morning coffee. She headed for the tea kettle and filled it with water from the kitchen sink and placed it on the stove turning on the heat. She waited patiently for it to boil and when it did she made the coffee knowing Destiny and Ethan would be up soon. As the coffee was brewing Ethan was the first to respond to the smell of coffee in the air. Good morning he said and how are you this morning he asked Madison as she turned to place a nice hot cup of coffee in front of him, she bent over to kiss him good morning. I am fine and what would you like for breakfast she asked him? Well how about some french toast for a change he replied smiling at her. Ok she replied and she started making the french toast. As the toast was cooking in the frying pan Destiny came into the kitchen, good morning everyone I slept very well last night, no noise or sounds to awaken us, hey she remarked!! Yes both Madison and Ethan replied at the same time. Yes. Would you like some french toast for breakfast Madison asked her with a smile on her face? mmm well, ok that will be just fine, thank you. As Ethan and Destiny sat at the kitchen table eating their breakfast, Uriel came running into the kitchen, he said what's for breakfast I am starved? French toast Madison replied do you want some she asked him? Oh yes please, he sat patiently waiting his plate piled high with french toast. Madison set it down in front of him along with a glass of orange juice. Madison also sat down at the table while everyone was eating their breakfast. Madison looked at Uriel and noticed he still looked terrible, his eyes were deep set with a reddish tint and they were black all around, his skin looked like it had the age of old man in his 90's, Ethan also noticed his appearance and said. Uriel was you feeling ok because you look like you just got ran over with a dump truck? A few seconds later Uriel looked up from his plate and with a glare in his eyes said, fine I am just fine. He finished his meal and grabbing his lunch bag ran out the door with no goodbye to everyone. Well replied Ethan, I guess it will take a few days for him to come around and act normal again hey? He looked up at Madison with a smile. Ethan finished off his coffee and breakfast and standing up headed for the counter, where he grabbed his lunch bucket and said well, I am off now you have a good day he told Madison as she headed towards him giving him a kiss goodbye you have a good day too she replied and he went out the door waving goodbye.

Destiny got up from the kitchen table as well, well it's off to school mom, you have a good day she told her mother as she past by her grabbing her lunch bag waving goodbye as she left the house. Madison once again found herself all alone. She decided to get another cup of coffee and sit at the kitchen table for a while. While sitting there she thought about Father Anthony, I have not heard back from him in a very long time, I wonder what he found out or what he is doing? As Madison finished off her coffee she decided to get up and clean up from the morning breakfast. Today I will clean the house once more she told herself. As she was at the kitchen sink washing the dishes she looked outside into the backyard. Oh my goodness, she said to herself, my flower bed is dug up again guess I will have to go out there and clean up that mess as well. When Madison got finished with the dishes she decided to go outside first and see to her garden. She headed for her bedroom where she changed into her garden clothes, old pair of blue jeans and an old sweat shirt. She then headed out to the kitchen and out the back door heading for the tool shed once, then the flower bed. She grabbed her garden tools and walked down towards the flower bed. Upon examining it she knelt down on the ground and found the whole bed was dug up, like a dog was there digging a hole to bury something, she moved the dirt around with her right hand and found a few bones just a few inches below the surface. She slowly brought them out to look further at them and examining them she found them to be small bones, maybe that of a small animal like a cat or small dog, mm she said to herself I wonder where these came from, they were not here before, I shall now have to dig them all out and replace my flowers. Madison started digging up the flower bed and as she did so found more small bones, she gathered them up and put them in a small plastic container, I shall have to show Agatha these bones and see what she makes of this. When she was finished she slowly re-planted the row of flowers which were just lying on the ground, like they were waiting to be replanted. About thirty minutes later she got to her feet and said to herself, well there, now this time you stay in there she told the flowers smiling at them. She picked up the mess and her tools and walked back to the small shed where she placed the tools inside along with all the garbage she gathered. She left the small plastic container which contained the bones just outside the back door, I will remember to show these to Agatha when she comes over. She then headed back into the house where in the kitchen she decided to make herself a cup of hot tea. Soon she was sitting at the kitchen table once again sipping on her tea. Well in about ten minutes I shall start cleaning, once again. She smiled at herself as she got to her feet and headed for the brook closet. She then took out all the cleaning supplies she would need along with a mop and a broom. She then head for her bedroom where she started making their bed, putting all the dirty clothes in the laundry hamper, and started to clean the room. She decided to open the bedroom and let in some fresh air, because soon it would be very very cold outside and she could not do that any more. She walked over and opened their bedroom window. There she said and took in a deep breathe of fresh air., I shall leave it open for a while and come back and close it. She then continued on with her cleaning, when she got done in their room she went down the hall to Destiny's room. Well maybe I shall open her window also and let in some of that fresh air. She did so and started cleaning Destiny's room.

When she was done she decided to go into the bathroom and clean that room next. She always knew it would be the worst room always in their house to keep clean. Soon Madison had finished cleaning the bathroom.She then asked herself, shall I go into Uriel's room and clean that, it could be a awful mess by now. She hesitated at the door to his room then finally decided to go inside and have a look around. She opened the door and to her amazement the room was not all that bad as she thought it might be. She stood there for a few seconds and said wow he kept his room tidy after all, she was surprised to say the least at the appearance of it. She decided to go about cleaning up his room. She headed for the window to open it, but it would not budge. She tried and tried and said to herself, what is wrong with this window it just will not open. Finally she gave up, oh well I will leave this window and she went about cleaning his room. When she was done she closed the door to his room and headed for the front of the house, cleaning from the front door back to the kitchen. Finally she was finished cleaning the whole house, and looking up at the clock on the wall noticed it was lunch time so she made herself a ham and cheese sandwich and another hot cup of tea to wash it down it. She sat at the kitchen table having her lunch when the telephone rang. She got up and walked over to the telephone and picking up the receiver she said, Hello. Hello Mrs. Appleby this is Father Anthony, how are you he asked her? Well I am just fine and how are you doing Father Anthony she replied? Father Anthony replied he was fine and in good health. I am sorry I did not get back to you sooner but we have been awfully busy here at the church. First there was a wedding and then there was funeral, one thing after another he said. Oh well Madison replied things happen, not to worry about it. He went on to tell her what he thought was her problem at home, about a evil vengeful spirit whom did not want to leave. He told Madison what he could possibly do for her. I am just not quite sure as to when Bishop Peter and myself could come by and perform the ceremony he told her. I will have to get back to you on that he told her.

Well Father Anthony that is fine, please do what you have to and get back to me when you can she told him. Ok and thank you for your patience Mrs. Appleby I will do that, and he said goodbye and hung up the phone. Madison went back and sat down at the kitchen table pondering over what he told her. Looking up at clock again she noticed soon the family would be home, what should I cook for supper today? Madison decided on chicken with vegetables and rice, and I shall make some rice pudding for dessert as everyone loves that she said to herself. Soon Madison was on her feet preparing supper. As the main meal was cooking away she started making the rice pudding. When it was all ready and put into a baking dish, she walked over to the oven and placed the baking dish into the prewarmed oven at 350 degrees. When all was still cooking away Madison sat at the kitchen table thinking about her day. Maybe I will call Agatha and tell her what I found in my garden, yes. She got up from the table and walked over to the telephone and started dialing Agatha's telephone number. After three rings of the phone Agatha answered the call. Hello Hello Madison how are you? I am fine Agatha and how are you she asked? I am a little tired but I am fine. Why did you call today has something else happened over there she asked? Well, no but I called to tell you what I found in my garden today. Something had upset my flower bed so I went out to fix it. As I was digging up the soil I found many small bones, they look like that of a small animal but I am not sure, so I was wondering if you're not doing anything tomorrow could you drop by for a short visit and have a look at them Madison asked her? Well Agatha replied, I do have to go into town tomorrow about 12:00pm to meet with another friend for lunch, I will stop by after we are finished lunch on my way home. Ok that would be great Madison replied, thank you I will see you tomorrow then and Madison said good bye and hung up the telephone. As Madison turned around to check on supper Destiny had come in through the back door. Hi she said to Madison I am home, what's for supper she asked with a smile on her face? Well chicken Madison replied. Ok Destiny replied I will be in my room I have homework to do she said. Ok replied Madison. About fifteen minutes later Ethan came in through the back door. Hello there how was your day he asked Madison as she walked towards him with open arms and hugged him and said my day was fine and how was your day she asked him? Ok just a normal day he replied. He turned and walked into the bathroom to wash up and change for supper. Then he went into the front room and turned on the television to watch the days news. About thirty minutes later supper was cooked so Madison took the pudding out of the oven and placed it on the counter top to cool. She went about setting the table and placed out four settings for everyone. Five minutes later she called out to everyone to come for supper. Two seconds later Destiny came running into the kitchen and sat down at the table then Ethan came into the kitchen and sat down at his place at the table.

Madison put the food onto each plate with one serving each, and she placed some out for herself, then she also sat down at the table. Ethan looked around and said, what no Uriel today, where is he do you know he asked everyone looking right at Madison? No he has not come home yet, Destiny he asked? Nope he was not at school today either, the teacher asked me where he was I told him I did not know. Don't tell me he is going to play this game again, what shall we do with that child and he shook his head . I thought we were finished with this non-sense he said. Madison and Destiny just looked up at him and shook their heads. Supper was over now so Ethan went off into the front room to watch some TV before going to bed and Destiny helped her mother clear away the supper dishes and put them away. When the girls were finished in the kitchen they joined Ethan for some television before going to bed. About one hour later Destiny went off to bed good night everyone she said and left the room. Soon Ethan stood up and said well it's bed time for me too I am very tired. Ok Madison replied and she went off to the bathroom to get ready for bed as Ethan went about the house turning the lights off and making sure all was locked up and secure for the night When he had finished Madison was also finished so Ethan went into the bathroom to get ready for bed then he joined Madison getting under the bed covers. He turned and kissed his wife good night rolled over and fell off to sleep instantly. Madison lay there for a while before she drifted off to sleep. On this the fifth evening after the cleansing Madison awoke to the sound of a very loud moaning sound. She did not know weather to get up and go have a look or not. She laid there for a while and decided yes I must get up and see what is making that noise. Madison slowly got up out of bed, opened her bedroom door and upon looking down the hallway she seen Uriel walking on all fours upside down. As soon as he saw Madison looking at him, he backed up into his room backwards slamming the door behind him. Madison stood there for a while just amazed at what she saw. Am I imagining this again she thought then slowly walked towards Uriel's room and opened the door. To her amazement she found Uriel sleeping in his bed, but she noticed the night stand beside his bed was pushed away to one side, and that there was a medium size hole in the wall about one foot square, inside she noticed there was a glowing blue light, as she gripped closer she noticed the glowing blue light was that of a small figure in the shape of a small head of some evil looking gargoyle, all of a sudden it stopped glowing. Madison backed away slowly thinking to herself...this I shall tell Agatha and Father Anthony of, then she slowly backed her way to her room and under the bed covers covering her face and soon after fell off to sleep.

   The next morning Madison awoke as usual and went into the kitchen to make the morning coffee. She stood at the counter beside the coffee pot waiting for it to be finished. Soon Ethan came into the kitchen with the smell of coffee in the air he ask good morning what's for breakfast? What, what would you like Madison asked him? Mm how about just some cereal and toast with coffee he told her. Ok that's easy she told him as she poured him a cup of newly brewed hot coffee. She then placed the bread into the toaster and placed the cereal out on the table. Soon the toast popped up and she handed it to him on a small plate along with butter and some jam. here you are she replied. Ethan looked up at her and said, is there something on your mind this morning?? Madison hesitated and replied, no not at all just trying to wake up she replied. Well ok he replied. Ethan ate his breakfast and said well, it's off to work we have a busy day today, he stood up kissed his wife good bye grabbed his lunch bucket and off he went. Soon Destiny came into the kitchen good morning she said, breakfast? We are having cereal and toast this morning she told her. Ok Destiny replied, so Madison got up to place some bread into the toaster and push it down. When it had finished toasting she place it on a small plate and took it over to Destiny, here you go she told her. Thanks mom she replied. Soon Destiny was finished and said well, it's off to school mother. She stood up from the table kissed her mother on the cheek and said, good bye mom I'll see you after school. ok have a good day dear Madison replied. Destiny was off and out the door. Madison was once again left sitting at the kitchen table alone. Thinking out loud she said to herself I hope Agatha comes by today. Madison sat at the kitchen for a long time sipping her coffee. She then decided to do some laundry while she was waiting to hear back from Agatha. She went into her bedroom took up the laundry basket and grabbed all the dirty laundry, then headed towards Destiny's room and did the same, then headed into the bathroom gathering all the dirty towels and placing them into the laundry basket. She headed into Uriel's room, as she opened the door to his room she found Uriel to be still sleeping in his bed. She went over to awaken him, giving him a small shake and calling his name, he did not stir, Madison turned and picked up all the dirty laundry she could find and headed out of his room closing the door quietly behind her. She then headed down to the basement where she put the lights on and put the first load of laundry into the washing machine. She always placed the whites in first because she would add some bleach to whiten them up. The machine was loaded with laundry soap, and bleach, she then closed the lid down turned the machine on. She then turned around to separate the rest of the laundry, then headed back upstairs to the kitchen where she made herself a nice hot cup of tea. She sat at the kitchen table sipping her tea and waited for the laundry.

About thirty minutes later she went back down to the basement, took the finished wet laundry out of the machine and placed them into the dryer closing the door and turning the machine on. She then went back to the washing machine and placed the next load of laundry into the machine with some soap, closing the lid down she turned the machine on once again. She then headed back upstairs to the kitchen. Just as she was about to sit down at the kitchen table the telephone rang. She walked over to the phone and picking up the receiver said, Hello, hello my friend Agatha here just wanted to tell you I am finished and I am now heading towards your place, I shall be there in about forty minutes she told Madison. Oh ok Madison replied, I will put the kettle on for us, see you soon then and Madison hung up the telephone. Madison turned and placed the kettle on the stove to boil and make a nice big pot of tea. She then headed to the pantry to find some nice sweets to go with the tea. She found a package of cookies so she took them out and placed them on a small plate and placed it on the kitchen table. Just then a knock came to the front door. Madison turned and walked to the front door and upon opening it saw Agatha standing there. Hello my dear friend, please come in Madison told her with a smile on her face. Hi Agatha replied, please come into the kitchen I have some hot tea for us Madison told her. You said you found some small bones in your garden out back Agatha said looking at Madison? Why yes I did, can you tell me if they mean anything or are they just misplaced Madison asked her? Stay here I will go and get them Madison told her leaving her at the kitchen table Madison headed out the back door, picked up the plastic container and took it inside and placed it onto the kitchen counter top near the back door. Agatha slowly got up from her chair and walked over to Madison, she then looked into the plastic container Madison had placed there. She put on a pair of plastic gloves she had in her pocket and started to examine them turning them over and over, and even picking some up and placing them into the day light, like she was trying to look through them, then placed them back into the container. Well if you don't mind, I will take them home and check them out further she said. Oh ok Madison replied, please, please do I don't know how or why they were there. When I planted my flowers they were not there then Madison told her. Oh ok replied Agatha I will return them if you wanted she asked with a smile on her face. Oh no no you don't have to do that Madison replied.

The ladies sat there for a while then Madison remembered. Oh there is something else Madison told her. What is it Agatha asked her? Come, come with me Madison told her and they walked over and went into Uriel's room. Slowly opening the door Madison noticed that Uriel was not in his bed any more, oh he must have left she told herself. Madison slowly entered his room and walked over to the wall where she found the opening the night prior. She bent down and pulled the night stand away from the wall. She exposed the small opening in the wall and said to Agatha, see come look she told her. Agatha bent down also and they found a small container inside the hole. Madison slowly reached for the item and slowly pulled it out of the hole and placed it on the floor beside them. The item was wrapped in some very old cloth, she carefully took it out of the container and started to unwrap it. Agatha still wearing her plastic gloves took the item and carefully looked at it, turning it over and over in her hands. It seemed to made of a resin matter, it was not very heavy but rather light in weight. I will check at the library tomorrow and see if I can find out what this is Agatha told her. She then was about to return it to the box when all of a sudden it started to light up a glowing blue light came from within it, Agatha dropped it and it fell back into the small container it came out, exactly in the same position. Well Agatha said, that is very strange, lets just put it back where we found it for now and I will check into it Agatha told her. Ok Madison replied they replaced it back into the wall and placed the night stand in front of it. Both women got to their feet and left Uriel's room, closing the door behind them and went back to the kitchen. That is a very ghastly looking item isn't it Madison told Agatha. Well yes it is, please don't touch it again until I find out what it is, ok Agatha told her. You got my word Madison told her I will definitely not. The two women finished off their tea then Agatha told her she had to leave. Ok replied Madison please call me when you find out anything. Yes, yes I will replied Agatha as they walked towards the front door. Madison opened the door and watched as Agatha left her house, down the path and got into her car. Madison waved good bye and went back inside closing the door behind her. She then headed back downstairs to the basement where she found her laundry to be done. She took the dry clothes out of the dryer and placed them into the laundry basket, took the wet clothes out of the washing machine and placed them into the dryer, turning the machine on. She then walked over to the washing machine where she placed the next load of laundry, placed some laundry soap into the machine and closed the lid down turning the machine on. Madison then went back upstairs to the kitchen where she sat at the table to finish off her tea and cookies. Looking up at the clock on the wall she noticed it was getting pretty close to supper time, my how time flies when having fun she told herself.

She decided to make some hamburgers today with french fries. She started to make the hamburgers and cutting up the french fries. As the hamburgers were cooking slowly the back door suddenly opened there was Destiny Hi mom hamburgers hey that's good how soon will they be ready she asked her mother, oh not for a while I will call you Madison told her. Ok Destiny replied and went off to her room closing the door behind her. Soon Ethan came in through the door. Hi there how was your day he asked her as he kissed her on the cheek? Oh just fine how was your day she replied? Oh just fine the day was not as busy as we thought, which was good for us he smiled at her and went into the bathroom to wash up and change for supper. Soon he came into the living room where he turned on the television to watch the evening news and sat down in his big comfy chair. About twenty minutes later supper was almost ready. Madison set the table for supper placing some condiments and plates. Soon the supper was ready so Madison took out the french fries and placed them on a platter setting them in the middle of the table. She then put the hamburgers together and placed them out on table, then called everyone to supper. Soon Ethan and Destiny came into the kitchen mm that smells very good Destiny said with a smile on her face and sitting down in her usual spot. Soon everyone was eating their meal. No sign of Uriel today Ethan asked looking at Madison? No he was sleeping this morning in his bed when I went in to get his dirty laundry so I left him there. Soon Agatha and I went into his room to check something and he was gone. Oh ok Ethan replied well I guess he is not eating again. That child is going to get very thin Ethan said with a smile on his face. Soon supper was over and Ethan retired into the living room to watch some television while Destiny helped her mother clean up after supper putting the clean dishes away. They soon followed Ethan into the living where they all watched television for a while. Soon Destiny got up and went off to bed, good night everyone she said. Good night Madison replied. Soon both Ethan and Madison got up and was headed off to bed. Madison got ready first then it was Ethan's turn. Soon they were both tucked under the bed covers and fell off to sleep. The next morning Madison woke with no interruption of sleep last night. Wow finally a good nights sleep she told herself and went out to the kitchen to make the morning coffee.

As soon as the coffee started brewing Ethan came into the kitchen rubbing his eyes, oh is it morning already he asked with a smile on his face? Why yes it is, did you sleep well Madison asked him? Yes I think I did finally he said. What is for breakfast today he asked Madison? Well what would you like this morning she asked Ethan? mmm what about some pancakes they really fill me up for the day he said. Ok pancakes it is Madison replied as she went about making them. As they were cooking Destiny came into the kitchen, wow pancakes great, can I have some she asked her mother? Why yes you can sit down and I'll stir some up for you. Destiny sat at the table awaiting her plate. Soon Madison came along with a stack of pancakes for her, here you go now eat them all Madison told her smiling at her. Both Ethan and Destiny were having their breakfast when Uriel came into the kitchen. Hey can I have some too he asked, I'm starved. Yes sit down and I'll fix you some Madison replied. Soon as Uriel was having his pancakes Ethan looked at him and asked how he was doing. I am fine father really. Ethan replied well you don't look fine to me maybe you should go to the doctor and get a check up he told him. No no he replied I am fine, and Uriel got up and left the house like he was in a hurry. Wow there is definitely something wrong with that boy Ethan said. Yes I suppose there is Madison replied. Well Ethan replied am off to work you have a good day and I'll see you later he told her as he kissed her good bye and picked up his lunch bucket and left then house. Everyone has left the building again Madison thought to herself. Well I should finish the laundry I started yesterday she thought to herself, so she got up from the table and went down to the basement. When she got to the bottom of the basement stairs she stopped dead in her tracks. Looking down at the floor she saw this small figure again, the one that was suppose to be upstairs in the wall of Uriel's room. She stood there for a moment then thought, there is a answer for this, so she just stepped over it and went over to the laundry room. She took the dry clothes out of the dryer and placed them into the laundry basket which was still sitting on the floor in of the dryer machine. She then took the wet clothes out of the washing machine and placed them into the dryer turning the machine on. She then placed the last of the laundry into the washing machine, added some laundry soap and turned it on. Stepping back she said to herself, there after these are done laundry will be done, she brushed off her apron turned and went back upstairs to the kitchen, as she past and looking down she noticed the small figure was gone, so she went into the kitchen where she put the kettle on for some tea.

When the kettle had boiled she made herself a nice hot cup of green tea and sat down at the kitchen table to sip on it. Madison sat there for about forty five minutes then decided to go downstairs and see to the laundry. As she approached the bottom of the stairs, and looking down she did NOT see the small figure again, it was not there this time. Scratching her head she told herself that is very strange, one minute it's there and the next it's gone. Oh well soon hopefully this will all be over with. She continued on over to the laundry area, took the dried clothes out of the dryer placed them into the laundry basket which was at her feet, and placed the wet clothes out of the washing machine into the dryer and turned it on. Closing the lid down she turned and headed back upstairs to the kitchen where she continued to sip on her tea. About twenty minutes later the telephone rang. Madison got up and walked to the telephone to answer it, hello she said hello. Hello Madison this is Agatha how are you doing today she asked? Well I am just fine and how are you she asked Agatha? I am good, I just thought I'd call you to let you know what I found out about that figure, Agatha continued. I found it to be a Greek Mythology called a "Chimera". It is suppose to be a horror monster believed to frightened away any evil spirit or spirits. This one in particular is a fire-breathing creature, it is made up of many other animals the head of a lioness, the back of this creature to be a goat and the tail of a snake like creature, it is supposedly originated from Italy. That is all I know at this point of time. Well replied Madison why is it in the walls of my house, I mean how did it get there Madison asked? I don't know Agatha told her, I really don't know but we will get to the bottom of this, I promise. Has there been anything strange going on since I left she asked? Well no, but this morning I went down to the basement to finish my laundry but before I got to the bottom of the stairs, I looked down and there laying on the floor was the figure from inside the wall. I stood there for a moment then I went about my business and forgot about it, and I went back upstairs. When I came back down again to finish my laundry I had noticed it was gone. I don't know what to make of that, do you she asked Agatha? After a moment of hesitation Agatha replied, no I really don't know but we will find out. Don't panic until I talk with you again Agatha told her just go about your business ok she told Madison. Well ok I will, I'll say good bye for now as I am still doing laundry Madison replied with a giggle in her voice.

Oh ok I will let you go do that and I will call you back when I find out anything Agatha told her and said good bye. Madison hung up the phone and went back to the table and sat down. About thirty minutes later Madison went back down to the laundry room to pick up the rest of her laundry. She did not notice anything out of place, so she turned the lights out and went back upstairs. Madison walked into her own bedroom to put away their clothes and linens, then she walked into Destiny's room and put away her clothes. She then walked into the bathroom where she put away a pile of towels she kept in the small closet near the bathroom door outside in the hallway. She then headed for Uriel's room, upon opening the door she walked in and found this horrible smell through the room like some one had died in there or something. Madison put away Uriel's clothes and just before leaving his room she glanced down at the hole in the wall behind the night stand, she stood there for a moment wondering...it has to be inside there it can't possibly come out and walk downstairs by itself Madison brushed it off and went into the kitchen where she made herself some lunch. Today she wanted some hot soup with crackers. Madison was sitting at the kitchen table sipping on her hot soup when all of a sudden the whole house started shaking like there was a earth quake or something. Madison held onto the kitchen table with both hands and both feet planted on the floor. After a few seconds it stopped. Wow what was that she asked herself, what was that?? Sitting there in deep thought Madison decided to call on Father Anthony see if he had heard anything yet. She walked over to the telephone picked up the receiver and dialed his telephone number. It rang about five times when finally a woman answered the call. Hello this is Family church of God how may I help you she said my name is Madison I am calling Father Anthony is he around or nearby Madison asked? No not at this time do you want to leave him a message she asked? Yes, could you please have him call me when he gets in, it is very urgent Madison asked. Ok the woman replied I will tell him, thank you for your call good bye and she hung up the phone.

Madison walked into her own bedroom to put away their clothes and linens, then she walked into Destiny's room and put away her clothes. She then walked into the bathroom where she put away a pile of towels she kept in the small closet near the bathroom door outside in the hallway. She then headed for Uriel's room, upon opening the door she walked in and found this horrible smell through the room like some one had died in there or something. Madison put away Uriel's clothes and just before leaving his room she glanced down at the hole in the wall behind the night stand, she stood there for a moment wondering...it has to be inside there it can't possibly come out and walk downstairs by itself Madison brushed it off and went into the kitchen where she made herself some lunch. Today she wanted some hot soup with crackers. Madison was sitting at the kitchen table sipping on her hot soup when all of a sudden the whole house started shaking like there was a earth quake or something. Madison held onto the kitchen table with both hands and both feet planted on the floor. After a few seconds it stopped. Wow what was that she asked herself, what was that?? Sitting there in deep thought Madison decided to call on Father Anthony see if he had heard anything yet. She walked over to the telephone picked up the receiver and dialed his telephone number. It rang about five times when finally a woman answered the call. Hello this is Family church of God how may I help you she said my name is Madison I am calling Father Anthony is he around or nearby Madison asked? No not at this time do you want to leave him a message she asked? Yes, could you please have him call me when he gets in, it is very urgent Madison asked. Ok the woman replied I will tell him, thank you for your call good bye and she hung up the phone.

    Madison walked into her own bedroom to put away their clothes and linens, then she walked into Destiny's room and put away her clothes. She then walked into the bathroom where she put away a pile of towels she kept in the small closet near the bathroom door outside in the hallway. She then headed for Uriel's room, upon opening the door she walked in and found this horrible smell through the room like some one had died in there or something. Madison put away Uriel's clothes and just before leaving his room she glanced down at the hole in the wall behind the night stand, she stood there for a moment wondering...it has to be inside there it can't possibly come out and walk downstairs by itself Madison brushed it off and went into the kitchen where she made herself some lunch. Today she wanted some hot soup with crackers. Madison was sitting at the kitchen table sipping on her hot soup when all of a sudden the whole house started shaking like there was a earth quake or something. Madison held onto the kitchen table with both hands and both feet planted on the floor. After a few seconds it stopped. Wow what was that she asked herself, what was that?? Sitting there in deep thought Madison decided to call on Father Anthony see if he had heard anything yet. She walked over to the telephone picked up the receiver and dialed his telephone number. It rang about five times when finally a woman answered the call. Hello this is Family church of God how may I help you she said my name is Madison I am calling Father Anthony is he around or nearby Madison asked? No not at this time do you want to leave him a message she asked? Yes, could you please have him call me when he gets in, it is very urgent Madison asked. Ok the woman replied I will tell him, thank you for your call good bye and she hung up the phone. Well yet another day gone and nothing else has happened that's good news right he said to Madison with a smile on his face? Yes replied Madison as she rolled over and kissed her husband good night, sleep well she said and Ethan turned off the light, they both fell deeply asleep.

CHAPTER SEVEN

The next morning Madison awoke first as usual got up out of bed, and went into the bathroom, washed up and got dressed. She then went into the kitchen where she put the kettle on to make the morning coffee. As the coffee was brewing and with the smell of coffee in the air Madison could hear Ethan get up and go into the bathroom to get ready and dressed for work. He then walked into the kitchen, good morning he said, good morning replied Madison coffee she asked? Yes please, she then poured him a big cup of coffee, as they both sat there Madison asked, what would you like for breakfast she asked? Well how about some bacon and eggs this morning, I am in the mood for some bacon he said with a smile on his face. Well, ok bacon and eggs it is, Madison replied as she got up from the table and walked over to the stove where she started to cook some bacon, then some eggs. She then made a pile of toast, as he was about to put some, bacon and eggs on Ethan's plate and put it on the table in front of him Destiny came into the kitchen, mmm bacon and eggs, can I have some she asked also with a smile on her face looking straight at her mother? Ok sit down and I shall get some for you. Do you want some orange juice with it Madison asked? Yes please Destiny replied as Madison poured her out a small glass of juice, there you go now eat up and go to school. Ok mother Destiny replied. As the family sat at the kitchen table having their breakfast Uriel came into the kitchen, just staring at his mother. Finally he said good morning may I have some also I am starving he said. Ok replied Madison sit down here and I'll get you some. As Madison prepared him some bacon and eggs he sat patiently at the table, not looking at anyone else. He finally got his breakfast and ate it up like there was no tomorrow, then ran out the back door, good bye. Ethan just stared at him as he disappeared out the door. Well I must be off to work Ethan got up from the table, and grabbing his lunch bucket kissing his wife goodbye he too disappeared out the door. Soon Destiny was off good bye mother have a good day she said as she went out the door. Madison was once again sitting at the kitchen table alone. As she sat there sipping on her coffee the telephone rang. Madison went over to answer it. Hello she said, hello. Hello Mrs. Appleby this is Father Anthony calling, how are you today he asked her. Well I am fine Father and how about yourself she replied? I am well thank you. My secretary told me you had called the other day, I am returning your call he told her. I was just wondering when you could possibly come by and help fix our little problem Madison told him. Well Father Anthony replied, I have talked to Bishop Peter, we are gathering up the things we will need and come by and perform an exorcism on your son Uriel. It took a long time to convince the cardinal of our wishes. At first he always told us no we could not do this, but eventually he reconsidered and decided to let us perform the art. I shall call you back with a date and a time Father Anthony told her, ok replied Madison but I sure hope it will be very soon, we are all going crazy here not knowing what to expect next she told him. Yes I understand he told her I will call you right away. I must say good bye for and prepare for the work, I shall call you back soon he said. Ok thank you again Madison replied good bye for now and she hung up the telephone. Madison went back to the kitchen table sat down and enjoyed her coffee and breakfast she finally prepared for herself. Madison decided to clean the house today as all the laundry was done and put away. She got up from the kitchen table and cleaned up the dishes from breakfast. When she was finished she walked over to the broom closet and took out the cleaning supplies she would need to clean the whole house, including the mop and a bucket. Madison started to clean the house starting from the front door, dusting and washing all the floors. She got to her own room and opened the door and started to clean, opening the window to let in some fresh air. When she opened the window she noticed the air outside seemed to be getting a little cooler now as it was the fall season and soon the winter snow would be covering the ground, she shook a little telling herself I don't like the winter. Madison went about the room dusting everything and she swept the floor ready for a mopping. Before she started to wash the floor she went over to the window and closed it, deciding it was getting a little too cold for comfort. When the window was shut she went about washing the floor, and backed out of her room closing the door behind knowing the freshly washed floor would soon dry on its own. Next she went into Destiny's room. Madison walked over to the window and opened it as well with a shiver to her bones, then she went about cleaning the room, picking up the dirty laundry which Destiny had just flown down on the floor, and putting them into the laundry basket. I wish these children would pickup after themselves, but I guess that is too much to ask Madison said to herself. When Madison was ready to mop the floor she once again walked over to the window and closed, then started to mop the floors, leaving the room as she was finished closing the door behind her.

The Possession Of Uriel

    Next she thought to herself is the worst room in the whole house the bathroom. Madison entered the bathroom and found dirty laundry laying about the floor, and the counter top was filled with Destiny's make-up, it was all over the place. Madison started to clean up the mess putting things away where they belonged. She cleaned the bathroom spending a lot of time on the bath tub scrubbing away as everyone used this bathtub and no one ever cleaned it. Finally she had finished cleaning the bathroom and was moping the floor on her way out the door, this time she left the door to the bathroom opened. She found herself very tired, so she decided to stop and have a cup of nice hot tea and a breather, rest period. Madison sat down at the kitchen table sipping on her hot tea having a rest. A half an hour went by when she decided to get up and finish her work. On my she thought, next is Uriel's room, should I dare go in and clean it she thought to herself. After a few minutes she decided to give it a go. She walked to Uriel's room and opened the door. She stood there for a moment just looking around the room, nothing out of place in here she thought to herself so she started to clean his room. She picked up his dirty laundry and placed them into the laundry basket, straightened out a few of his things and dusted the room completely, not even noticing the hole in the wall behind the night stand. She then swept and moped the floor backing out of his room when she was finished closing the door behind her. She straightened up and said there that wasn't too bad, nothing happened. She then walked over and into the kitchen. Madison dusted the whole kitchen area then swept and moped the floor. When the job was completed she put away all the cleaning supplies, and noticing the kitchen floor was dry she decided to make herself some lunch. She decided on a ham and cheese sandwich, which she prepared for herself along with another hot cup of hot tea. She sat down at the kitchen table to have her lunch. I wonder how Agatha is making out, wonder if she found out any more news on that object we found. She sat there for a while pondering over the thought. When the whole house was completely cleaned and very quiet, she was sitting at the table when all of a sudden she heard this very loud crashing sound like a plate glass window had been shattered. She did not know whether to move, go and look or stay where she was, soon the sound stopped and the house was very quiet once again.

She decided to get up and go have a look around the house, she checked every nook ,and cranny and every closet in every room. mmm she thought to herself nothing, I found nothing at all, could it be just my imagination. she thought about it for a while then went and sat back down at the kitchen table. About half an hour later the telephone rang. Madison got up and went to answer it. Hello she said Hello. Hi Mrs. Appleby this is Father Anthony calling, how are you today he asked her? Well I am I guess and how are you Father she asked him? Have you decided when you will be coming around she asked? Why yes that is why I am calling he replied. I wanted to know if tomorrow evening around say 7:00pm is ok with you and your family he asked her? Oh my yes that will be just fine Father Anthony, Madison replied. Oh ok then we shall come by tomorrow evening around 7:00pm and offer our services, he told her we shall perform a exorcism on Uriel and this will or should get rid of all evil spirits in your home Mrs. Appleby. Oh my goodness that sounds just fine, thank you Father Anthony we look forward to seeing you tomorrow evening around 7:00pm then replied Madison, good bye for now then she replied and hung up the telephone. Looking up at the clock on the wall she noticed again it was getting to be near supper time. She decided to cook some pork chops with potatoes and vegetables for their meal today. She went about the kitchen preparing and she took out the frozen pork chops there were in the freezer. When they had thawed, she started cooking, first the pork chops as they would take the longest time she thought, then she prepared the vegetables, as she was about to start cooking the vegetables Destiny came in through the back door. Hi mom how are you she said as she walked past her mother and into her bedroom, have homework to do let me know when supper is ready she said. Ok replied Madison as she stood at the kitchen stove watching over the meal as it cooked. About twenty minutes later Ethan came in through the door. Hi dear and how was your day he asked her as he kissed her on the cheek walking past her? Just fine and how was your day she asked him back? Oh just the usual. I'm going to clean up before supper he said and went into the bathroom to wash up. When he was finished he then walked into the living room and turned the television on to watch some news before supper.

About ten minutes later Madison called out, supper is ready everyone. Destiny came running into the kitchen and sat down at her usual spot and asked what's for supper? You will see in about thirty seconds Madison told her as she placed a pork chop, and some vegetables on a plate and handed it to her here you go she told her with a smile on her face. Destiny smiled back and said mm, smells good as usual. It is just eat Madison told her. Next Madison put two pork chops out on a plate with lots of vegetables and placed it down in front of Ethan, then she went and prepared her own plate then sat down at the table. No one looked up or said one word until Madison spoke up and said. I am having Father Anthony and Bishop Peter come by tomorrow evening to perform a ceremony to help rid us of any evil being in this house. Madison looked up and straight at Ethan. Oh well that sounds great dear and what time will this happen he asked her? He told me about 7:00pm tomorrow evening Madison replied, so I want supper and the mess to be cleared away before they arrive she said looking at Destiny. Oh ok mother I will help you she replied. The family finished their meal and before leaving the kitchen Ethan asked Madison and where is Uriel today, not home I suppose. No Madison replied I have not seen or heard from him, have you Madison asked Destiny? Why no mother I have not seen him at school either, but a friend of mine has seen him, so he was at school today. Oh ok Ethan replied out loud at least he is at school. As Ethan got up and went into the living room Madison and Destiny started to clear away the mess and dishes from supper, and then they went into the living room to join Ethan. About one and a half hours later Destiny got up and said good night everyone I am off to bed. Good night dear Madison replied. Soon Ethan stood up and said I am tired and going to bed he told Madison, ok she replied. They turned the television off as Ethan went about the house checking to make sure all was secure and turning off the lights Madison went into the bathroom to get ready for bed then went into their bedroom and got under the bed covers where she waited for Ethan. About ten minutes later he came into the bedroom and got under the bed covers, rolled over kissed his wife and said good night dear. Good night Madison replied and they both fell off to sleep. There were no sounds or excitement that night so the family slept well through the night. Morning came and Madison got up first as usual and went into the kitchen to put the kettle on to make coffee.

As the kettle boiled Madison made the morning coffee and as it was brewing and with the smell of coffee in the air soon Ethan got up and came into the kitchen. Good morning he said. Good morning replied Madison and what would you like for breakfast today she asked him? Maybe some boiled eggs and toast he replied. Ok coming right up Madison replied and went about fixing his breakfast. Soon Destiny came into the kitchen and sat down at her usual spot, she looked at her father and said what are you having for breakfast she asked him? Eggs and toast sweetie. Oh ok she replied maybe I will just have some cereal and juice Destiny said. Ok replied Madison, you know where the cereal is help yourself she said looking at Destiny with a smile on her face. Destiny got up from her seat, went over and took out the cereal box along with a bowl and the milk jug sat down and poured herself out a bowl of cereal, and sat eating it. Soon Ethan got up and said ok well, it's off to work for me, I will see you later then he told Madison kissing her good bye have a good day he said. Madison replied don't forget Father Anthony is coming by tonight so don't be late please, ok he replied and off he went. Soon Destiny was on her way out the door too grabbing her lunch bag, good bye mother see you after school and left closing the door behind her. Madison poured herself the last cup of coffee and sat down at the table, thinking about her day ahead. I wonder what will happen tonight I hope only good news comes of it whatever they are going to do I really do she told herself. Madison sat at the kitchen table for a long time thinking about the day ahead. Maybe I could make some biscuits for the boys when they arrive, yes I shall make some biscuits she told herself. (She called the Father and Bishop boys) because she thought of them as young men, not men of the cloth. Madison went about the kitchen gathering up the ingredients for the biscuits and she started to mix and put together the mixture and put them into the oven at three hundred degrees for about fifteen minutes she thought. Soon she could smell the biscuits baking and when they were done she took out of the oven. Mmm well done they are she told herself with a smile, I think they will like these. As the biscuits were cooling on a wire rack on the counter top Madison cleaned up the mess she had made and sat down at the kitchen table just staring outside . By this time it was getting pretty close to supper time so she decided to make a early meal consisting of chicken, rice and vegetables. As she took the frozen chicken out of the freezer to thaw, she thought she saw, looking out the into the backyard, a small animal of sorts or could be a dog too, digging up her flower bed again. She placed the frozen chicken into the kitchen sink to thaw and ran outside into the backyard, and as she got closer to the small animal it had taken off, she saw it had once again started to dig up her flowers and as she got closer and upon inspection she saw that there were once again a bunch of small bones laying in the dirt where the animal was digging, with her newly planted flowers once again dug up and scattered about. mmm she thought to herself I will leave this mess and show Agatha when she comes to visit, I don't have time for this right now she told herself. Madison turned around and headed back to the house where she brushed off her clothes before going inside. Once in the kitchen she noticed the chicken had thawed out and looking up at the clock on the wall decided to start cooking supper. She prepared the chicken and the vegetables and placed them into a pot for the vegetables and a frying pan for the chicken. Shortly there after Destiny came home, see mom I got home early is there anything I can help you with for supper she asked her mother Well you can set the table dear Madison replied.

Ok Destiny said and went about setting the table. Soon Ethan came home hi everyone I am home how was your day he asked Madison as she was cooking supper at the stove, just fine how was your day she asked him? Just fine. He walked into the bathroom where he washed up and changed for supper then went into the living room to watch television until supper was ready. About ten minutes later he could hear Madison call supper is ready. He quickly got to his feet and went into the kitchen where he sat down at his usual spot and the family had their meal. The family ate their meal, and as usual Ethan went back into the living room while Destiny helped her mother clean up the mess and dishes from supper. Once the kitchen was clean again both Madison and Destiny went into the living room to join Ethan until the boys showed up. About five minutes to 7:00pm there came a knock to the front door. Madison got to go answer it and said they are here, I guess you can stay right where you are she told Ethan and Destiny. Madison walked to the front door and upon opening the door saw Father Anthony and Bishop Peter standing there. Please, please come in she told them. The two gentlemen came in and walked straight towards the kitchen table with Madison following close behind them, and placed their stuff down on the table. Madison noticed that both Father's were wearing long black robes. Father Anthony wore a long purple sash wore round about his neck, and both men were carrying some kind of black prayer book. Father Anthony told Madison to tell the family just to stay where they were until they were finished. While Madison walked back to sit with Destiny and Ethan in the living room Father Anthony and Bishop Peter walked over to Uriel's room and went inside slowly chanting a prayer in Latin and closed the door behind them. Many loud screeching sounds came from within but Madison, Destiny and Ethan sat on their couch nervously holding their hands over their ears. A few minutes later there came silence. Madison saw Bishop Peter come out of Uriel's room heading for the kitchen. Madison got up and walked over to him, what, what is it she asked him? I was wondering if you could possibly make us a hot cup of tea I could really use it about now he said looking at her? Oh why yes please come and sit down here I will make it for you Madison replied.

The Possession Of Uriel

Soon the tea was made and as Bishop Peter sat at the kitchen table sipping on it, he told Madison it would be a long tedious journey but that eventually it come to an end. He then stood up and thanking Madison for the tea, said I shall return to Uriel's room I do not want to leave Father Anthony in there all alone, it is important that there be two of us in the room at all times, thank you he told her and walked back into Uriel's room while Madison went back to sit with her family in the living room.

During the next few hours there came the same various weird sounds and noises coming from Uriel's room now and then there would be a very loud bang, then a few minutes of silence. All of a sudden there came a very loud bang with a shaking of the whole house, a few minutes later a loud crash sound, then all had stopped, silence throughout the whole house. After a few minutes Bishop Peter came out of Uriel's room but Father Anthony did not. He walked slowly towards Madison whom had by this time walked towards him. I think we have everything cleared up Mrs. Appleby, the exorcism went well though Father Anthony did not survive. After the smoke cleared he just vanished into thin air, gone. I looked for him everywhere but only your son Uriel came out walking towards me. Bishop Peter turned around to find Uriel standing about three feet behind him. He walked slowly towards his mother then ran into her arms, saying mother, mother. He slowly raised his head and looked into Madison's eyes, Madison looked back at him noticing his face had gone back to normal. His eyes seemed normal colour and his skin had returned to the normal glow a child should have. As they stood there holding each other Bishop Peter finally said, Mrs. Appleby I must take my leave now, my job here is done he smiled as he past the both of them in a embrace. As he headed for the hallway to leave Madison noticed his clothes and appearance had changed from very clean to a very dirty look, like he had just been through a ringer washer. I hope he will be ok Madison said under her breath. Just before he got to the front door, Ethan stood up and walked towards him, his hand extended to shake Bishop Peter's hand, while shaking hands Ethan said, Bishop Peter we are very very grateful for what you and Father Anthony had done. We shall be forever in your debt, we did not know what would become of us had you two not come by this evening, again we are very grateful and thank you from the bottom of our hearts. Ethan smiled at Bishop Peter and allowed him to leave, waving goodbye as he walked down the street to his car. Ethan and Destiny walked into the kitchen area where they found Madison and Uriel still in a good embrace. All of a sudden Uriel looked up at this father and sister and ran over to them hugging them intensely. After all was said and done, Madison put Uriel to bed and so did everyone else go to bed. The whole family slept well that night. The following morning Madison awoke as usual to make coffee, and as everyone was getting up and coming into the kitchen everyone seemed back to normal. Everyone had their usual remarks about each other and laughed about it. Yes, Madison thought my family is finally back to normal. After everyone had left for work and school, Madison cleaned up the morning mess and dishes and decided to go into Uriel's room to clean up, after all she thought to herself that room must be a terrible mess by now. Madison finished up in the kitchen and walked over to Uriel's room and went inside. She opened the door and looking around, found the room to be normal again, and there was no terrible smell either. She walked over to the night stand and pulled it away from the wall. What she saw threw her off her feet!!! The hole that used to be in the wall there was completely gone, no sign anything had ever been there. Madison ran her fingers across the wall and found nothing, the only thing she did find was the long purple sash from Father Anthony's neck, it was just laying on the floor under the night stand.

Madison picked it up, went into the kitchen washed it and hung it up to dry. I shall call Bishop Peter and tell him what I found and will try to return it as soon as I can. With that said and done Madison finished cleaning Uriel's room and left, closing the door behind her. She walked into the kitchen put the kettle on to make herself a nice hot cup of tea. As she sat at the table sipping her tea, she decided to call Bishop Peter and tell him of the sash she had found and that she wanted to return it. All she got was a answering machine so Madison had left a message for Bishop Peter to call her when he returned then she hung up the telephone and went back to her seat at the table sipping on her tea. She still had not heard from Agatha about the small bones that were found in her flower bed, maybe after I finish my tea I shall go out there and have another look, maybe they too are gone she thought. Madison continued on with her day as usual, then looking up at the clock on the wall she noticed it was getting near to supper so she decided to make some supper. She decided on a pot roast, so she went about preparing the roast, placing it into a large pot and placing it on the stove to cook. A few hours later she would add the as soon as I can. With that said and done Madison finished cleaning Uriel's room and left, closing the door behind her. She walked into the kitchen put the kettle on to make herself a nice hot cup of tea. As she sat at the table sipping her tea, she decided to call Bishop Peter and tell him of the sash she had found and that she wanted to return it. All she got was a answering machine so Madison had left a message for Bishop Peter to call her when he returned then she hung up the telephone and went back to her seat at the table sipping on her tea. She still had not heard from Agatha about the small bones that were found in her flower bed, maybe after I finish my tea I shall go out there and have another look, maybe they too are gone she thought. Madison continued on with her day as usual, then looking up at the clock on the wall she noticed it was getting near to supper so she decided to make some supper. She decided on a pot roast, so she went about preparing the roast, placing it into a large pot and placing it on the stove to cook. A few hours later she would add the vegetables and they would have a good supper. After all she thought to herself Uriel must be starving I know he will eat well today as she filled the pot with lots of vegetables. Soon the whole family had come for supper and everyone was once again happy having a normal life. A few months went by and nothing, nothing at all had come back to haunt them. Madison was very happy. The family never heard any more noises or seen any more strange sightings, whatever was in their home had now disappeared was gone forever, or at least that is what they all thought.

CHAPTER EIGHT

Ten years past with no incidents. Uriel was now twenty three years of age and still living at home. Destiny was right behind him in age but she had finished school and had her first job. She was hired at the same prison her father worked at for so many years, but she was only working in the front office doing a lot of paper work which she loved. Her father, now in his late sixties had retired for about two years now, finding it very hard to stay home and do nothing except working about the house, repairing things, fixing things, doing some gardening work, which Madison had tried to get him to do a long time ago, but he refused. Now, it seems he has a change of mind, you can find him outside in the garden everyday doing something, or just sitting in his chair looking out into the backyard. Madison, getting older like everyone else, now had some mild illness, arthritis in her legs and a muscle discomfort in her right arm. She found it very hard to do much of anything any more, but there was no one else in their home to do the basic chores, like cleaning and do the laundry.

Ethan helped her whenever he could, but found that work to be very tedious. He would take out the trash, clear the driveway, cut the grass but when it came to house work he put his foot down and said, I don't have time for such work. Destiny, when she was at home helped her mother out whenever she could. She would go to work leaving the house about seven thirty in the morning and come home about six o'clock. Uriel, on the other hand was his normal self, didn't want to go back to school to finish his education, nor did he want to find a job. Ethan told him day after day that if he wanted to stay living at home he would have to at least find a part-time job to help out. Humming and hawing, after a long period of time, finally found himself a part-time job, working at the local supermarket, stocking shelves and cleaning up. He did not really care to be doing this but he stuck it out.

One day when Uriel returned home. It was very late this one day, Uriel did not even look at his parents who were sitting in the kitchen at the table, having their afternoon coffee and cookies, both Madison and Ethan looked at him and said, well hello to you too. Just then Destiny came into the kitchen looking for a drink, she saw Uriel standing in the doorway and said well Mr. Sad face, how was your day? Uriel just glanced up at her but said nothing and stormed off into his room. The three family members just sat there in the kitchen staring at each other, after a few minutes Ethan said, well, I hope this non-sense is not returning. I hope he is just angry for something that happened at work today. Madison got up from the table and decided to make some chicken and vegetables for supper. Looking up at the clock on the wall, she noticed it was almost 5:00pm, so decided to start supper.

Madison took some chicken out of the freezer to thaw and took some vegetables from the refrigerator. After the chicken had thawed, she started cutting it up into pieces, covering them with some flour and seasoning and placed them into her huge frying pan that was on the stove warming up. She then turned her attention to the vegetables, started cleaning and cutting them and throwing them into a pot she had boiling on the stove. Also she thought she would make a nice green salad. She went back to the refrigerator and took out some salad greens. Turning to the kitchen counter top, she placed them all on the top and started to wash and cut them into the big salad bowl she had waiting. Soon the salad was finished, so placed the bowl in the refrigerator to keep them cool until the rest of supper was ready. Mean while the chicken was cooking on low heat, then she started the vegetables, soon they were boiling and cooking. About thirty minutes later, the chicken was cooked and so were the vegetables. She then took them out of the pot and placed them onto a large plate. When all was ready she placed all the food out on the kitchen table, which Destiny had set up for supper. She went back to the refrigerator and took out the salad and the salad dressing which she placed on the table. She then called out to everyone…supper is ready come and get it. Everyone came into the kitchen except for Uriel. Ethan called and called him but he never showed. After a few minutes he said, never mind Ethan he is not coming for supper leave him alone.

After the family finished supper, Destiny helped her mother clean up the kitchen and put the dishes away while Ethan did he usual, went into the living room to watch some television. When the girls were finished in the kitchen Destiny joined her father in the living room, and shortly after Madison joined them. Sitting there quietly they could hear Uriel walking about in his room. Madison thought to herself, he never did come out for supper, maybe he is not hungry today. About two hours later, Destiny said she was very tired and wanted to go to bed, off she went, Ethan stood also and said, well that's a night for me and started towards the kitchen area. Madison stood up, shutting off the television, then headed for the bathroom where she went in and got ready for bed before Ethan came for his turn. Soon she was finished and went off to their bedroom, knocking on Destiny's door she said good night Destiny, to which Destiny replied, good night mother, sleep well. Soon Ethan went into the bathroom for his turn, and when finished hen soon joined his wife in bed. Getting under the bed covers he gently rolled over, kissed his wife on the cheek and said, good night love, good night replied Madison, and they fell off to sleep.

That night Madison woke to this very strange sound, and looking at the clock on the night stand noticed again, it was 3:00am. She sat up in bed and listened again, she could hear this very strange sound, like a thumping noise, someone very big and heavy walking down the hallway, but yet she knew no one like that lived in their house. She listened closely for about twenty minutes, then the sound disappeared. Madison slowly slid back under the bed covers, and fell back to sleep. Early the next morning Destiny was the first to get up, go into the bathroom to shower before going to work. While she was in the bathroom Madison got up and headed for the kitchen to put on the coffee and start breakfast. This morning she would make some bacon and eggs with buttered toast. As the coffee was brewing and with the smell in the air, soon Ethan came into the kitchen wearing only his pj's, is coffee ready he asked looking at Madison? Soon, sit down and I will pour you one when it is ready Madison told him smilingly. Ethan sat at the head of the kitchen table and waited. About twenty minutes later Destiny had finished in the bathroom so Ethan was the first to get up from the table and head for the bathroom, me first he told Madison, me first and off he went.

Destiny Madison asked, do you want some breakfast this morning? Yes Destiny replied, I have time to sit and eat this morning, I am in no particular hurry. Soon Ethan had finished in the bathroom and when he got dressed came into the kitchen where his cup of hot coffee sat waiting for him at the table. About ten minutes later breakfast was ready, Madison placed some of everything on a plate and handed it to Destiny, and one for Ethan laying them on the table in front of each of them. Toast is coming Madison said out loud. Soon you could smell toast, toasting in the toaster and popping up, with a slight pop. Madison buttered the toast and brought it over to the kitchen table, where both Ethan and Destiny dug into the plate. Wow, you would think everyone is starved around here the way you people eat Madison stated with a smile on her face. Everyone was having their breakfast, and when they were almost finished Uriel came into the kitchen. Looking quite normal to everyone said, can I have some breakfast, I am starved looking directly at his mother. Yes, sit down and I will get you a plate Madison replied. Uriel sat at the table, not looking at his father and Destiny. His food arrived and he ate it so quickly he almost choked on it, then indistinctly took off out the door not saying one word to anyone.

Ethan spoke up, now, what is his problem? Don't tell me he is going through the same thing as before years ago he said looking at Madison with a frown on his face. Destiny just lowered her head and said nothing. Well she said I am off to work, see you folks later, she got up from the table kissed her mother and father good bye and left through the back door. Madison still said nothing but got herself some breakfast and sat down at the kitchen table to eat. Ethan finished his breakfast and said, well my dear I am off to do some gardening, there are a lot of weeds out there today and I aim to get rid of them, he said with a smile on his face. Ethan got up from the table, put on his gardening boots and went out the back door, leaving Madison to sit alone in the kitchen having her breakfast, she is always the last one to eat she thought to herself, always. With that she smiled, finished her breakfast then got up from the table to clean up after breakfast. Today she thought to herself, I must do some laundry, everyone is out of clean clothes.

After she was done in the kitchen, she turned to go down the hallway to gather up all the dirty clothes, First she went into her own room, pulling the linens off the bed and laying them into the laundry basket, next she went into Destiny's room. Just look at this mess she thought to herself, this child does not pick up her clothes at all I do not know which is dirty and which is clean, so I'll just take everything. She gathered up all the dirty clothes then pulled the linens off Destiny's bed, turned and went down the hall to the bathroom. She gathered up all the dirty towels and dirty clothes that were laying about on the floor, and put them into the laundry basket. She then went down the hall to Uriel's room. When she entered his room she noticed there was this awful smell, the same smell she smelt before those many years ago. She quickly gathered up his dirty clothes and pulled the linens from the bed and left his room quickly not looking back, closed the door behind her.

Madison headed for the basement door, opening it and went down the stairs thinking to herself, oh I hope this nonsense is not coming back upon us, I really hope not. Once downstairs Madison turned on the lights and sorted the clothes, whites from the darks and all the time talked to herself, about what was going on in her home now. The first of white clothes was put into the washing machine, then she added some soap, and a little bleach to help whitened the clothes, closed the lid and turned the machine on to wash. There she said to herself that will take about forty minutes then I shall return. Madison then turned around and went back upstairs to the kitchen where she put the kettle on to make herself some nice hot tea. Sitting there at the table with her very hot tea, she was thinking about the past and what the family went through. Madison shook her head, no I refuse to believe that it would happen to us again, no, she kept repeating to herself. Sitting there in silence and watching Ethan working outside in the backyard, she heard this loud bang, again and again, oh maybe some one is at the front door. Madison got up from the table and went to the front door and upon opening it found no one there, she looked around left to right, right to left no one. Mmm she said, no one, she then closed the door behind her and went back to the kitchen and sat at the table.

About ten minutes later Ethan came into the kitchen, I need a drink he told her, got any coffee left he asked? No Madison replied but I can make some more she said. Oh ok, yes please I need coffee he replied smiling at her. Ok I will make some. Madison headed to the coffee pot to make some more coffee. Soon the kitchen filled with the smell of freshly brewed coffee, and even before the coffee had finished brewing Ethan grabbed the coffee pot and poured himself a big cup, putting the pot back on the brewer. He then went and sat down at the table eyeing Madison. What are you going to do today he asked her? Madison looked at Ethan and said, well since no one has any clean clothes I am doing laundry she replied. Oh ok he said. I will continue bout in the garden after I finish my coffee, then it will be lunch time, right? He looked at Madison as if to say what's for lunch, but he did not. Ok Madison replied, I will call you when lunch is ready but it won't be for a while yet, ok. Ok Ethan replied finished his coffee and went back outside. Madison sat there for a minute or two to figure out what she will make for lunch. Then she decided to go down to the basement and check on the laundry first. Once downstairs she noticed the washing machine had finished its cycle, she went over took the wet clothes out of the machine and placed them into the dryer along with a dryer sheet, then turned the machine on, there that will take about one hour she told herself then turned to the washing machine and placed another load of laundry into the machine, along with some soap, then closed the lid down and turned the machine on. Madison turned around and went back upstairs to the kitchen, well, maybe I will make grilled cheese sandwiches and some hot soup, yes that is what I'll make for lunch.

Madison went about heating up some chicken noodle soup, and preparing the grilled cheese sandwiches. About twenty minutes later their lunch for ready, Madison opened the back door and yelled out to Ethan, lunch is ready. She seen Ethan stop working, brush off his pants and walk towards the house. Madison placed the hot soup into bowls placing them on the table, along with the sandwiches she made. Soon Ethan had come in went and washed his hands and came to the table sitting down in front of his bowl. Oh he said this looks pretty good, thank you Madam. Oh you are welcome Sir Madison replied with a smile on her face. As they sat there having their lunch Madison remembered about the loud banging noise she had heard earlier, but said nothing to Ethan. It might get him started she thought to herself. They sat there quietly having their lunch. Ethan was finished first, he sat back In his chair, and said oh I am full now, got to get back to work, there are a whole lot of weeds out there, and now I got raking to do. He stood up from the table, turned around and went out the back door. Madison sat there for a while just thinking, then realized, oh my goodness, my laundry must be finished by now. She got up from the table and went down to the basement where she found her laundry to be done as she thought. She took the dry clothes out of the dryer and put them into the laundry basket, then took the wet clothes out of the machine and placed them into the dryer and turned it on. She then placed the last load of laundry into the washing machine, along with some soap and closed down the lid, turning the machine on. There she said, that should take about forty to fifty minutes, then I shall return. With that she turned around and went back upstairs to the kitchen where she put on the tea kettle to make some hot tea.

All of a sudden there came a knock to the front door, this time she thought that was a real knock, so she got up from the table and went to the front door. Upon opening the door she saw the mailman standing there with a parcel in his hand, I have a parcel for a Uriel he said and handed it to Madison, thank you she replied, then the mailman turned around and walked away. Madison looked down at the parcel, it was very roughly wrapped with harsh cord, it was made out to just Uriel. Oh she thought to herself I wonder what he is ordering without telling us about. Madison thought no more about the matter and went into the kitchen and found the tea kettle had boiled, so she made herself a cup of tea. She placed the parcel for Uriel in front of his door so he would not miss seeing it. Madison thought to herself the parcel was not very heavy so it could not have been much she thought. She sat there for about twenty minutes, when Ethan came in through the back door, hello again he said, I am done working for the day, I'm going to wash up now he said and walked off. Madison turned her thoughts to the laundry downstairs, thinking it has to be finished by now, she got up from the table and went down to the basement. She found both machines to be finished so she took the dry clothes out of the dryer placing them into the laundry basket and placed the wet clothes into the dryer and turned the machine on. Madison turned around and went back upstairs to the kitchen, where she found Ethan with his head in the refrigerator, what are you looking for she asked him? A drink he said, what have we got to drink? Well Madison replied, I think we have one last beer left, it is in the very back of the second shelf. Ethan dug around and found it, oh good he said, guess I'll have to go out tomorrow and get some more. Ethan then headed for the living room where he turned on the television and sat down. After thirty or forty minutes had past Madison went down again to the basement to see to the laundry, this time all was finished so she took the laundry out of the dryer placing them into the laundry basket and went upstairs, closing the basement door behind her, but then all of a sudden the door swung open again, like someone had pushed it open, well, Madison thought to herself what was that all about, maybe I did not close the door correctly, yes that was it, so she continued on to her own bedroom where she placed the clean laundry back where it had come from and placed clean linens on the bed, once she had finished in her room, she then went into Destiny's room, place her clothes back in their places and put clean linens on her bed. She then walked into the bathroom where she placed some clean bath towels and face clothes, she also placed some clean towels on the towel shelf, just above the sink there was a cabinet just for that. She then had to go into Uriel's room, when she approached the door the parcel was still on the floor so she gently stepped over it and into the room. As soon as she entered the room it felt very very cold, she quickly placed Uriel's clothes away and put clean linens on his bed as fast as she could then just as quickly left the room, slamming the door behind her.

Ethan stood up and said, what is going on in there? Oh no worries Madison replied its just me, I slammed the door shut by mistake, sorry. She then headed for the kitchen to make supper. What should I make today she thought to herself, just what? She stood there at the kitchen counter scratching her head. Ok, I'll cook some pork chops with rice and vegetables. Madison walked over to the freezer and took out four pork chops, she knew Ethan would have two then one for her and one for Destiny.

It was getting close to supper time, so Madison started thawing out the pork chops, then she started washing and cutting up the vegetables. She decided on some carrots, broccoli, and Brussels sprouts, along with some rice. When the pork chops were thawed, Madison coated them with some flour and seasoning, then placed them into the large frying pan she had on the stove, heating up. As the pork chops started to cook, she then placed the cleaned washed vegetables into a large pot on the stove, and turned on the heat below them. Slowly they started cooking, and so were the pork chops, which she turned over a few times as she sat in the kitchen waiting for them to cook. Soon Destiny came in through the back door, Hello mother I am home, how was your day she asked Madison with a smile on her face? Madison turned to her and said oh my day was just fine, and how was yours she replied? Oh my was ok they gave me a lot of work, to do today but I muddled through it she said with a smile on her face. Ok good Madison replied. How soon is supper Destiny asked her mother, well it will be another half hour or so Madison replied. Ok just give me a call she said, and went off to her room closing the door behind her. Ethan yelled from the living room, how soon is supper I am starving he asked? Be patient Madison replied, you are always hungry, it will be about thirty minutes or so she told him. About twenty five minutes later, she found the pork chops to be cooked through and the vegetables were almost done, so she started cooking the rice, which will take another twenty minutes she thought to herself. As the rice was cooking Madison set the table, always including Uriel she set out four settings. As the rice was cooking Madison decided to make some green salad to go with supper. She went to the refrigerator took out the greens and tomatoes, and started cutting up the greens for salad placing them into a large bowl, then she tossed them and placed the bowl on the kitchen table. She also put out a small plate of bread. Soon the rice was fully cooked, so Madison called out that supper was ready. She placed the pork chops on a plate and set them out on the table, and then she placed the vegetables out into a bowl and set them out on the table, finally she placed the cooked rice into another bowl and set that bowl out. Soon everyone was seated at the table, of course Uriel was no where to be seen, but everyone else was. They started their supper with Ethan asking, what? No Uriel again, what is going on with that boy? IS he home from work yet, or did he quit his job already he asked looking straight at Madison with a frown on his face?

About ten minutes into their meal, Uriel came running in through the back door, right past everyone not saying one word, almost knocking Destiny off her chair, Hey she yelled, watch where you're going, but she got no reply from Uriel. He went straight into his room, slamming the door behind him. Well, pipped up Madison, that was really rude of him. Ethan go into his room after you eat and talk with him, please. Well ok Ethan replied, I'll see what is going on with him. Soon the family was finished their meal, and Ethan stood up and walked over towards Uriel's room. Once there he knocked on the door,,,no replied he knocked harder, still no reply. He screamed out, Uriel, Uriel you open this door right now he demanded. Ethan knocked harder, almost bringing down the door. He stood there for a moment then decided to open the door with his foot. He went through with a bang. He found Uriel crouched down in the far corner with his arms hugging his knees and his head down. Hey young man Ethan called out, what is wrong with you? Uriel did not reply, Uriel he said again, what is wrong with you? Slowly Uriel raised his head, and as he did so he gazed right at Ethan and Ethan saw bright red eyes gazing back at him. Ethan stumbled backwards staring at Uriel and he fell backwards, landing on his rear end with this strange look on his face.

He stayed there for a few moments, then quickly got to his feet and left, slowly went into the kitchen where he found Madison at the sink washing the supper dishes. Before turning around to look at Ethan, Madison asked, well, what did he say? A few seconds past, then Madison turned around to see Ethan's face as white as a ghost. Wiping her hands on her apron, she walked over to him and said, wow what is wrong, what happened she asked? Ethan shook himself and sat down at the kitchen table, slowly turning to Madison told her what had happened. Both of them sat there wide-eyed and thoughtless. After a few minutes had past, Destiny came into the kitchen wanting a drink and grabbed some juice from the refrigerator. Wow she said, what is going on here, did someone die she asked jokingly? Madison looked up at her and said, your brother is acting strange again, so if you hear anything tonight, just ignore it please. Oh Destiny replied, ok and off she went to her room, good night everyone I have a early start tomorrow, I have a lot of work they want done. Ok good night Destiny Madison replied sleep well. Ethan and Madison sat at the kitchen table just thinking, soon they got up and Ethan said, lets go to bed, maybe this will be gone tomorrow. Ok Madison replied, you lock all the doors, and I will go into the bathroom. Ethan went one way and Madison went the other. When Madison was finished in the bathroom she headed for their room, where she got undressed, got into bed and waited for Ethan. About twenty minutes Ethan came into the bedroom, all is locked up he said as he got into his pajamas. The two lay there for a while staring up at the ceiling. Soon Ethan drifted off and Madison soon followed.

A few hours later Madison woke to this strange smell, rolling over she noticed the time on the clock, next to her bed it was exactly 3:00am. She sat up and sniffed at the air. Mm, now what is that smell, smells like gun powder or sulfur, should I get out of bed and go check, or should I stay put??? Madison thought, to be safe I will just ignore that smell and go back to sleep. She lay there for a long time sniffing the air. Soon she fell off to sleep.

CHAPTER NINE

The next morning Madison was the first one to get up, go into the bathroom, then head for the kitchen where she made the morning coffee. As she stood at the kitchen counter waiting for the coffee, she looked out into the backyard. Madison thought her eyes were deceiving her. Rubbing her eyes and looking outside again, she thought she could see a person standing in the flower bed. It was a tall dark figure wearing a long dark robe of some kind, but was like two feet from the ground. All of a sudden Destiny came into the kitchen and grabbed her mother by the shoulders saying, good morning. Madison jumped five feet from then floor. OMG don't scare me like that. What? Destiny replied, what is wrong? Madison turned to her and told her what she saw out the kitchen window, or what she THOUGHT she saw. Destiny replied, with a smile on her face, oh that was just your imagination mom, what's for breakfast she asked? Madison replied, what would you like? Well, how about some bacon eggs with toast, do we have that today? Yes, yes we do Madison replied slowly going about the kitchen. Soon Ethan came into the room and helped himself to a cup of coffee, good morning everyone he said, good morning replied Destiny, did you sleep well? Yes I did but I don't know about mother there, hey Madison how did you sleep he asked her? Well not too bad, I woke thinking I could smell something, but soon put it to rest. I am making bacon and eggs for breakfast, Ethan do you want some also she asked? Yes please. Madison went about cooking breakfast and when it was ready she placed it out on a plate, one for Destiny and one for Ethan. As they sat down to eat Ethan asked, where is Uriel this morning, not up I suppose he said looking at Madison. Nope I have not seen him yet Madison replied, Destiny how about you, have you seen your brother today? No I have not he can stay in his room for all I care. Well that is not nice Madison replied.

Soon Destiny was finished her meal, then she stood up from the table and said, well, I must be off, got to be there early today have a busy day. She grabbed her coat, kissed her mother and father said, I'll see you two later good bye now and off she went. Madison and Ethan sat at the table finishing off their breakfast. Neither one had much to say this morning, just deep in thought. Ethan finally said, well I have to go into town and pick up a few things, do you need anything at the store while I am there he asked her? Oh yes Madison replied, here is a list of things that we need, could you get them for me please she replied. Yes give me the list I will get them. Ok thank you she replied, Ethan headed for the front door, gathered his coat and went out the door, leaving Madison alone in the kitchen to clean up. When Madison had finished cleaning up after breakfast, she could hear Uriel moving about in his room. She made herself a nice hot cup of tea and sat at the table waiting for Uriel to come into the kitchen but he did not. All of a sudden she could feel this very cold draft, it seemed to be coming from the direction of Uriel's room, Madison thought to herself, there are no windows open where is that draft coming from. She grabbed her shoulders and shook, then she went into her bedroom and grabbed a sweater from the closet. As she got closer to Uriel's room it seemed like the north pole, around the door to his room, there seem to be a line of frost or ice forming.

Madison thought to herself, what is going on in there. She got up enough nerve to knock on Uriel's door. Uriel she called out Uriel are you in there? But no answer, no reply, she kept knocking then decided to leave. As she got to the kitchen table she sat down and drank her tea. Thinking about Uriel and the cold air. She wore her sweater and drank her tea. Well, maybe I will just clean the house today she told herself, this place could use a good cleaning.

After she finished her tea, she went to the broom closet and took out the cleaning supplies along with the bucket, brought them into the kitchen. As she was filling the wash bucket in the kitchen sink, once again she saw this black figure standing out in the flower bed. A few seconds later, she thought she could these bright red eyes staring back at her. In disbelief and shock, she had filled the bucket and it was running over all over the floor when she wised up, looked down saw the water all over the floor and turned the tap off. Looking up again, the figure she saw had now gone, disappeared. Madison commenced to clean up all the water and start her cleaning. With shaking hands she thought about the tall dark black figure she thought she saw. Madison said to herself, I swear there was someone or something standing out there watching me from the yard, I know there was. Madison went about doing her cleaning of the house, she started from the front door, down the hallway, past the door to the basement, then she stopped. Standing up straight, she froze again, there was this feeling of someone's hand laying on her left hand shoulder, then it started to squeeze and squeeze, until Madison let out this terrible scream. All of a sudden as quickly as the hand came, it left, leaving Madison, standing there in the middle of the hallway bent over like she saw something on the floor. A few seconds later, she calmed down enough to pull herself together and go into her bedroom where she started cleaning like nothing had happened but she knew in the back of her mind that there really WAS a hand laying on her shoulder, she could really feel it!! Next Madison headed down the hall to Destiny's room, she stood just inside the doorway and looked about, wow she thought Destiny is starting to become like her brother very messy throwing her clothes everywhere and not picking them up and put them where they should be. I'll have to talk to that girl she told herself with a smile on her face. Madison was standing at the window looking out into the year next door, when she noticed yet another odd figure or statue of some kind standing in the front yard of her next door neighbors, she stood there for a moment just gazing at it. I will have to go out there and have a closer look, she dropped her duster and broom, dusting off her apron, she grabbed her sweater and headed for the front door. She opened the door and went outside, walking towards her neighbors house. As she approach the driveway and got a closer look, there was nothing there but a very big rock, she went over to touch it to make sure, oh my goodness she thought, silly me my imagination is running away with me, just as she was about to turn around and walk away her neighbor Mrs. Brownson came out to greet her, well Hello there, and how are you this morning she asked Madison? Madison looked up very surprised and said, well good morning Mrs. Brownson I am fine, I thought I could see a person standing in your front yard here, but as I got closer it was just this very big rock you have here in your front yard, she smiled at her neighbor. Oh yes, that was my husband's idea, he thought if there something big and hard there, like a rock, and there was car crash on the road out there, that the accident would not hit our house. You see that has happened to us before, about five years ago before we moved here, we lived over there in Allison, a little ways down the road, our house was about five feet from the main road and one night there came this very loud crashing noise. We both jumped up out of the bed and came running in to the front room to see what it was, sure enough there was this very big truck, all smashed up heading for our front door, it had hit one of the beams in the garage that was how close it was she said. That was what stopped it from hitting our house, so we decided to move away and get a house that was the farthest from the road, so it could not happen again. We could not find one so we settled here, the house is not quit far enough away so Harold, that's husband decided to put that rock here.

Oh replied Madison I see why he decided to do such a thing, I just find it very odd he would, but hey, each to his own I guess Madison replied. Yes Mrs. Brownson replied with a shake of her head, hey we should go out to lunch one of these days, go downtown and have lunch at that cafe', she smiled at Madison. Why yes, ok I'll check my calender and let you know when Madison. Ok that sounds fine I'll see you later then Mrs. Brownson replied, turned and went back inside. Madison felt so silly, thinking she saw something out there but it was just a big old rock. Smiling as she left the property she headed home and back inside. Once in her house, Madison continued on with her cleaning, next was the bathroom the worst room in the house she thought. When she opened the door she almost let out a yell, OMG what a mess in here. Madison starting cleaning the bathroom, then headed down the hall, just looking up at Uriel's door she decided not to go in there today so she headed for the kitchen.

Once in the kitchen she cleaned up a little bit then made herself a nice hot cup of tea, and sat down at the kitchen table. Looking up at the clock on the wall she noticed she had missed lunch, mm, I will have to make some supper soon, so she chewed on some biscuits instead of lunch and quickly went about making a roast for supper today, which she took out of the freezer. She thawed the roast out, placed it in a big roast pan, seasoned it and placed it in the oven, set at three hundred and fifty degrees. Closing the door she told herself it would take about 3 to 4 hours to cook, so she sat back down at the kitchen table and sipped on her tea. About thirty minutes later she decided to put her cup in the sink and go dig out some vegetables to go with the roast. Standing at the kitchen sink, looking outside, she once again saw the tall dark black figure just standing in the flower bed. She gazed at it for a while, then looked down then back up again, noticing the figure had gone. Oh she told herself it's just my imagination, it has to be. First I see it then I don't. This is just crazy. When the vegetables were ready, Madison placed a few potatoes in the roasting pan with the roast, then added some carrots and onions, then closed the oven door, there that will be yet another forty five minutes, then I will make some salad to go with it. Madison went and sat down again at the kitchen table, what should I make for dessert today she said to herself. MM well, maybe I will put together some rice pudding, everyone loves rice pudding. So Madison went about making the dessert, and when it was ready she placed that in the refrigerator. Madison sat at the table, just thinking when Destiny came in, hello mother and how are you she asked with a smile,? Oh I'm just fine dear and how was your day she replied? Busy busy as usual she replied, but it's nice to be busy and not bored, with that said Destiny went into her room closing the door behind her. Just then Ethan came into the kitchen, here are your groceries he told her, placing them on the counter, how soon is supper he asked, smiling at Madison, Madison replied it will about one hour can you wait that long she asked smiling at him? Oh well I guess so he replied and went into the living room to watch some television. Mean while Madison had to put away the groceries Ethan had brought home,then she sat down at the table.

The Possession Of Uriel

About forty five minutes later Madison knew that the roast and it's contents were cooked and ready for serving. She took the roast and the vegetables out of the big pan and placed them onto a big plate, then she started to make some gravy, with flour and milk, soon everything was ready, and she called out supper is ready. Everyone came into the kitchen and sat down. Madison had placed the roast and vegetables on the table ready for Ethan to cut up for them, and as he did so Destiny watched him wide-eyes, just waiting for the food. Ethan noticed her staring at it and asked, what, are you hungry or something he asked her smiling at her. Destiny replied yes dad I am starved will you please hurry it up, come on now she said. Soon the meal was ready and Ethan served up the food, giving Destiny her's first, here you are you poor starved child he said smiling at her. Destiny smiled back and started swallowing down her food. Take it easy Madison told her you are going to choke on it. Oh no no Destiny replied I won't. The family except for Uriel of course sat having their. Soon everyone had finished and it was Ethan who first got up and went into the living room to watch some more television. Well Destiny replied lets clean up this mess, it was a great meal mother it really was. Oh thank you Madison replied, and the two women went about cleaning after supper, putting away all the dishes.

About twenty minutes later Destiny went into her room and Madison went into the living room to join Ethan to watch some television. Two hours later, Ethan stood up and said, well, I am tired and going to bed, are you coming Mrs. He asked Madison? Yes, you lock up and I will go wash up she replied. Madison went into the bathroom while Ethan did his usual tour around the house locking up all the doors. When he was finished went into the bathroom, as Madison had finished and went into their bedroom awaiting Ethan. Soon Ethan had finished and came into the bedroom, he sat on the edge of the bed and said, well, I wonder if we will get interrupted tonight while we sleep he asked Madison looking at her with a frown on his face? Oh I don't really know Madison replied, hopefully we won't hear anything tonight and have a good nights sleep she said. Soon Ethan fell off to sleep and soon Madison followed him.

Again it was 3:00am when Madison woke to yet another strange sound. It sounded like the roar of a big cat like a lion or tiger in the woods, Madison thought for a minute, then she got up out of bed and started slowly and cautiously walking down the hallway, four feet from Uriel's doorway she saw this very bright blue light running from under his bedroom door, she approached very slowly but hesitated when she got closer. Mmm no I will NOT go any further. She turned around and quickly went back into her room, got under the bed covers beside Ethan who seemed unaware of everything, still that strange sound kept up, but got lower and lower and soon disappeared. It was very late when Madison finally dropped off to sleep.

The next morning Madison woke first, went into the bathroom and when finished she went into the kitchen and put the coffee on. As the coffee was brewing the smell drifted throughout the house, and woke Ethan. Soon she could hear him in the bathroom, then all of a sudden his face appeared in the kitchen. Well good morning to you, want some coffee she asked with a smile. Ethan walked over to her put his arms around her and said softly, yes please. What is for breakfast he asked out loud? What would you like this morning Madison replied? How about some poached eggs on toast, I have not had that for a long time. Oh ok yes I can prepare that Madison replied, and she went about preparing the eggs, putting them into the poacher and turning on the heat very low. Then she put some toast into the toaster and push it down. About twenty minutes later, Madison placed the poached eggs on top of the toast, on a plate and handed it to Ethan. Here you go sir, enjoy she said with a smile on her face. Soon Destiny came into the kitchen, what's for breakfast she asked as usual? Poached eggs on toast this morning, do you want some she asked Destiny? Mm why ok, Destiny replied and sat down at the kitchen table waiting for her breakfast. Soon her breakfast was ready and Madison brought it over to Destiny and placed it down in front of her. Soon they were all eating when all of a sudden guess who appeared in the kitchen. Uriel came into the kitchen rubbing his eyes like he just woke up. He sat down at the table and asked may I have some breakfast? He sat across from his father who looked at him in a very strange manor, Uriel quickly looked away when his breakfast was placed down in front of him.

He ate very quickly, got up from the table and ran out the back door, late for work was all he said and was gone. I don't know about that boy, don't tell me he is in that crazy mood again like before Ethan said. Madison glazed at Ethan from across the kitchen, and said, well I don't think so, maybe he is just upset at someone or something. Destiny pipped up and said, well folks I am off to work, straighten him out will you please before I punch him one. Destiny smiled and quickly left before mom or dad could say anything. These kids are acting very strange, don't you think so, Ethan asked Madison? She just smiled and said nothing. She poured herself a cup of coffee and sat down at the table. What are you going to do today Madison asked Ethan? Well, I have to go into town again and get some oil and stuff for the car and some weeding mix, do you want to come with me he asked? Madison looked at him and said, no I have things here to do today, you go ahead and I will see you when you get back she replied. Oh ok Ethan replied, then and grabbed his coat and went out the back door, passing Madison he kissed her and said good bye for now see you when I return. Ok drive safe Madison replied. Ethan was out the door, leaving Madison once again sitting alone in the kitchen. She sat there for a while thinking what she would do for this beautiful looking day, noticing the sun was shining today, a little chilly but very nice. Madison decided to pick up the telephone and call her neighbour and see if she wanted to go into town and have lunch at the cafe'. Madison dialed Mrs. Brownson;s number and waited. After four rings she picked up the phone, Hello she said. Hello Mrs,. Brownson this is Madison from next door, are you available today for lunch in town Madison asked her? Well she replied, yes, I think so I have all my errands done, what time did you want to go and I will come and pick you up? What time is good for you Madison replied, oh how about 12:30pm Ok yes that will be fine, see you then Madison replied and hung up the phone. Madison went and changed her clothes and got ready for lunch in town. About 12:25pm Madison could hear this car horn outside. She went to the front door and upon opening it saw it was Mrs. Brownson, she yelled out I'll be right there.

    Madison got into her neighbors car and off they went. In town was this small cafe where everyone who knew one another gathered for gossip or for just lunch. It was called Barbara's Cafe' Shop. The ladies parked the car and went inside and found a seat by the window, here Madison replied, here is fine. Both ladies took their coats off and sat down. The cute restaurant held about thirty people with reddish colored booths on each side of the room, and had light green table coverings made of plastic. The waitress come over to their table and asked, do you want a menu? Yes please replied Mrs. Brownson, the waitress left two menu's one for each of them. Both ladies looked over the menu and decided on what they wanted. After they had ordered, Madison said, well this is very nice coming out here today, it gets me out of the house for a change, how about yourself she asked Mrs. Brownson? Yes, it is good to get out once in a while. About twenty minutes later their lunch had arrived, pipping hot too Madison thought. Oh this looks very good she told Mrs. Brownson. Madison had order the lunch special which was the Club House sandwich with a bowl of cream pf mushroom soup, and a coffee. Mrs. Brownson had order just a BLT sandwich with fries.

The ladies sat having their lunch and not said one word between them. When they had finished however that was when the talking began and never ended. Soon they stood up and walked over to cash register and paid their bill, leaving a generous tip behind. Both ladies went out and got into Mrs. Brownson's car heading for home. Soon they had pulled into her driveway where Madison got out and said, well thank you so much for lunch, it was a pleasure she smiled at her neighbour and closed the car door. Mrs. Brownson smiled back, got out of her car and went into her house. Madison headed home and went inside. She took her coat off, and hung it up in the hallway closet and went into the kitchen where she put the kettle on for tea. Madison thought to herself, I drink too much tea, In will have to find something to drink instead but I don't know what. She smiled to herself as sat down at the kitchen table sipping her tea.

She must have sat for some time because she suddenly looked up at the kitchen clock and said to herself, oh my it is almost supper time, what should I cook today. Madison thought for a few minutes and decided on chicken, with vegetables, vegetables are very good for you she told herself. She took some chicken out of the freezer to thaw out placing them into the kitchen sink. Madison sat there just thinking to herself, sipping her tea. All of a sudden, the hand she felt on her shoulder the other day, was suddenly back, like someone wanted to talk with her but when she turned around, no one was there. This is very spooky she thought just spooky. Soon Destiny came in the back door, Hi mother how was your day, good I hope? Why yes dear, it was a good day how was your day she asked Destiny, busy at work? Oh no not today she replied just a normal day. I see we're having chicken for supper when will it be ready she asked her mother? Oh about thirty or forty minutes. Oh ok then Destiny disappeared into her room closing the door behind her. Soon Ethan came in. How soon till supper mother, he called her mother every once in a while? About thirty minutes or so. Oh ok he replied and disappeared into the bathroom to wash up, then headed for the living room where he sat watching the television until supper time.

Exactly thirty minutes later the supper had been cooked, and Madison was placing it on the table when Destiny came into the kitchen, can I help you she asked.? Why yes please, help me put out the meal, so Destiny helped out then sat down at the table calling her father as she did so. Soon everyone was seated at the table, spooning out their share of the meal. How was your lunch today with our neighbor Mrs. Brownson is it Ethan asked her? Well I must say, it was a very good outing for us, we thoroughly enjoyed our lunch, very pleasant people work there Madison replied. Oh that's good to hear, maybe one day we can go out there and have lunch, Ethan replied. Yes, that would be very nice Madison replied as they sat having their supper. Soon they had finished their meal, and Ethan went off to the living room where he sat down in his arm chair. Madison and Destiny cleaned up after supper and put away all the dishes. Destiny headed for her room while Madison joined her husband in the living room to watch some television before going to bed. Soon both were very tired, so Ethan said ok bed time, I will go lock up all the doors he said, ok rep;lied Madison and she went off to the bathroom, their regular routine for the evening. Soon Madison was in bed under the covers waiting for Ethan whom came in directly behind her. He rolled over and kissing his wife said good night, sleep well, then he fell off to sleep. Madison lay there for a while, until she finally drifted off to sleep.

Again it was 3:00am when Madison was waken. This time it sounded like there was a party going on in Uriel's room, many many people talking very loudly and banging on things shaking the whole house. Madison got up out of bed, and went down the hallway towards Uriel's room. When she reached two feet from the door, the sounds stopped. She found her bare feet to be very very cold from walking on the cold hardwood floor, she walked very fast and got back into her bed pulling the covers up over her head. She lay there for a few minutes until the noise and sounds subsided, soon she drifted off to sleep.

Early the next morning even before Madison was awake she could hear people out in the kitchen, talking very loudly, walking about, stomping their feet, then she could hear the sound of dishes being broken, like someone had thrown them across the room. Looking at the clock beside her bed Madison saw it was like 4:30am, what is going on now she told herself. She slowly got out of bed, sliding into her slippers and quietly heading towards the kitchen. Sense it was still early morning it was very dark outside, as she got closer to the kitchen, she saw no one, there was absolutely no one in the kitchen, Madison quickly turned the light on to make sure. No, no one was in there. Wow she thought to herself, I must be hearing things again, I'm going back to bed for another few hours. Madison turned around and headed back to her room closing the door quietly behind her and slide into bed beside Ethan, trying not to wake him.

About two hours later Madison woke, got up out of her bed and headed into the bathroom. When she was finished she then went into the kitchen where she put the kettle on to make the morning coffee. As the coffee was brewing Ethan got up and Madison could hear him in the bathroom, soon he came into the kitchen, is that coffee ready yet he asked Madison, with a smile on his face? Yes she replied, I will pour you a cup. Madison got a cup from the kitchen cupboard and poured a cup for Ethan then took it over to him, sitting at the table. What would you like for breakfast this morning she asked him? Ethan looked at her very concerned, mm maybe some french toast he said. Well I think I can manage that she replied with a smile and wink. Madison walked over to the refrigerator and took out some eggs, she then took a big bowl out of one of the cupboards and placed it on the counter. Sitting it down she thought to herself, well Destiny will be in here soon so maybe I should make enough for everyone. Sure enough Destiny came into the kitchen and walked over to her mother, well french toast this morning she said with a smile. Why yes Madison replied would you like some? Oh yes please Destiny replied then went and sat down at the table. In the mean time Madison had a few eggs scrambled up in this bowl, then she walked over to the stove turning on the big front burner. Waiting for it to warm up, she then placed one piece of toast at a time into the egg batter, then slid it into the frying pan which was now heated up, she then placed two or three pieces of toast into the frying pan, and started cooking them. Soon she had a plate with four toast slices on it and placed it in front of Ethan who was sitting there waiting for his breakfast. Oh that looks very good, thank you he told her. Madison then walked back to the stove where she placed another few toast slices in to the hot frying pan cooking a few slices up for Destiny who was anxiously waiting for her's. Where is the maple syrup she asked Madison? It is in that cupboard over there could you please get it, I forgot about that she told her, grinning at her. Destiny got up from the table and went over to the cupboard where she took out the syrup and placed it on the table. Father she asked, could you please open this for me, it is very hard to open she said? Destiny handed the bottle to Ethan then he tried to open it. With a funny look on his face, like he was going to fart or something, he quickly opened the bottle and handed it to Destiny. Here you go he told her. Destiny took the bottle and said thank you, and she returned to her spot at the table. Soon everyone was sitting at the table having their breakfast.

About fifteen minutes later, Uriel walked into the kitchen and standing in the doorway he stopped, and held onto the walls like he was going to fall over or something. Ethan, Madison and Destiny stared at him, noticing the red eyes, black space around his eyes, and his very pale complexion. Ethan was the first to speak up, are you ok son, what is wrong with you he asked? Uriel did not reply but instead he fell to the floor. Ethan ran over to pick him up, and in doing so noticed his skin was very cold to the touch. Ethan looked up at the girls and said I will take him to his room and Ethan picked Uriel up off the floor and carried him to this room. Once in his room Ethan put Uriel on his bed and covered him up with a blanket. Slowly Ethan backed out of his room, leaving him to sleep on his bed, or at least that is what Ethan thought Uriel was doing.

Back in the kitchen he told Madison that he put Uriel to bed and covered him up. Let him sleep for a while, maybe he is just sick, if he does not get any better we will call the Doctor. Ok Madison replied and the three family members finished off their breakfast. Destiny went off to work and Ethan went out the back door going about his gardening duties. Madison was once again left alone at the kitchen table, sipping on her coffee and wondering what was wrong with Uriel. He looked so poorly she thought to herself, like he saw a ghost or something, if he is not any better by this afternoon I shall call the Doctor. When Madison was finished she got up from the table and started cleaning up after breakfast. Madison thought she would do some laundry today as she was running out of clean clothes.

When she was done cleaning up the kitchen, she headed for her room, where she grabbed the laundry basket which was by this time half way full already. She then stripped the bed and added that to the basket. She continued on down the hallway to Destiny's room where she did the same thing, stripping the bed linens, and taking up all the dirty clothes she could fine, including some clothes she could not identify, she placed them into the laundry basket and headed down the hall to the bathroom. Upon opening the door she could see that every towel in there was dirty and thrown on the floor, very wet. Madison gathered up everything and placing them into the basket she headed towards the kitchen, she thought she would skip Uriel's room for today, she could always come back later or even tomorrow.

When all the laundry was gathered, she even took dirty clothes and towels from the kitchen.She headed for the basement, turning on the light that led down to the laundry room machines. Madison separated the clothes whites from the darks, and placed the first load of laundry into the washing machine where she added some soap and a little bleach for the whites she thought would bring the whiteness out. She then closed the lid down and started the machine up. She then headed back upstairs to the kitchen where she thought she would make herself and Ethan some lunch while waiting for the laundry. Think I will make us a bacon sandwich with some onion soup. Madison started preparing the lunch for the both of them, frying up some bacon, cleaned and washed some tomatoes and lettuce, then placed the soup into a pot to heat up on the stove. Soon the sandwiches were made and the soup was hot, Madison placed the soup into bowls and placed them on the table, she also put the sandwiches on small plates and cutting them in half, placed them on the table. She then opened the back door and yelled out to Ethan, lunch is ready come and get some she told him. Soon Ethan came into the kitchen and went over to the sink to wash his hands and face. Then he sat down at the table to have his lunch. Well, how is the gardening coming along Madison asked him? Well, pretty good, but I will have to get some fertilizer for the grass for next year as it is starting to look very bad with lots of weeds he told her smiling at her. Oh ok she replied and continued eating her lunch. What do we have to drink with this delicious lunch he asked? How about some water, or juice Madison said? Oh ok I will have some juice please he told her smiling again at her as she poured out the juice into glasses she had set out on the table. What are you doing after lunch he told her, I am doing laundry she said, everything appears to be dirty again. Oh ok, I will finish up outside and then come in. Ok Madison replied, and soon Ethan finished his lunch and went off outside to finish his work.

    Madison turned her thoughts to the laundry and decided to go downstairs to see to it. Once downstairs she found the laundry to be finished, so she took the wet clothes out of the machine and placed them into the dryer along with a dryer sheet and closed the door turning the machine on. She then placed another load of laundry into the washing machine added some soap, closed the lid down turned the machine on. There she told herself, brushing off her apron that will take at least one hour then I shall return. Madison was half way up the stairs when all of a sudden she once again felt this strange hand on her left shoulder. It had a very cold sensation to it, but yet it did not seem to want to hurt her in anyway. Madison continued up the stairs and went into the kitchen, where she put the kettle on to make herself a cup of tea. Once the kettle was boiled she made herself a cup of tea and sat down at the table, thinking about the hand that always seems to target her. I wonder what the ghost or whatever it is she told herself wants from me. I don't think it means to harm me but I don't know what it wants. Madison sat there for a while pondering on the thought. One hour had past when she decided to go back downstairs and see to her laundry. Sure enough the washing machine had finished it's cycle so she turned to the dryer, found the clothes to be dry so took them out and placed them into the laundry basket, then put the next load of wet ones into the dryer and turned it on. She then placed the last load of clothes into the washing machine, added some soap, closed the lid down and turned it on. Madison told herself to come back in one hour and the laundry will be done.

She then headed back upstairs to the kitchen, and looking up at the clock on the wall she noticed it was almost supper time. Well, what should I cook today she asked herself? I think something light like chicken, vegetables and some rice. Dessert I shall make some rice pudding, everyone likes that. Madison went to the freezer and took out some chicken, enough for everyone, placing them into the kitchen sink she run some cold water over them to thaw them out. Soon the chicken had thawed. Madison took out some vegetables from the refrigerator and started cleaning them and washing them. She coated the chicken, which she had cut into strips with flour and seasoning and placed them into the frying pan, turning on the heat to start cooking. Next she placed the vegetables into another pot with some water and a little salt and started cooking them. Next she took out the rice cooker which she placed on the kitchen counter top, and turned it on Madison thought she would use the cooker for the rice today. She cooked a lot of rice because she was going to make the rice pudding also. As the chicken was cooking and the vegetables, she started preparing the pudding, adding the ingredients, then the rice and cinnamon, and some raisins, then she placed it into the oven which she had turned on at three hundred and twenty five degrees. Soon everything was almost cooked when Destiny came in through the door. Hello mother how are you, how was your day she asked with a smile? My day was fine and how was yours? Oh just good, not to busy. Destiny went past her mother and went into her room, then came back out, where is my linens for the bed she asked her? They are being washed as we speak they will be ready for you soon, ok Madison told her. Oh ok, Destiny replied.

Supper will be ready very soon too Madison told her. Ethan came in through the back door also. When is supper ready he asked, with his clothes all covered in dirt. Soon Madison replied, but get cleaned up first she told him. Ok he replied and went into the bathroom to wash and get cleaned up. Soon the oven rang ding ding, telling Madison the pudding was cooked. Madison it took it out of the oven and placed on a plate on the counter top to cool. When Ethan had cleaned up and came into the kitchen he asked about Uriel, how is he doing, feeling better now he asked? Well, I don't really know he has not come out of his room yet Madison replied. About twenty minutes later Madison had called everyone to the table as supper was ready and being put out. Ethan was the first to show up and then Destiny. They both sat down at the table as Madison had placed the food out for them on their plates. Oh I see we have rice pudding for dessert Destiny said. Why yes we do Madison told her. Soon Ethan, Destiny and Madison had finished their meal and Destiny helped her mother dish out the pudding into small bowls. Oh why thank you Ethan told Destiny. You are welcome Destiny replied. They sat there eating their dessert and when they finished, Ethan went into the living room to watch some television while Destiny helped her mother clean up after supper, putting the dishes away. When they had finished Destiny went off to her room, while Madison went to the basement to gather up the clean clothes. When she reached the top of the stairs, she headed for Destiny's room first and knocking on her door said, clean linens are here open up please. Destiny opened the door and took her clean clothes and linens from her mother. Thank you mother I can manage the rest, ok dear then Madison headed down the hall to their room, where she put away their clothes and made their bed with fresh clean linens.

Madison returned to the living room where she found Ethan still sitting watching some television. She joined him for about one more hour then said, well I think it's bed time, yes me too Ethan replied, I will go and lock up. Madison headed for the bathroom first to wash and get ready for bed, then headed to their room where she put on a clean pair of pajamas, and got under the bed covers awaiting Ethan. Soon he arrived, put his clean pj's;s on and got under the covers to join his wife. He rolled over and kissed Madison on the cheek, good night dear, sleep well. He then rolled back and fell off to sleep. Madison lay there for a few minutes before she fell off to sleep.

Again the clock on the bedside table read 3:00am. A very strange sound woke Madison out of her deep sleep. She woke up but did not get up out of bed as of yet. She lay there for a minute or two just listening. It was a voice speaking a new or different language which Madison did not recognize. She slowly sat up in her bed listening. Madison decided to get up out of bed and go check it out. She slowly slid into her slippers, and very cautiously got out of bed and started walking towards their bedroom door. She slowly opened the door and looking down the hallway to Uriel's room, she saw there was this very bright white light coming from underneath the door to his room. Madison thought that Uriel had gone to sleep, so why should there be any light in his room, she was very surprised to say the least. She slowly and as quietly as she knew how walked towards Uriel's room, when she got within three feet she could hear these strange voices speaking yet she did not know what they were saying. She placed her ear to the door without making a sound to see if she could hear anything further. Madison could pick out a male voice, speaking she believed in ancient Hebrew, again not knowing what was said. She knew it could not be Uriel's voice as he only spoke English, at least as far as Madison knew. She listened for a while and when the door suddenly flung open, Madison startled, fell backwards landing on her backside on the hard wood flooring. She put her arms out behind her so she wouldn't hit her head on the floor. She did not care if she had hurt herself or not all she wanted to do was flea and run back to her room. She quickly got to her feet and backed away, just staring into the bright white light that was still coming from within Uriel's room. She slowly backed away and went into her room closing the door quietly behind her, not wanting to wake Ethan, she got under the bed covers, pulled them up and over her head and tried to go back tom sleep. Soon Madison saw the sun light coming in through their bedroom window, oh my she thought to herself, it must be morning already. Rolling over and looking at the clock she saw it was almost six o'clock in the morning, oh I must get up now and put the coffee on.

    Madison got to her feet, and slid into her slippers again, which were still warm from the night before, she headed into the bathroom to wash up. When she had finished she then walked into the kitchen to start up the coffee. When the coffee was almost finished brewing she could Ethan in the bathroom and soon he appeared in the doorway to the kitchen. Good morning, is the coffee ready yet he asked her? Just about I will pour you cup, sit down please. She poured out a cup for Ethan and a cup for herself,as she sat at the table facing Ethan, he noticed she was deep in thought and had this very strange look upon her face. Hey hello there Madison, is there something wrong with you he asked? Madison slowly replied, well last night I thought I could hear a weird noise. I got up out of bed and walked towards Uriel's room where I saw this bright white light coming from under the door to his room. As I got closer I could this male voice speaking in a foreign tongue, it sounds like Hebrew but I couldn't be sure. Do you know if Uriel can speak another language she asked Ethan? Ethan stared back at her and took a moment to think. No, I don't believe so, but hey we could be wrong, why what did you hear he asked? Like I said Madison replied, a male voice speaking I believe was Hebrew, I don't know what was said, then, as I was standing there at the door, it suddenly flung open and it knocked me off my feet and I fell backwards onto the floor. Very surprised I got to my feet and went back to bed, I got to tell you I did not sleep for the rest of the night, I am getting very nervous. What do you think we should do, we can not be afraid every night in our beds she asked? Ethan stared back at her for a few minutes then said, well,, maybe you should call your friend Agatha I think is her name and her friend…what's her name again, I can't remember he told her. Madison sat there for a few seconds then said, oh ok maybe I should, I just don't know what to do any more Madison told him. Ethan replied, call her and see if they can come over here again and help us, because we can not do this for much longer.

The Possession Of Uriel

Madison suddenly looked up from her coffee cup and said, ok I will call her this morning, hopefully she will come over again, along with her friend, Madam Ashley I believe is her friend's name. What would you like for breakfast this morning Madison asked Ethan and as she did so, Destiny came into the kitchen, may I have some of that coffee she asked. Why yes dear you can, sit down there and I will pour you a cup then make breakfast for us. How about some pancakes this morning we have not had them for a long time now, he smiled looking up at Madison. Ok she replied, then Madison went about the kitchen making a very big plate of pancakes. Soon the pancakes were cooked and she asked Destiny to come help her put them out on the table, and as Destiny helped her mother she then asked, maple syrup anyone she asked looking straight at her father? Yes please he replied with a smile on his face, yes. Destiny placed the bottle of syrup on the table and they all sat down to eat. Soon Destiny had finished her breakfast first and said, well folks, I am off to work, got another busy day today. She got up from the table and kissing her mom and her father goodbye grabbed her coast and purse and went out the door, slamming it very hard as she left .Madison jumped then sat back down again. Looking over at Ethan Madison noticed his face had changed drastically, what, she said, what is wrong? Turn around he told her turn around but don't get out of your chair he said. Madison slowly turned around and they were both staring at the figure in the doorway to the kitchen. There stood Uriel, or at least what was left of Uriel. He had very white skin, cuts and bruises on his face and arms, his finger nails were very long, sharp looking, and his mouth, and eyes were black in colour. He opened his mouth, which Madison could see his very dry lips cracked and peeling off. No sound came out, but after a few seconds, this very loud harsh sounding voice said, something like, let me out, let me out, I demand you. He stared down at Madison with one arm out stretched as if to drag her off somewhere, but then turned around and went back into his room, slamming the door very hard behind himself.

Well, said Ethan after a few minutes of silence, what was that for heaven sake's, just what was that, was that our son he asked Madison??? Madison sat there in silence as well but said nothing. I,I am going to call Agatha right now and see if they can come over right today, I can not wait any longer she told him. They both sat in their chairs for a few more minutes, then Ethan got up and was about to walk over to Uriel's room, but Madison grabbed his arm and said, no I wouldn 't go there if I were you, please don't go there. Ethan stood there for a few more moments then changed his mind, ok I will go outside and do some yard work, please he said, please call Agatha right now and see what can be done. Oh ok Madison replied I will like right now.

With that said, Ethan walked out the back door and went about doing his gardening, Madison stood there for a moment, then headed for the telephone and dialed Agatha's telephone number. As she past the window looking out into the backyard, once again she thought she could see this tall dark figure just hovering around the gardening. She could not make out any features of this person could not even make out a face, she just stared at it for a moment, then turned to the telephone on the wall and dialed Agatha's number. After about eight rings Madison got the answering machines, Hello Agatha this is Madison, could you please call me when you get in, you have my number, thank you, then she hung up the phone. Madison went about the kitchen cleaning up after breakfast and while doing the dishes in the sink, she looked, outside but did not see that figure again, just Ethan out there working in the garden.

When Madison was finished cleaning and putting away the dishes from breakfast she made herself a nice hot cup of tea and sat down at the kitchen table. It was about two hours later when the telephone rang, and upon picking up the receiver, Madison said Hello, Hello. Oh Hello my dear friend, how are you Madison asked? Agatha replied that she was fine and wanted to know how Madison and her family was doing as they had not talked for a very long time, since the last time this happened. Well, that is the reason for my call Madison said, we think that ghostly figure or demon or whatever it was that was here before is now back again, Well why do you think that Agatha told her? Madison went on to tell her of the goings on in their house, what they saw and what they heard so far. Agatha listened intensely and to every word Madison spoke. After the two women had talked for about one hour, Agatha telling Madison that she would try and call her friend Madam Ashley and see what they could do, Madison hung up the phone and walked back to the table where she sipped on her hot tea. She was too very nervous to do anything today, so she decided to just stay in the kitchen and clean out of the cupboards. As she was cleaning out the cupboards, all of a sudden she heard this rumbling sound, like there was train about to come through their house, everything shook and even some dishes fell from the opened cupboards. Madison held on to one of the cupboard doors with her life, until eventually the rumbling stopped. Well she said to herself what in heavens name was that all about. She finished cleaning the last cupboard, and decided to make some lunch. She decided on just a bacon sandwich today with some potato chips. When she was finished she called Ethan to come inside for lunch, soon Ethan came in through the back door, went into the bathroom to get cleaned up and came back into the kitchen, sat down at the table and had his sandwich. Well how is the gardening coming along Madison asked without a word of the shaking of the house. Mmm well, its coming along just fine, I am just about finished, then I will have to find another project to do. Maybe I should get myself a hobby he told her. Madison just smiled back at him. And what praytell would that be she asked him with a smile on her face? Don't really know yet, but I will find something to fill my time he replied. Oh replied Madison I called Agatha and she will check with her friend to see if and when they could come over and visit our home again. Well ok replied Ethan I hope they can come up with a cure, as I am getting pretty tired of all of this nonsense he said. Yes, me too replied Madison, me too. Do you have any idea what you would like to have for supper today she asked him with a smile on her face? How about a nice pork roast? Do we have one in the freezer he asked? Well, I don't know I will go and check and if we do that is what I shall cook for today. Well that is settled, any more question for me today he asked with a smile? No, that was it Madison replied. Ok he said, and Ethan got to feet, and said well I'm just about finished so I will go and do that while you put on a nice roast for us. He smiled at Madison as he went out the back door again. After Ethan went back outside Madison headed for the freezer where she dug around and around and finally found a nice size pork roast. She took it out of the freezer and put in the kitchen sink running some water over it to thaw out for supper.

About thirty or forty minutes later the roast was finally thawed, so Madison seasoned it, browned it and placed it into the big roasting pan, added some onions, put the lid on it, closed the oven door, and turned on the heat to three hundred and seventy five degrees. There that will take about four hours she told herself. I wonder if we have any applesauce to go with this lovely roast. Madison went about looking through her pantry shelves, when she finally came upon a can of applesauce. Oh this is just great, it will go with the pork. She took the can out of the pantry and placed it into the refrigerator to get cooled. Madison once again sat at the kitchen table, sipping on her tea. She wondered what kind of vegetables to have with this nice roast. She finally decided on some potato's, pea's and green beans, yes we shall have that.. Now for dessert? Mmm, why is it always ME who has to decided what to have for these meals, why can't anyone else decided for me, she asked herself.

Eventually she decided on some chocolate pudding with whipped cream for the topping. As the roast got closer to being done, she cleaned,washed and cut up the vegetables. She put all the vegetables together in a large pot and turned the heat on below them and brought them to a boiling point. Soon the roast was cooked, so Madison took it out of the oven, placed it on a large platter, and started making the gravy. Soon the vegetables were cooked as well. As everything started cooling down enough to cut, Madison started making the dessert. When it was finished she placed it into the refrigerator to keep cool. Soon Destiny came into the kitchen, hello mother how was your day she asked with a smile on her face? Oh just fine honey, and how was your day? Oh very very busy she replied, I am bushed she told her mother. Oh too tired to eat supper then she asked with a giggled in her voice? Oh definitely no, how soon till super she asked her mother. About ten minutes, I will call everyone when it is ready Madison told her. Ok, Destiny went off to her room. Soon supper was ready, so Madison placed the roast out on the table, called for Ethan to come in for supper. He did so very quickly, went into the bathroom to clean up and change and came back to the table where he started carving up the roast. Madison then put all the vegetables out on the table in a big bowl, along with a plate of bread. Also she brought out a bowl full of gravy which she had made. Soon everyone except for Uriel was seated at the table preparing to have their meal. Oh this looks great mother and tastes just as good Destiny remarked while dishing out some of the meat on her plate with some vegetables and poured a little gravy on her meat. Soon the family was having their supper, and talking about their days. Well work is getting pretty busy lately Destiny told everyone, maybe some more new inmates will be arriving soon, and we are over crowded now, where will they put everyone she asked her father staring him down? Oh, don't look at me my darling I don't work there anymore remember he told her!! Oh I thought you might have an idea she told him. Mmm nope I do not and I don't care anymore, done with that line of work he told her. Oh ok Destiny replied. I will tell you if there are more inmates coming in weather you want to hear it or not told him. She smiled at him, as they were just finishing up, Ethan stood up and walked into the living room to watch some television before going off to bed.

Soon the two women were cleaning up the dishes from supper, as you know with a big dinner such as this, there were a lot of dishes to be washed. Soon they had finished and Destiny went off to her room and Madison went into the living room to sit with Ethan to watch some television for a while before going to bed. About one hour and half later Ethan stood up and reported that he was very tired and was going off to bed. Are you coming Madison he asked her? Yes, right behind you she told him , as they both got up, Madison turned the television off, and headed for the bathroom to get cleaned up and change before going to bed. Soon Ethan followed her going into the bathroom to wash up and get ready for bed. In his pj's Ethan walked into their bedroom closing the door behind him he got under the bed covers, and laying down beside his wife, rolling over kissed her on the cheek and said, good night my dear and please, sleep better tonight. Good night dear and yes, I hope I do, believe you me, I hope I do. With that said Ethan turned off the lights and he soon fell off to sleep, with Madison close behind him.

CHAPTER TEN

It was again 3:00am, when something woke Madison. She thought she could hear the same foreign Hebrew language spoken again but this time it was quit loud. She slowly got out of her warm bed, slid into her slippers and as quietly as she knew how stood up and walked very softly towards their bedroom door. She slowly and causionly opened the door. Standing in the doorway of their room, Madison saw this tall dark figure once again hovering in the middle of the hallway, looking at Uriel's bedroom door, and seemingly shouting out at him in Hebrew, or that is what Madison took it to be at the time. She put one foot in front of herself and when it hit the floor this tall figure, turning around and started coming towards her inching closer and closer. As he got about five feet from her door, it stopped, with a out stretched arm and a very long pointy finger he motioned Madison to come towards him speaking at her in this harsh male voice which Madison did not understand. The longer Madison ignored him, the louder the voice became. Madison closed her eyes very tightly thinking that when she opened her eyes again this figure would be gone. She counted to ten then opened her eyes again. Looking down the hallway she noticed this tall figure had vanished, disappeared. Madison calmed down a little thinking oh, this figure has gone, but she could still hear voices in Uriel's room. With her last will of nerves she managed to get within two feet of the door to Uriel's room.

She stood there for a few seconds, trying to decided should she knock on the door, should she just push the door open or should she just simply back away. Madison found herself frozen to the spot, she was about to turn around and leave when the door suddenly flung opened like there was a hurricane in the room or something. Madison felt this very cold chill run through her body, and closing her eyes again felt something or someone grab her arm and started pulling her into the room. She grabbed the frame of the doorway and held on for dear life just repeating the Lord's prayer as if she was in Church over and over again. Finally the cold chill left her and the hand that was gripping her arm let go. Quickly and rapidly she turned ran down the hallway to her room, closing the door behind her gently as to not awaken Ethan, walked around the bed and quietly got into bed and under the bed covers. She lay there for the longest time just shivering no way was she going to go to sleep now she thought to herself. But soon enough just before dawn she did fall asleep. At six thirty the alarm clock went off and woke her up out of a very deep sleep. Madison opened her eyes thinking, wow did I just dream that last night or did that really happen, she did not have a answer. Madison got out of bed and once again slid into her warm slippers, she headed for the bathroom down the hall where she washed her face, then bringing her head up to meet the mirror with the towel in hand, she caught a glimpse of something in the mirror. It surprised her so she quickly stepped back from the mirror, thinking I thought all the mirrors in this house were broken, but not this one, why not? Madison did not have an answer but stood there for a moment thinking I did see something there a minute ago, where has it gone? Whatever it was, had completely disappeared, vanished like the tall figure in the hallway. Madison stood there for a while longer when she heard a knock on the bathroom door. Is someone in there I'd like to have a turn please called out Destiny. Yes dear it is mother I will be out in a minute ok. She could hear Destiny say ok but hurry up please. Two seconds later Madison opened the door and said, well, ok there you go, you can't rush an old lady don't you know. She smiled at Destiny and laying a hand on her shoulder headed for the kitchen to put on the morning coffee. Soon the coffee was brewing and filled the room with the aroma. She could hear Destiny coming out of the bathroom and head towards her, good morning mother and what is for breakfast this morning she asked with a smile on her face? What would you like dear Madison asked? How about some scrambled eggs and toast, with some of that very nice coffee you just brewed. She smiled at her mother again. Well, ok think I can manage that. Soon they could hear Ethan in the bathroom and soon he appeared in the doorway to the kitchen. Good morning ladies how is everyone this morning he asked looking right at Madison?

We are just fine dear and how are you this morning Madison asked him expecting to get a reply like, oh what was that dammed noise I heard last night, but he did not say that. Ethan replied I am just fine and well slept like a baby last night he told them. Oh good replied Madison, we are having some scrambled eggs and toast this morning would you like to have some with us, or do you want something else she asked him? Mmm Ethan mumbled, well, guess I have no choice, yes that will do just fine thank you was his replied. Madison went about making enough scrambled eggs and toast for everyone, including herself as she found herself very very hungry this morning for some reason. Soon the eggs and toast was ready so Madison put them out on a plate for everyone and a smaller plate of toast in the middle of the table.

Here you go help yourself she told them and sat down herself to have some breakfast. Well, what is everyone up to today he asked first looking at Destiny, well work is just fine, we are still very busy which I don't mind at all she told him, well that is good he replied, Madison what are you up to today he stared at her expecting a surprisingly good answer?

I have a lot of laundry to do again. Will you be going into town today she asked Ethan? Not really, but if you need something let me know and I will go and get it for you, you know I would, he replied with a smile. Oh ok yes please, I have a list there on the counter Madison pointed to the list on the kitchen counter close to the back door where she knew Ethan would see it for sure. May I have some more coffee first then I will go into town he told her. Ok coming right up she replied. As Madison reached her arm out to fill his coffee cup Ethan noticed the mark on her left arm just below the elbow. Hey, Ethan grabbed her arm and held it examining the mark. What in heavens name is that and where did it come from he asked her? I don't really know, I was dreaming last night about something I can't remember but I do remember that someone grabbed my arm and pulled me back from the side of very high cliff she told him. Are you sure he asked again because it looks real to me and it looks like it hurt a lot. Oh no Madison replied with a smile on her face, no it does not hurt at all,I barely notice it she told him.

Soon Destiny got up from the kitchen table and upon kissing her mother and father said good bye mom and dad have to get to work,I will see you later she told them and off she went. Good bye Madison yelled back have a good day. As she turned around to go back to the table and sit down she noticed Ethan had got up and was getting ready to leave and go into town. As he grabbed his coat from the hook on the wall, he kissed Madison good bye and said I am off to town is this your list he looked at Madison and she replied yes, please don't forget anything on that list as I need everything please. Ok he replied and off he went. Madison was once again left alone in the kitchen to clean up after breakfast. When she had finished cleaning up and putting away all the dishes she sat down at the table to finish up her cup of tea she had made for herself. Madison had finished stood up and walked over to their bedroom and opened the door. She walked towards the laundry hamper, and grabbed the laundry basket and filled it with all their dirty clothes and pulled the linens off the bed to wash as well, she then walked down the hallway to Destiny's room where upon opening the door found her clothes and stuff scattered around the room just like before, oh I will have to talk with that girl she said to herself. After she picked up all the dirty clothes and pulled the linens from the bed, she then turned around went down the hallway to the bathroom, where she gathered up all the dirty towels, face cloths and clothes that were thrown about the bathroom floor.

Madison headed down the hall towards Uriel's room,but before opening the door she stopped and knocked on the door. No reply, she knocked again only this time harder. Mmm still no reply she thought. Oh well, I will NOT venture in there without some backup she told herself, then continued on towards the kitchen where she gathered the towels and any clothes that were in there. Once Madison thought she had everything she headed for the basement, turning on the light that led downstairs. Once at the bottom of the stairs she walked over to the laundry room area, and pulled the string to put on the light so she could see what she was doing. Madison separated the clothes like she always does, then put the first load of laundry into the washing machine. She then added some detergent and some bleach as this was the whites. She closed down the lid and pushed the start button. There she told herself, wiping her hands on her apron, that will take about forty five minutes, then I shall return. With that said Madison turned around then headed back upstairs to the kitchen where she put on the tea kettle to make herself another cup of nice hot tea. When the kettle had boiled she poured some hot water into her cup and waited while the tea seeped a bit. Soon the tea for ready as she tested it with a spoon, yes it is right. Madison just put the cup to her lips when the telephone rang. She jumped up to answer it. Hello she said, Hello. Hello my dear friend it is I Agatha and how are you doing today she asked Madison? Well, I guess I am fine, and how are you my friend she asked Agatha? I am just fine thank you for asking she replied.

Has there been anything odd or weird going on over there lately she asked Madison? Well, yes and we were wondering if you and Madam Ashley could possibly come back and help us out again Madison told her. Oh I see Agatha replied, like what kind of things happened she asked? Madison told her of the events that had happened so far, most of the goings on were at 3:00am in the morning, or early evening. Most of the things that happened I did not tell Ethan about, but I know he knows some how I just know it Madison told her. There was a silence on the phone for a few minutes then Agatha said. Let me see what we can do. Last time we talked I could not reach my friend Madam Ashley, so I will try again and if I still can not reach her I will try another friend of mine, a true person, one I can trust. I know she will be able to tell you what is going on over there if anything at all, her name is Marybeth she is a clarvoyent from Boston, Massachettes. She just moved here recently and lives not too far from your small town, I will try to call her, ok? Oh, ok that would be very good, and please get back to me as soon as you can, I don't know for

The Possession Of Uriel

how much longer we can hold out this time Madison told her. Ok don't worry my dear friend I shall find out right away and get back to you as soon as I can. Good bye for now and I will call you don't worry. Good bye my friend and Madison hung up the telephone. Oh I hope she finds out and soon Madison said to herself, this is starting to worry all of us.

Madison sat back down at the table when all of a sudden she heard Uriel calling out to her, mom, mom can you come in here please I need your help Uriel said. Madison quickly got to her feet and ran towards Uriel's room and upon opening the door she found Uriel, walking utterly up the wall and across the ceiling like he was glued there. Mom I can't get down help me please he shouted!! Uriel, Uriel what is going on with you, what she yelled back at him. Suddenly he stopped and just turned his head to look at her and said, get out of here bitch get out now. Madison could feel the walls starting to shake and the floor beneath her feet shook like there was a earth quake, but yet she knew there wasn't one. Madison backed out of the room screaming Uriel I will come back for you, I promise I will, Madison quickly left the room with Uriel still on the ceiling snarling at her like some kind of animal would. She slammed the door shut and went back to the kitchen. She sat trembling at the table, what in heavens name is going on here, really she asked herself, but she had no answer. Agatha will surely help us I know she will. When she calmed down she went down to the basement to tend to her laundry. She put the wet clothes into the dryer along with a dryer sheet and closed the door and turned the machine on. Then she placed another load into the washing machine, adding detergent, closed the lid and turned it on. Standing back she told herself, that will take at least one hour, then she turned around and went back upstairs to the kitchen where she sat down at the table once again.

Soon Ethan had returned she could hear his car engine turn off and the door being slammed shut. He walked in the back door carrying a few bags of groceries. Here you are Mrs. Madam and he laid them down on the kitchen counter. What is for supper today he asked her with a smile. Looking up at the clock on the wall she noticed, oh my goodness its almost supper time. Well I am not sure yet, But I will let you know she told him with a grin on her face. Ok Ethan left the kitchen and went into the living room where he turned on the television to watch until supper was ready. Madison decided on chicken, with some vegetables and rice. She walked over to the freezer and took out enough chicken for everyone and put it in the kitchen sink to thaw. Soon the chicken was ready for cooking, so Madison took out the vegetables she wanted to have and cleaned, washed and cut them into a pot to cook. Mean while she coated and seasoned the chicken cut them into strips and started cooking them in a large frying pan she had on the stove. Soon Destiny walked in through the back door. Hi mother I am home. Yes I see that Madison replied, how was your day she asked her? Good she replied very good, no mishaps today everything went smoothly. Oh ok I am going to my room until supper, let me know when it is ready she asked? Yes ok I will dear. Madison decided to also make some green salad so she took out the green lettuce, cucumbers tomatoes and other green items she wanted in the salad and tossed it into a big bowel and set it on the kitchen table. Soon the chicken was cooked along with the vegetables. She then cooked the rice, she always did last because it took the least amount of time cook. When all was ready she placed everything on the kitchen table and called out, supper is ready everyone! Soon Destiny came running into the kitchen and Ethan followed behind her. They both sat down at the table, and started digging in. Wow mother this supper looks really good thank you she said. Madison sat down in her seat and replied why thank you, now eat she told her. Destiny told her mother and father of her day at work and how easy it was. I wish my job there was that easy he pipped up, laughing at Destiny as she filled her face with food.

Madison how was your day Ethan asked her as he was in town at the market? Oh just fine, I am still doing your laundry though she pipped up and told them, looking around at each one of them with a smile on her face. Soon the family had finished their meal and Madison stood up and went down to the basement to finish the laundry, while Destiny started cleaning up after supper. Soon Madison returned from the basement with a basket full of laundry, I will help you finish up when I return she told Destiny. Oh don't worry about it mother I will finish Destiny told her. Ethan on the other hand went into the living room where he watched some television until bed time. Madison headed for their bedroom where she put away the clothes and put clean linens on their bed, then she headed for Destiny's room where put away the clothes but left the clean linens out for Destiny to finish up. Madison then headed for the bathroom where she laid out clean towels and face cloths. Then she headed back to her room where she put the laundry basket away, until next time she spoke to the basket, giggling as she left. Madison returned to the kitchen where she found Destiny had just finished cleaning up after supper and put away all the dishes. Why thank you Destiny Madison told her, you are a good daughter I must say, with that Madison smiled at Destiny. Destiny then told her mother she was going to take a good math then go to bed early. Oh ok dear sleep well. Madison then walked into the living room to find Ethan almost asleep on the couch as she sat down beside him.

After about twenty minutes Madison shook Ethan and told him to go to bed he was already sleeping on the couch. Oh, why

The Possession Of Uriel

no I was not he told her with a smile on his face. Oh yes you were now go. Madison stood up turned the television off and went to the bathroom to wash up and get ready for bed. Soon she was in bed and under the clean linens waiting for Ethan. About fifteen minutes later, Ethan had come to bed slid under the bed covers, rolled over and kissed his wife good night then turned over and went off to sleep like right away. Madison could hear him snoring within five seconds. She laughed to herself trying not to disturb him. Soon Madison found herself falling asleep so she rolled over, and turned off the light, sliding under the bed covers and fell off to sleep instantly.

It was again, 3:00am when Madison felt this tug on her blanket. It woke her instantly,and Madison sat up and looked to the bottom of her bed. To her surprise, she saw nothing, she lay back down I her spot and covered up with the blankets once again. Five minutes later another tug on her blankets. Madison laid there in disbelief trying to ignore the matter. A few seconds later someone or something had tugged the blanket so hard, that it came off of Madison, and onto the floor at the foot of the bed. This did not in any way disturb Ethan he was fast asleep with no bed covers on him at all. Well Madison thought he could sleep through a storm and never know it came and went. Madison slowly but very nervously got out of bed and slowly went to the foot of her bed and looked down. There were the bed covers all in a big pile on the floor. Madison went to bend down to retrieve them but couldn't, so she got down on her hands and knees, and upon peering under nether the bed, saw this terrible black, gray face, with red eyes staring back at her. Madison could not move, slowly this figure under the bed came towards her, crawling on its hands, it seemed to have no other body parts but just the head and parts of its shoulders, where these long very bony like arms came first, then she saw long pointy fingers, with what appeared to be drops of blood, dripping onto the floor.

Madison quickly got to her feet and scurried back to bed, pulling the bed covers, which she had picked up on her way from the floor, up and over her head, thinking this image is not real, can't be real. With that thought, she closed her eyes very tightly and started praying …Our Father who Art in Heaven… but before she could finish, she fell off to sleep. She woke quickly a few minutes later to find herself choking on the blankets. Oh this is very silly she thought to herself, tossing the top blankets off, and as she did so woke Ethan. What, he said what is going on he asked rubbing his eyes? Oh, oh nothing Madison replied, I just had a bad dream but I am fine now, please, go back to sleep. Mmmm he said ok, night and he fell back to sleep right away. Madison lay there for a while thinking her actions were quit fictitious, but yet they seemed so real to her. Shortly afterwards she fell off to sleep.

Before she knew it, the alarm clock on her bedside table went off telling her it was 6:30am time to get up. Madison sat up in bed, scratching her head. I feel like I never got any sleep last night but I know I did. She slowly got out of bed and slid into her slippers which were on the floor beneath her feet. Stood up, stretched yawned, and walked around the bed, out of the bedroom and down the hallway to the bathroom, where she washed her face in the sink and as she was about to stand up, grabbing the closest towel, she saw this tall black figure again just floating behind her. She dried her face quickly and turned around, just to find the figure had disappeared. I must ask Agatha about this figure I keep seeing, maybe it is just my imagination she told herself, it has to be. Madison finished up in the bathroom and hurried down the hall to the kitchen, where this morning she found Destiny making the morning coffee. Well good morning Destiny, you are up very early this morning aren't we Madison said. Yes mother, I have to leave very early this morning I have a meeting to attend she told her mother, so early in fact, I won't have time for breakfast. I will just grab something in town to take with me. She turned around, walked over to her mother, kissed her on the cheek and said, well, I'm off I will see you later, have a good day, ok and off she went out the door waving her hand at her mother as she left. Good bye Madison replied, knowing Destiny could not hear her now. As the smell of freshly brewed coffee lingered, Madison poured herself a cup and as she did so Ethan came in the kitchen. Good morning to you my dear, think I'll have a cup of that. Ethan poured himself out a cup and sat down at the kitchen table. How are you this morning he asked her with a smile? Oh I am just fine, did you sleep well she asked him? Yes I suppose I did until you woke me with that dream you said you had. What was that all about he inquired? Oh I was dreaming I was being pulled under the water, we were out in a small boat and I fell over board, yet you would not save me she told him, so guess I was trying to save myself she told him, knowing this was not the truth.

  Oh he replied, ok. Hey what is for breakfast this morning and where is Destiny? Well what would you like for breakfast she asked him? How about some french toast this morning that sounds good to me. Ok Madison replied. As for Destiny she had to leave very early this morning, up and gone before we even got out of bed, something about a meeting she had to attend. Oh ok replied Ethan. Madison walked over to the kitchen counter and starting preparing the french toast. She took a few eggs from the refrigerator, and broke them into a bowl then stirred them up really good. She put the frying pan on the burner of the stove and set it to medium heat. As the pan was heating up she took a piece of bread from the bag, soaked it into the egg mixture then another slice of bread and then a third slice, then placed them into the frying pan, fried them on one side slightly and then turned them over to toast the other side, this apparently is what they call French Toast, at least this is what Madison calls it. Soon she had a stack of four pieces of french toast on a plate, and took it over to Ethan, whom was still sitting at the table. She then headed over to one of the cupboards and took out the maple syrup and took it over to the table, placing it down in front of Ethan. Then she went back to the frying pan and made a few slices for herself, then turned the burner off, and set the frying pan aside so it could cool down. She picked up her plate of toast and went over to the table and sitting down across from Ethan started eating her breakfast. What are you going to do today she asked Ethan who was still filling his face with breakfast? I have to do some work on the car then I am going to clean up the tool shed and the yard a bit. Oh ok that should keep you busy all day then she said with a smile on her face. Well maybe he told her, and hey by the way what has happened to our son, you know Uriel? Have you seen or heard from him Madison he asked? No, no I have not, but I have to do some cleaning today so I will probably try and go into his room, maybe he is still in there yet doesn't want to come out and talk with us, I will check this today and let you know what I find she told. Ok. Soon they were both finished their breakfast, so Ethan got up to his feet first and headed outside through the back door. Let me know when lunch is ready he told her. Is that all you think about is your stomach she replied, waving him out the door?? Ok I will she said as the door closed behind Ethan. Madison cleaned up after breakfast first then went over to the broom, and took out the cleaning supplies she would need for the days job along with the mop bucket and broom. She decided to start in the front doorway. She went about dusting down all the cobwebs she could find, then dusting all the furniture. She liked to use Hawk's Lemon oil for all the wooden furniture, she said it smelt really nice and like lemons she thought to herself. When she had completed the front entrance and down the long hallway, she placed the cleaners in the kitchen on a counter top, then went back to sweep all the floors and then to mop them down. She had finished the front entrance way so she then headed for her bedroom, she always started in there then headed back to the kitchen. She started off by dusting everything, she opened the curtains to let in some sun light so she could possibly see things better. She found cobwebs she never knew existed, then completed dusting her room, she then headed back to the kitchen where she grabbed the broom and mop bucket. She went back to her room, where she swept the floor and then washed them down. Madison always put a little Pinesol cleaner in the washing bucket because it made the floors smell so much better and cleaner. Once she had finished in her bedroom, she headed down the hallway to Destiny's room.

She opened the door and found all of Destiny;s belongings scattered all over the floor again. She bent down to start picking everything up and then decided to just put everything on Destiny's bed for she did not know weather they were clean clothes or dirty ones. She then opened the curtains again to let in some sun light and brighten up the room. Madison dusted everything she could possibly dust and took down some cobwebs she found up in the corners of her room. She then put all the cleaning supplies out in the hallway and took up the broom and swept the floor, then when she had finished she mopped the floors, closing the door behind her and on to the next room. Oh no it';s the bathroom, the worst room in the whole house she thought to herself, well I guess someone has to clean it, she then giggled to herself. Madison went inside the bathroom and started to clean and disinfect every square inch of the room, she even cleaned the bathroom mirror so well, she thought she could see clear through to China. Once she had finished cleaning the bathroom, she gathered up the dirty towels and face cloths, and put them into the laundry hamper, and placed out some clean ones, then she washed the floor, closing the door behind her.

Next she thought was Uriel's room. Madison hesitated at the door, then decided to knock first to see if Uriel would answer. No. Still no answer. Well Madison decided I must get in there and clean up his room, it must be a terrible mess by this time. So with a lot of caution Madison reached for the door knob and opened it. As the door opened wider Madison got this terrible scent of sulfur, or very wet dirt. She remembered Uriel calling it goofer dust or some such thing. To Madison it smelt like the graveyard after a heavy rain fall.Madison held her nose and walked into hie room. She reached for the curtains to open them when Uriel all of a sudden screamed out, NO NO please don't open the curtains, please he told her. Madison turned around to see Uriel sitting on the floor in a corner hugging his knees, looking down at the floor. Hey hey young man, what is wrong with you lately, I have to get in here and do some cleaning since you won't, now let me clean please she told him with a harsh angry voice. In reply as Madison turned around to start cleaning near the window area, she could hear this very scary harsh male voice say….esse non poteris experiri et adepto mihi mulier,si hic nunc interrogo ego then he repeated it over and over.

Madison did not know what to make of this, she finally had to leave the room, as his voice got louder and louder, closing the door behind her. She went back to the ,kitchen then she headed for the book shelf to find a book on Latin. She remembered the words, they were very clear in her head, so she could translate them. He said thou shalt not try me woman get out of here right now I demand you. Madison was very shocked so she wrote down these words she found to give to Agatha when she got here, yes she would show Agatha and tell her what had happened and ask if there was anything she could do about the situation. As Madison sat at the kitchen table, she thought to herself, I did not know Uriel could speak so fluently in Latin or any other language for that matter, Madison was shocked to say the last. Maybe I should study the language so I can speak to it or him, and find out what it wants from us, after all, I know it is not Uriel speaking to me, I just know it she told herself. Madison thought for a minute then said to herself out loud, I saw his face, hands and feet, they were very white in colour, had many many cuts but yet was not bleeding I just don't understand. Don't understand at all.

After Madison had composed herself, she finished doing the cleaning of the kitchen and back porch, then she put all the cleaning supplies away and as she stood at the kitchen sink getting rid of the dirty water from washing the floors, she looked outside into the back yard, where once again, she saw this tall dark figure. According to Madison it was floating at least two feet above the ground, it did not show any feet at all, as she got a closer look, the place where the face SHOULD be, was gone, like it was just a black hole, yet it had two glaring bright red eyes looking right back at her. Madison stood there for a few seconds, then discovered she had overflown the sink again and looked away to stop the water from running over onto the floor, but when she looked up again the figure was gone, just like behind.

Looking up at the clock on the wall Madison noticed it was lunch time. Oh my what should I make Ethan will be in soon looking for his lunch. Quickly Madison decided to put together some sandwiches, so she made some ham and cheese and some corned beef on rye, all of which she toasted. There that should do him. She walked over to the back door and yelled out to him Ethan come get your lunch please. Soon Ethan came in through the back door, he walked over to the kitchen sink and washed his hand thoroughly with soap and water, then sat down at the table. He dug into the sandwiches like he was starved or something. Madison looked at him and said, are you hungry or something, don't eat so fast you will get indigestion, He looked up at her and laughed, no, no I won't I am very hungry, what do you have to drink, I need a drink now he told her. Well how about some juice or water that is your choice. Well, I guess juice will do, I don't want beer just yet, I still have some work to do on the car and I had better do it right he told her staring in her direction. Yes, yes you should. Soon the two of them had finished their lunch, as Ethan stood up and said, well I must go finish my work. I will check in at supper time. Madison just looked up at him and smiled, always food is on your mind, nothing else she asked him? Nope, not right now he said and off he went. Madison did not tell him what happened in Uriel's room or of the tall dark figure she keeps seeing.

Madison was expecting to hear from her friend Agatha today but I guess not, she must be really busy or is still looking for her friend to come and help her, I will wait Madison told herself. I am going to start writing down all the things that happen around here so I won't forget to tell her about, Madison said to herself. Starting right now. Madison headed over to one of the drawers in the kitchen just before you come to the back door. She opened it and took out a note pad, along with a pen and went back to the table to write down a few things. Today she wrote down what happened in Uriel's room and the Latin words he spoke, then tell her about this tall dark figure she keeps seeing, then tell her about this image she thought she saw under her bed the other night. Soon Madison list got longer and longer, she now remembers other things that happened before that were just coming back to her, Agatha has to know these things she told herself.

Soon Madison found herself to be getting hungry again, and looking up at the clock on the wall seen it was getting to be supper time. Oh why oh why do we need to eat so often she said to herself. I am always either cooking or cleaning there is no stopping this madness,,,she giggled to herself. Madison thought for a minute then decided on some pork chops, with vegetables and mashed potatoes today. She then walked over to the freezer and took out enough pork chops for everyone, then placed them in the kitchen sink with some water to thaw out. I shall cook them with some cream of mushroom soup, that will make a nice warm sauce, yes I shall do that. Now what shall I make for dessert today. Madison thought for a while then discovered she had a frozen berry pie in the freezer, I shall thaw that pie out and we'll have that, we have some vanilla ice cream to go with it, I shall warm it up in the oven, yes, that is what we will have today.

About one hour later as the clock on the wall read 5:30pm, Madison took the pork chops out of the sink and laid them in the frying pan with a little cooking oil, and started cooking them, When they are almost done she will add the mushroom soup to it. While the pork chops were cooking she then cleaned and cut up some vegetables to go with it. She peeled enough potatoes to make mashed potatoes,and started cooking them. Soon she added the soup to the pork chops and vegetables, potatoes were cooked, so she started mashing them up. She had taken the frozen pie out before this and it was out thawing on the kitchen counter top. Destiny came into the kitchen, hello mother how are you doing? How was your day? Oh my day was fine, and by the way,

I cleaned your room today, please pick your stuff up off the floor so next time I can clean your room better, ok Madison told her with a smile. Ok mother I will and off she went to her room. Soon the meal was cooked and ready for serving. Madison set up the table and placed the bowl of vegetables out on the table along with a platter of pork chops, she also put out a plate of bread I case anyone wanted it. She called out to Ethan who was still outside, and soon he came running into the kitchen then headed for the bathroom to wash up. Soon everyone was sitting at the table having their supper. There was complete silence for a while then Madison spoke up and told Ethan she had not heard from Agatha has of yet, but I know she will call. Destiny, Ethan asked, how was your day I heard you are very busy at work right now? Yes father we are, we are all glad to be busy other than sitting there doing nothing and getting paid for it, Destiny let out a giggle. Yes I suppose so he replied. Soon the family had finished their meal and Ethan retired to the living room to watch some television before going to bed. Destiny helped her mother in the kitchen to clean up after the meal. How is Uriel doing mother I have not seen him in quite some time, has he come out of his room yet she asked?

Madison replied no I was in there today to clean up and he literately told me get out and in Latin of all things she told her. What Destiny replied, I did not even know he knows how to speak another language, with that she laughed out loud. Neither did I Destiny neither did I, but he did. Don't know what is going on with him but we are going to find and find out soon she told her. Soon the two woman were finished and Destiny went off to her room while Madison joined Ethan in the living to room to watch some television before going to bed. Soon Ethan said he was very tired and that he was going off to bed, are you coming dear he asked her? Yes Sir I am, you go and lock up and I will hit the bathroom, so off they went. Madison took only a brief few minutes in the bathroom so Ethan followed quickly behind her, getting ready for bed. Soon Ethan joined Madison in their bedroom, and he got underneath the bed covers, rolled over and kissed his wife good night, rolled back to his spot and fell off to sleep right away. Madison rolled over and looked at him about to tell him something when she noticed he had already been asleep. Madison lay there for a short period of time and soon she too, fell off to sleep.

The next morning Madison awoke bright and early before the alarm went off. Wow she thought to herself as she headed for the bathroom to wash her face. I slept through the night nothing woke me, maybe that's a good sign. Madison stood at the bathroom mirror drying her face, and when she had finished walked into the kitchen to make the morning coffee. She stood at the kitchen sink overlooking the backyard, and staring outside told herself, this is a very nice looking day, maybe I shall go for a short walk today. Just then Destiny came into the kitchen, good morning mother is the coffee ready yet, and what is for breakfast, I am starved this morning. Yes, coffee is ready I shall pour you a cup and what would you like for breakfast today she asked Destiny?

Destiny hesitated, then said, how about some ham and eggs, I am getting pretty tired of bacon these days she said smiling at her mother who was still standing at the kitchen window staring outside. Madison turned around, what, what did you say sweetie, I am sorry I was not listening Madison told her! Mother, what are thinking about Destiny asked her? Nothing, Destiny really, nothing. Oh, oh ok ham and eggs it will be Madison told her. As Madison was preparing and cooking the ham, Ethan came into the kitchen, good morning everybody, what a nice looking day out there. Ethan walked mover top the coffee pot and poured himself a cup. What's for breakfast he asked with a smile on his face? Take a guess Madison told him, looking into the frying pan. Oh, ham and eggs for a change, that will be great, don't burn them please he commented to Madison with a smile, who in return slapped him one, go away and sit down at the table she told him, right now, or you won't get any she told him.

Oh someone is not in a very good mood this morning hey my dear!! Madison turned to him and smiling replied, go, go and sit down, it will be ready soon she told them. The ham was almost cooked so Madison started cooking the eggs. She knew Destiny would eat two eggs, while Ethan will eat three. Madison placed six eggs in the frying pan, and walked over to the toaster and place four slices into it and push the button down. Just as the eggs were done, the toast had popped up. Destiny came over and helped her mother, she buttered the toast and put it on a plate and walked it over to the table, placing it down, then she sat down. Thank you Destiny Madison told her, as she put, a plate in front of Ethan and a plate in front of Destiny. Then she walked back to the counter and picked up her own, and went sat down at the table to join the others.

Well pipped up Ethan, what is everyone doing today he asked, staring at Madison? Well, first I thought I would enjoy a nice walk, just to get some fresh air she told him with a smile on her face. Then, I am not too sure. We know Destiny here is off to work, so I am going to work o the car for a while, as I need to winterize it for the winter which is quickly approaching he said. Oh ok replied Madison. With that said Destiny stood up and reported that she was on her way to work, I may be a little late coming home today as there is a big meeting after work, in which everyone has to attend, I don't know how long the meeting is mother, so if I am late for dinner, please don't wait for me, I will get something on my way home, ok! Well ok dear, have a good day at work. Then Destiny waving her arm good bye mom and dad will see you later and off she went. Ethan and Madison sat at the table sipping their coffee. Ethan stood up and said, I am off to work, he smiled at Madison, who smiled back at him, ok she replied. After I clean up after breakfast you shall see me going out for a walk, if you want to join me, let me know, I will welcome the company she told him. Ok Ethan replied and went out the back door. Madison was left once again alone in the kitchen to clean up after breakfast. She cleaned away the mess, washed the dishes and put them away. She then walked over to her bedroom, opened thew door, went inside and grabbed a sweater from the closet. It must a little chilly out today, I shall wear this sweater just in case she thought to herself.

Madison then turned around, and walked out towards the kitchen. She opened the back door and went outside and as she did so, felt the chill in the air. She shook a little then wrapped the sweater a little tighter around her waist. She walked up to Ethan and said, I am off for a walk, do you ant to join me she asked? Mmm no, not right now, if you are not back by the time I am finished I will come look for you he said with a smile. Well ok replied Madison and off she went down the driveway out to the road headed for town. Madison walked slowly taking in the fresh air and looking around the area. About thirty feet down the road, she just happened to look down at her feet and saw this shiny object just laying in the dirt. She stopped, looking around, no one watching her so she picked it up. Oh it is a silver chain it had an odd shaped medallion attached to it. It was a circle with a six sided star in the middle Madison examined the shiny medallion, and turning it over noticed initials engraved on the back along the one edge, " UEW". Madison put it on her pocket to take home and look at it more thoroughly. Madison walked for another sixty feet, and was starting to get quit cold, so she decided to head back. Madison turned around and headed for home and looking up saw Ethan coming towards her. Oh you did not get very far he told her with a smile. No I am getting cold so I decided to come back home and get a warm drink she told him. Ok, he replied and put a arm around her to warm her.

They reached home and walked up the driveway and into the back door. Madison went and put the kettle on to boil and make herself a nice hot cup of tea. Would you like some she asked Ethan. Ok yes please, that would be nice. When Madison put the kettle on, she remembered the necklace she found in her pocket, and took it out. Hey Ethan, look at this I found in the dirt on the side of the road, I wonder if it belongs to some she asked him? Madison handed it to Ethan who took it in his hand. Upon examining it Ethan said, UEW, who's initials is that I wonder? I don't know either Madison told him. What should I do with it she asked him? Oh it's up to you he told her, either keep it or throw it away, I am not really sure Madison The tea was made, so both Madison and Ethan sat at the kitchen table dipping on the very hot tea. Madison had the medallion in her hand and was examining it again. It looks very old, don't you think so? Ethan did not reply. She gazed at it for a while, then Ethan pipped up, what's for lunch I am hungry now. Oh ok what about a nice corned beef sandwich she told him? Oh do we have some rye bread he asked. Why yes we do. Ok ok then that's what I want he told her with a smile. Madison got up from the table and headed for the refrigerator, taking out the corned beef and , then headed for the cupboard on the other side of the kitchen and took out some bread. She started making the sandwiches. Do you want another cup of tea to go with the sandwich she asked him? Oh ok yes please he replied. Soon the two were sitting at the table having their lunch. All of a sudden Madison dropped her sandwich and looking up saw Uriel standing in the doorway to the kitchen. He stood there, with many cuts and deep lines all over his face like he had been in an accident or something, and his skin was very white in colour. Ethan looked up and said, what, what is wrong with you he asked Madison. Turn around Madison told him, turn around, with that Ethan turned in his seat and saw Uriel standing there, with his pale skin,many cuts and deep set lines on his face.

Ten seconds had past then Uriel pointed with his right arm,. and index finger extended at Madison and said in a harsh Latin voice …..I cibus, cibi mei et ego dabo vobis comedent. NUNC postulavit eum. !!

Neither Madison or Ethan knew what he said, so he repeated it over and over, then his voice got louder and louder. Covering his ears Ethan said, What does he want, what did he say?? Madison replied I have no idea, I will have to look it up. They both just sat there covering their ears trying to block out the sound of his voice. With both covering their ears and looking down at the floor, all of a sudden Uriel disappeared, and the sound of voice vanished. Madison was the first to look and seen Uriel had vanished, gone. She uncovered her ears and said, he is gone Ethan he is gone. Ethan lowered his hands and looking around saw Uriel had gone. What, what in God's name was that all about he asked, getting very upset at this point? What did he want he said looking at Madison? I don't know but I will look it up in one of our books. We have a book on Latin and I am trying to learn it she told him. Oh ok Ethan replied, but please hurry it up. They both finished off their lunch. Ethan went back outside to work on the car, while Madison went into the library room, that is what she called. It was but a small room with two book shelves. It had contained many many books, most of which were reference books. Madison located and grabbed the book on Latin language. She took the book into the kitchen and tried to translate what Uriel had said.

She sat there for along time and finally figured out what he said and she wrote it down so she could remember to tell Ethan when he came back into the house. Madison wrote …..I need food, give me food or I will eat you, RIGHT NOW, he demanded…..

Madison sat at the kitchen table reading and reading on the Latin language. She got tired, she stretched and looking up at the clock on the kitchen wall noticed it was getting to be supper soon. Oh, she said to herself what should I cook today for supper. She stood up from the table and walked over to the window under the kitchen sink. She stood for a while thinking. I think I will cook some chicken and make some chicken Cacciatore. Madison went to the cupboard above the stove and took down her cook book to find the recipe. Sifting through pages and pages she finally found a good one. She noticed that she needed so much chicken cut into mouth size bites,she also needed some green or coloured peppers, garlic and some union, along with seasoning and some totatoe sauce. Madison went and looked in her pantry and found all the ingredients she needed and placed them on the counter. She then walked over to the freezer and took out enough chicken to make a good size meal. She placed the chicken in the sink along with some cold water to thaw out.

Soon the chicken had thawed so Madison started to cut up the chicken into smaller pieces, coated them with flour and seasoning, and placed them into the frying pan, which she had on low heat. As she read through the recipe she noticed it would take about one hour to make this, so while it was cooking she decided to make some custard pudding for dessert, and add some cherries which she had plenty of for taste. When the chicken was almost cooked through, she added the rest of the ingredients, then started cooking the rice, which take another twenty minutes or so. As the chicken and the rice was busy cooking she started to make the custard pudding for dessert. After the pudding was ready, she poured out the servings into each bowl then added the cherries, and then added a little whipped cream to the top of it all. Then she placed them in the refrigerator for later. Soon the meal was almost ready. About five minutes later Destiny came in. Well hello mother how are you she asked? Well I am just fine, I thought you had to work late today Madison replied. Oh oh no, they canceled the meeting and moved it until next week as one of the big bosses couldn't make it out today. Oh ok well that was good, you are home in time for supper then Madison smiled at her as Destiny walked past her mother and into her room. Call me when it is ready please she told her mother. Ok I will Madison replied.

About thirty minutes later the meal was ready. Madison called out back to Ethan telling him that supper was ready come and get it she demanded. Ok he replied I'll be right in. Three seconds later he came in through the back door, went past her and into the bathroom where he washed up for supper. In the mean time Destiny came into the kitchen and sat down at her usual spot. In the mean time Madison had made some green salad to go with the meal, so she placed the big bowl out in the middle of the table, along with three smaller bowls one for each person. She then served up the meal placing the rice on the plate first, then adding some of the chicken with sauce. She did so for each person, then herself. Madison finally sat down to have her meal. Destiny was the first one to speak, how was your day father she asked Ethan first? Well, not too bad, at least it is not too cold yet hey, to work outside,. he smiled at Destiny. Oh good, and mother how was your day as I asked the second time she told her. Oh just fine, I went out for a walk and along the way found a necklace with a silver medallion which had the initials "UEW" on it. Do you know anyone with those initials she asked Destiny? Destiny thought for a moment then replied, why no I don't know anyone mother, maybe someone just dropped it Destiny replied. Yes, maybe you are right. The family continued on with their when.

Just before they were finished Madison speaks out, Ethan I looked up those words Uriel spoke to us, earlier today and I found their meaning. Well woman, what did he say, he gazed at her with wonder in his eyes. He said ... I need food give me food or I will eat you. RIGHT NOW he demanded. Ethan stared at Madison like she had lost her eyes or something. What, what was that he repeated.... Madison repeated the words. Ethan sat there with his mouth wide open not knowing what to say next. Then Destiny pipped up, is Uriel speaking Latin now mother, when did he learn that she asked? And you how did you know what he said she gazed at Madison. Madison replied, I had to look it up in one of our books we have in the library room, and then I wrote it down so I wouldn't forget it. Oh well, replied Destiny maybe we all should learn how to speak Latin, then maybe Uriel will talk to us.

Neither Madison or Ethan said a word. Oh well it was a thought Destiny said out loud then got up from the table as they were all finished their meal, I will start to clean up mother she said. Madison stayed in her seat for about ten seconds then got up and went to help Destiny clean up, while Ethan, scratching his head, headed for the living room to turn on the television to watch before going to bed. Madison started talking with Destiny about the necklace she had found, what do you think I should do with it she asked her? Well, mother I would clean it up and keep it. It does look very good and until we find out whose initials they are, I would keep it, maybe in a box all by itself, at least for now, Destiny smiled at mother, then turned and said I am going to my room now and I'll be saying good night because I think I will fall off to sleep early today. Well ok Destiny good night then and off she went to her room, while Madison went into the living room to join Ethan.

Neither Madison or Ethan said one word, as they sat there and watched some television, until Ethan got up and said, well my dear, I am tired and I am now going to lock up and head off to bed, are you coming he asked her? Yes dear I am coming. Madison stood up and went into the bathroom where she got ready for bed, then she headed into their room where she changed into her pajamas and waited for Ethan to arrive. About twenty minutes later Ethan came into the room, got into his pj's and got under the bed covers beside his wife, he rolled over and said good night my dear sleep well please he told her then rolled back over and fell off to sleep, like instantly. Soon Madison fell off to sleep.

CHAPTER ELEVEN

That night Madison had a very strange dream. She found herself on a very big boat, sailing away to somewhere she did not know, but yet knew she had to get there and a soon as possible. Looking around on this boat Madison saw no one, no one at all, not even her husband. She started calling out to him Ethan, Ethan where are you Ethan. It seemed to her that it had been many days she was there, just walking around this boat, from one end to another and back, seeing no one. All of a sudden she heard this big bang like a bolt of lightening had hit somewhere, it was so loud that Madison fell to her knees and found herself kneeling on the floor of this boat, but when she looked up she saw Uriel standing before her, speaking in Latin or it could have been very old Testimony style Greek, she could not make out the words that were being said, nor did she understand them. She stared up at this figure, that supposedly looking like Uriel, but yet it wasn't. Madison stood up and said, who are you and what do you want of me she asked? All of a sudden this figure hit her across the face and she fell backwards, and kept falling until she reach her bed. She looked over and seen Ethan fast asleep. H my word she said to herself, what a dream, I wonder what if anything does it mean??? She had no answer.

Just then there was another very loud bang. Looking at the clock on the night stand told her it was 3:00am again. There was yet another loud bang, and yet another until it woke even Ethan. He sat up in bed and rubbing his eyes said, what in the hell is that? Madison turned to him and said, I don't know, should we get out of bed and go find out, or should we just stay put. About ten minutes later there came yet another very loud bang, followed by some person or thing speaking in Latin again. It did not sound like Uriel's voice, but then again, both Madison or Ethan did not know what Uriel's voice sounded like anymore. They just stared at each other sitting there. The whole house then seemed to shake at this point like there was an earth quake yet they knew there was not one there. They just froze to their spot and did not move. Both Madison and Ethan shut their eyes tightly and held hands, thinking what, what is going to happen to us? About thirty seconds later, the shaking and loud banging noise and voices stopped, just as suddenly as it came and the house was calm once again.

 They both lay back down in their bed, still shaking with fear and not knowing what was to happen next. They lay there so long that eventually they both fell off to sleep again. Very soon thereafter the alarm clock on the night stand went off and woke Madison. Looking at the clock she noticed it was that time again, time to get up and start a new day. Madison slid out of bed and slid into her slippers that were underneath her feet. She slowly got out of bed and gently walked down the hall and into the bathroom, where she washed up and combed her hair, then left the bathroom and headed for the kitchen where she started the morning coffee. The smell of freshly brewed coffee filled the air and soon Ethan came into the kitchen, and walked straight towards the coffee maker and poured himself a big cup and sat down at the kitchen table. Morning was all he said with his head down. Well good morning to you to. Just then Destiny came into the kitchen, walked over to the coffee pot and poured herself a cup, then went and sat down at the table. No on e said a word for about fifteen minutes, then Destiny said, what was all that noise about last night, I heard this big crash like a bolt of lightening, but when I looked outside there was no storm, then the house shook and woke me up, what was that all about she asked? Madison replied, we don't know, we did not get out of bed to find out, we were too scared she told her. Wow Destiny replied, we should find out what is going on here and soon, she stared at Madison.

Yes Madison replied, I have called Agatha and she is trying to find out when she and her friend can come by and help us out, hopefully real soon. If she does not call me today I will call her again, don't worry about it Madison told her. Ok mother, now that that is out of the way what is for breakfast she asked with a smile on her face? Well how about just some boiled eggs with toast? Destiny thought about it for a while then replied, ok yes that is fine. Ethan is that fine by you too she asked him? Ethan replied, mmm yea. Madison went about preparing enough eggs for the three of them and put some bread into the toaster to toast. After about ten minutes past, Madison knew the eggs were done, and in the mean time the toast had popped up tree times. Madison buttered enough toast for everyone and took them over to the table and placed them down. She then placed a small bowl and small plate down in front of Ethan then one in front of Destiny. The finally Madison place one egg and some toast in front of herself and sat down. All three members were eating their breakfast, and soon Destiny was the first to finish and say well, folks I am off to work, please get this situation fixed, the sooner the better for me she said smiling at her parents. Good bye mother father see you later she said and off she went out the door.

Ethan said he will work on the car today, so after he had finished his breakfast he put on his dirty old coat and went outside, let me know when lunch is ready he said on his way out the door. Madison just smiled at him and said, ok dear. She sat there for a while thinking about the different languages Uriel seemed to be speaking, so she decided to go into the library room, at least that is what she called it, and look up the different languages that Uriel seemed to speak, like Spanish, Latin and Lithuanian. Madison wrote down on a piece of paper what she wanted to say to him, she wrote …Uriel, if you are in there, what is going on with you? Please tell us what we can do to help you…. Soon Madison found the page where first the language of Spanish was spoken. On her piece of paper she wrote down.   Uriel, si esta's alli', Que te pasa? Dig'anos que' podemos hacer para ayudarlo ….beside the English words.

Then she found the Latin words….Uriel, si illuc quod agatur apud vos ut faciam tibi dic nobis placere non possant which she wrote down on the piece of paper beside the English words.

Then she found the Lithuanian words   Urieai, jei tu ten esi, kas su tavimi vyksta? Pras'au papasakokite , kq galime padaryti, kad pade'tume jums … which she wrote down beside the English words.

Madison sat there for a few more minutes trying to say the words as she understood them, over and over in her head thinking all the time, I need someone who can tell me how to pronounce them correctly, I don't even know if I am saying the words correctly or not… then thought, oh my I have laundry to do. She book marked the page of this book she was reading, closed it up, and walked into her bedroom and picked up the laundry basket, and started collecting all the dirty laundry, she decided not to replace the linens this day as they were already washed last week. She then headed into Destiny's room, where she gathered up all the dirty clothes, and placed them into the laundry basket.

The Possession Of Uriel

She then headed into the bathroom where she gathered up all the dirty towels, and face cloths, this day she decided to pick up all the scatter mats on the floor as they really needed a was. Madison then walked out towards Uriel's room. No she thought I will not enter there, at least not until Agatha and her friend has helped us to do something. Madison headed towards the kitchen area, where she found dirty towels, and some of Ethan';s dirty shirts he had left on the floor near the back door, and put them into the basket then she headed for the basement. As she started down the stairs she switched on the light so she could see where she was going, headed for the laundry machines which were in the far back corner. She then turned on the lights above her head, and started to separate the laundry. Madison then placed all the white clothes into the washing machine, adding some bleach to whiten and some laundry detergent, then closed the lid down and started up the machine. She then separated the rest of the laundry and laid them in the basket for the next wash load. Madison then headed back upstairs to the kitchen where she put the kettle on for a nice hot cup of tea.

When the kettle had boiled Madison made herself a cup of hot tea and sat down at the kitchen table. She had forgotten about the piece of paper she was writing on before so she got up and headed for the reading room, opening the door she seen the piece of paper she had left behind, and grabbed the paper then left the room and headed back to the kitchen and sat down at the table. Madison tried to read the words, first in Spanish, which she kind of got, but wasn't sure, then she tried the Latin words. Again she was not curtain she was pronouncing the words right, she read them over and over. When she tried the Lithuanian words, she fumbled over and over again, soon she just gave up. Madison laid the piece of paper down on the table and just sat there. She then

The Possession Of Uriel

remembered the laundry downstairs, so she headed back down to the basement. Se walked over to the washing machine and took out the wet clothes and placed them into the dryer and closed the door, turning the machine on. She then headed back to the washing machine where she placed the next load of laundry into the machine, she then added some laundry detergent, closed down the lid and turn the washer on. She stood back and brushing off her apron said to herself, there that will take at least one hour, then she head back upstairs to the kitchen.

In the kitchen she looked up at the clock on the wall and noticed it getting to be lunch time. Madison decided to make some corned beef sandwiches today, so she walked over to the refrigerator and took out the corned beef, then walked over to one of the cupboards and took out a loaf of bread. She then started making the sandwiches when Ethan came in the back door. Oh oh good I was about to ask about lunch but I guess you read my mine he told her smiling at her. I'll wash up first he said and went into the bathroom to wash his hands. When he came back to the kitchen he found his sandwich on a plate placed down on the table where he usually sits, and sat down. Starting his sandwich he asked, what about some fresh coffee to wash this sandwich down with he told her. Oh ok Madison replied I will start the coffee pot. As Madison came back to sit down at the table Ethan watched the coffee pot, and when it was almost done, he walked over and grabbed himself a cup of hot coffee. He turned around and said, do you want a cup of coffee while I'm here? Oh ok yes please Madison replied with a smile. Both Ethan and Madison sat at the table having their lunch. Ethan had finished up first stood up and said, well, I'm off to work again, I am just about finished with the car Oh good Madison replied and watched as he walked out the back door and disappeared again leaving her sitting alone in the kitchen.

Madison remembered her laundry again and got up from the table and headed down to the basement. She headed over to the laundry part where she found the laundry to be finished their cycle. She took the dried clothes out of the dryer and placed them into the laundry basket, then she returned to the washing machine, taking the wet clothes out of the machine and placed into the dryer, along with a dryer sheet, closed the door and turned the machine on. She then placed the last load of laundry into the washing machine, added some detergent, closed the lid and turned the machine on. She turned around and headed back upstairs to the kitchen area. She sat down at the table and sipped away at her coffee and about fifteen minutes later the telephone rang. Madison got up and walked over to the telephone and picking up the receiver said, Hello.Hello my dear friend this is Agatha, how are you doing she asked? Well not good, not good at all she replied. We have had many odd things happen around here and wanted to know if and when you ladies could come over and help us out? Well replied Agatha that is why I am calling you. I finally got in touch with my friend and she agreed to come out and help us. Her name is Miranda, but she lives very far away. She told me she would come out and help, but won't be able to get here until late tomorrow afternoon. You see she lives in Los Angles, California, so it is a very long drive for her, but she will come. She will stay at my house for a few days or until this matter is settled. Oh ok well that is good news. Madison told Agatha about the different languages Uriel was now speaking in and that she was trying to figure out what he was saying. She has this one book, she told her that has several different languages so she had written down some of the words she thought would come in handy but did not how to pronounce them correctly.

Agatha just laughed a little and said, well, don't worry about that we will help you figure this all out ok. Oh we definitely hope so Agatha, Madison told her, please, please come as fast as you could, even Destiny is getting afraid of what's going on in here Madison replied. Ok my dear friend we will help. I will call you tomorrow. Good bye for now, and please take care and don't do anything until we get there, ok? Ok Agatha I won't. Good bye my friend and call me tomorrow, don't forget, Madison's voice sounded very uncertain as she hung up the phone. Madison remembered the laundry so she went back downstairs and found the laundry to be finished. She took the dry clothes out of the dryer and placed them into the laundry basket, then she took the last load of wet clothes out of the machine and placed them into the dryer, closed the door and turned it on. Madison then headed back upstairs to the kitchen and sat down at the table. She sat there for quit some time just thinking. She happened to look up at the clock on the wall and it told her it was almost supper time. Oh my how time flies when you're having fun she told herself with a giggle in her voice. What should I cook for the family today?

Madison decided on some pork chops, she walked over to the freezer and took out enough pork chops for the family, walked over to the sink and placed them into the sink and ran some cold water over top of them to thaw them out. Madison sat back down at the table waiting for the laundry to finish and the pork chops to thaw out. About forty five minutes later she decided to go back downstairs and check on the laundry, sure enough the laundry had finished its cycle, so Madison took the remaining clothes out of the dryer, placed them into the laundry basket turned around, switched off the light, then headed back upstairs before closing the door to the basement she turned off the over head lights then closed the door behind her. She then headed for her bedroom, where she put away all the clean clothes, and upon leaving the room she shut the door behind her and headed for Destiny's room. She put Destiny's clothes on her bed thinking oh she can at least put her own clothes away, then Madison headed for the bathroom, where she hung up some clean towels and a clean face cloth and put the rest in the linen closet, the closet was close to the door where you come in, it was only a small closet so she could only place a few towels in it at one time. The she headed for the kitchen where she placed a few clean tea towels and hand towels and put the rest into the bottom drawer in the kitchen. She then walked back to her bedroom and placed the empty laundry basket on the floor, turned around and left the bedroom closing the door behind her. Madison got into the kitchen just as Destiny was coming home and walked through the back door. Oh Hi mother how was your day she asked? Oh just fine sweetie, and how was your day? Oh very busy but at least that is how we like it Destiny told her mother and smiled as she past her telling her she would be in her room until supper was ready. Ok I will let you know.

Madison returned to the kitchen sink where she found the pork chops to be thawed. She took them out of the water and placed them into the frying pan where she turned the heat on to start cooking. In the mean time she went and got some vegetables brought them over to the sink where she washed, and cut them and threw them into the pot of boiling water to cook. Soon everything was cooking nicely when Ethan came in through the back door. Oh I smell supper, I will go and wash up hen told her, you tell me when it is ready. Ok dear I will Madison replied. When Ethan had finished cleaning up he went and sat in the living room to watch some television until supper time as he usually does.

About thirty minutes later Madison yelled out, supper is ready come and get it. She had placed a big bowl of vegetables out on the table, along with the platter of pork chops which were cooked to perfection. Madison also had made a big bowl of green salad which she also placed on the table. Everyone sat down to eat and soon the conversation started up. Destiny started first, well dad how was your day, I know how you like to keep busy, even though you don't work any more? She smiled at Ethan waiting for a reply. Well, if you must know I worked on that old car most of the day, and how was your day he asked? Well my day was again very busy but we manage. Then Ethan turned his attention to Madison, well Mrs. M, which he liked to call her sometimes, how was your day? Well, I finally heard from my friend Agatha, she is waiting for another friend to come help us out, her name is Miranda, but she lives in Los Angles California so it will take a while for her to get here.

Agatha said she will arrive tomorrow late but will call me and let me know when they can come over. Well, maybe that will be some good news, any news of Uriel himself? Has he not shown his face yet Ethan asked looking around at both Destiny and Madison? Both women shook their heads, nope we have not, and I hope not to hear anything further until Agatha gets here. Did you happen to see the weird symbols he has drawn on the door to his room? Yes Destiny spoke up, like some kind of circles with six pointed stars, what do they mean, do you know she asked? No, we don't know yet but I am hoping Agatha and her friend can tell us. Everyone sat in silence for a few minutes then finally Ethan got up from the table, I'm going to watch some television he said and walked away. Destiny helped her mother in the kitchen clear up after supper, wash and put away all the dishes. Well I am off to my room I am very tired today, too much work I guess she told her mother. Ok dear good night then sleep well, please and off she went.

When Madison had finished up in the kitchen she went into the living room to sit with Ethan until bed time. They sat here for about one hour then Ethan stood up and said, well I'm very tired too so I am going to bed now are you coming he asked Madison? Yes dear you go first and lock up. Madison then headed for the bathroom where she washed up then walked into their bedroom, got into her pajamas and slid under the bed covers waiting for Ethan. About ten minutes later Ethan came into their room changed into his pj's and got under the bed covers. He rolled over and kissed his wife good night, rolled back and went off to sleep, like right away. Well, that was quick she thought. Madison just lay there for a while until she drifted off to sleep as well.

That night Madison slept very good until something woke her at exactly 3:00am. She did not get out of bed, but she rolled over to look at the clock on the night stand and it read 3:00am. She laid there for a few minutes, listening very closely. After about thirty minutes she could hear voice again, the same very harsh male voice again speaking in Latin she believed. Madison decided to get up and go have a look down the hallway. She got to their bedroom door, and upon opening it saw this very bright blue light coming from underneath the door to Uriel's room. Madison slowly walked towards the door, listening, then stopping, listening, then stopping. About three feet from the door she could hear.... Nituntur ejicere nos audeat quis? Dicere nomen meum, dicit nomen peccati, n. a,b,c,d,e,f X,X... over and over, it did not make any sense to her, not at all, she was tempted to get closer, but as she was about to step forward, the door to Uriel's room flung wide open. Madison stood there in disbelief, she could not believe what she saw, or thought she saw. With the door to his room wide open she saw all the walls, or part of them that she could see, all were dripping with what appeared to blood like substance, dripping down from the top of the wall to the floor, and this very potent smell, it was like some one had died or something. Madison decided to back away and holding her nose, slowly crept back down the hallway, turning around half way and went back into her room closing the door tightly behind her. She slowly went and got under neath the bed covers, and pulled the blankets up over her head still holding her nose.

She laid there for what seemed to be the longest time ever. She felt herself slowly calming down, settling down to the point where she found herself sitting up in bed, she slowly grabbed a pencil and some paper off the night stand beside her and wrote down the words she thought she heard…Nituntur ejicere nos audeat quis? Dicere nomen meum, dicit nomen peccati, n. a,b.c,d,e,f X,X… over and over, she did not know the words in English. But tried to translate them to ..who dare try to cast us out, who, say my name, say my name, no, no…a,b,c,d,e,f,,10,10…. then she sat back and thought, who is "US", and what does this mean?? Madison could not figure this out, she just lay there for a while and soon fell off to sleep, not realizing it, she fell asleep with paper and pencil in hand and the light on the night stand was still on.

The next thing Madison knew was that the alarm clock on the night stand went off to wake her. What, time to get up already she thought looking at the clock, she reached over and turned it off. Madison looked around and noticed she still hand the pencil and piece of paper laying beside her under the bed covers and that the light on the stand was still on. Wow I must have fell off to sleep right away, I don't usually leave the light on. She put the pencil and paper on the night stand and turned the light off got out of bed, slid into her slippers that were laying on the floor beneath her. She slowly and quietly left the bedroom and headed for the bathroom to wash up and comb her hair. She stood at the mirror just looking at herself thinking, wow, what was all that about last night, did I dream it all? Madison was uncertain. She then left the bathroom and headed for the kitchen to put on the morning coffee. As the aroma of coffee filled the air she could hear Ethan and Destiny get up, and the slamming of the bathroom door. She turned around to see Ethan coming at her, good morning mother is the coffee ready yet? Destiny beat me to the bathroom so I must wait he told her smiling at her. Just about dear, sit down and when it is ready I will pour you a cup she told him. Ethan went and sat down at the table waiting for his morning coffee and about three minutes later Madison brought over his coffee cup, there you are. Ethan looked up at her and said, thank you. Madison also poured herself a cup and sat down at the table with him. Twenty minutes later Destiny came into the kitchen, good morning everyone and how is everybody this morning she asked with a smile on her face as she walked towards the coffee pot and poured herself a cup, then turned and sat down at the table. My you are up very early this morning, you DO know it is Saturday right Madison told her? You don't have to go to work today. Yes I know, but my friend Brenda and I are going into town to do some shopping, I am in need of some new dresses and skirts for work, and my friend is just coming along for the company. Oh ok Madison replied.

What would everyone like to have for breakfast today Madison asked? Hesitating Ethan replies, bacon, and eggs please, and looking at Destiny she shook her head in a yes motion. Well, ok bacon and eggs it is. Madison got up from the table and walked over to the refrigerator and took out some bacon and the eggs. She then took out the big frying pan and heating it up place some bacon strips onto the pan. As the bacon started sizzling, she walked over to one of the cupboards and took out a loaf of bread which she placed on the counter top near the toaster. She then heated another smaller frying pan and cracked four eggs into it, as that was all it would really hold. As the eggs started to cook,she then checked on the bacon and turned it over, then she headed for the toaster and placed four slices of bread into it bushed the bottom down to toast the bread. The bacon was now cooked so she took it out of the frying pan and placed it on a separate board and padded it with some paper towel to get rid of some access oil, then turned the burner off. She noticed the eggs were done as well, so she placed two eggs on one plate and some bacon, then placed the other two eggs on another plate along with some bacon. The toast had popped up so she buttered the toast and place all of it on a smaller plate, and took everything to the table where Ethan and Destiny sat waiting. Here you go Madison said, eat up. She then returned to the stove and cracked two more eggs into the pa to cook for herself, along with two more slices of bread. Soon the eggs were cooked so she placed them onto a plate along with the rest of the bacon then buttered the popped up toast and place them on the same plate, then walked over to the table and sat down to eat.

As they sat having their breakfast Destiny asked her mother if there was anything she need in town? Madison thought for a moment then said, well why don't you surprise me and buy me something nice she smiled at Destiny waiting for a answer. Ok Destiny replied. After everyone had finished their breakfast Ethan told Madison that he was going out to do some gardening, so he got up from the table, grabbed his old jacket and went out the back door. Madison was once again left alone sitting at the kitchen table sipping on her coffee. I hope Agatha calls me today Madison told herself. She sat there deep in thought. Today she thought I will do some cleaning and listen for the telephone to ring, still in deep thought she told herself, I will do some more research on that language I heard the other night and try pronouncing the words, yes that is what I shall do today. Madison stood up from the table and started cleaning up the kitchen from breakfast. She washed the dishes and put everything away, then she walked over to the broom closet and took out the cleaning supplies she would need, along with a bucket a mop and broom. Madison stood at the kitchen sink to fill the bucket with hot water as she was standing there, looking out into the backyard once again she saw this tall dark figure just floating above the ground, he seemed to be standing right over Ethan's head, but Ethan had not even noticed it. He must be blind she said to herself with a giggle in her voice. She looked down just in time to see the bucket was almost over flowing and quickly turned the water off, dumping out about the bucket of water.

    Madison always start to clean in the front doorway, she walked down the hall to the front door, where she started to dust down cobwebs, and dust the furniture with a nice smelling wax, she dusted all the hallway and everything in it on her way towards the kitchen area where she left the cleaning supplies. Then she went back and started sweeping the floors, when she got to her "Library room", she opened the door to find all the books and any loose papers scattered all over the place, like a hurricane had hit the room, but yet she had just dusted it a few minutes prior. What, what on earth is this all about, she scurried about the room picking up all the books and loose papers and placing them back where they had come from, then she finished sweeping the floors. She then headed back to the front door where she started washing all the floors, knowing no one would come in just yet to step on her wet floors, she continued down the hall until she reached the kitchen and stopped. She still had not heard the telephone ring, but she will continue to listen for it. Madison then headed for her bedroom where she started to dust everything down and used that nice smelling wax to wax all the wooden furniture, then she swept the floor.

She thought she would dust and sweep the floor in Destiny's room and then come back to wash all the floors. She entered Destiny's room and noticed a awful lot of cobwebs, wow this child does not do anything to clean her room Madison thought, I will have to get after her and tell her when she had finished she swept the floor. She then headed for the kitchen where she grabbed the washing bucket and went off to her room. She starting mopping the floor and then went into Destiny's room and mopped that floor closing the doors behind her. She took the washing bucket back to the kitchen because she decided to put some clean water into it, this water is very dirty already she thought. She walked over top the kitchen sink and dumped out the dirty water and replaced it with clean hot water, she also added some floor cleaner to make the place smell nice, Murphy's Oil soap is what she added as Madison loved the smell of it.

When she had replaced the washing bucket she placed it down on the floor in the kitchen, then headed for the bathroom where she knew this is the dirtiest room in the house ad it needs a real good cleaning she thought. As soon as she opened the door she could tell that it truly was the worst room in the house, maybe because everyone used this room the most she thought. Madison started to clean and disinfect the toilet, the bathtub, this time it even had a dirt ring around the top of it, she giggled to herself as she went about cleaning it, then she cleaned the mirror and the sink area, then she swept the floor. She headed back to the kitchen to get the wash bucket and wash the bathroom floor. I think it needs two washing's this time she told herself, so Madison washed the bathroom floor twice. When she had completed that room, she washed the hallway floor right up too Uriel's room, which she was not going to bother with, after thinking about what she saw the other night. No I will not enter this room she told herself. She headed for the kitchen. I think I need a good cup of hot tea before I do any more work, so she put the kettle on to boil and when it had boiled she made herself a cup of hot tea and sat down at the table to sip on it. Five minutes later Ethan had come in through the back door, what is lunch there cutie? How about some soup today Ethan that will be quick she replied, ok that is fine he replied as he headed for the kitchen sink to wash his hands and wait for his lunch. Madison had opened a can of vegetable soup and heated it up on the stove, and about five minutes later she had poured Ethan a bowl of hot soup, along with a pile of soda crackers, as she knew he would crumble them up and put them into the soup, he liked it that way she thought, and sure enough that is exactly what he did, then he sat there and ate his lunch. Madison also had a small bowl of the same soup, with a few crackers. Both Ethan and Madison sat there having their lunch.

Boy, this place smells really really clean he told her with a smile on his face. Well I hope dear as I am still cleaning it. Are you done working outside yet she asked him? No, not quite but I am almost done, does that garden not look great to you he asked? Madison stood up ad walked over to the window to look outside and have a look, well, I believe it does it looks really good, then she returned to table to finish her lunch. Has your friend called today yet he asked her? No, not yet but I know she will,because she told me so, she always keeps her word Madison replied. Oh ok, well I am off to finish my work he said and off he went out the back door. Madison sat for a few more seconds then got up and cleaned up after lunch. Soon she was back at it, cleaning the kitchen area, she even washed down the kitchen cup boards as they were real messy she thought. Soon Madison had finished her job, and was putting away all the cleaning supplies and emptied the washing bucket and put it away. She decided to make herself yet another cup of tea, and when it was ready she sat down at the table to sip on it.

As she sat at the table she read the different Latin words over and over again, she still did not understand what any of this meant, but she was going to for sure ask Agatha about, I know Agatha will know what this means she said to herself as she gazed down at the words in front of her. Madison sat there for the longest time and wondered what she would make for supper today. Looking up at the clock on the wall she saw it was getting pretty close to the time, but what she asked herself, what?? I think some chicken, with vegetables and rice, yes that will be quick and easy to make, and for dessert…mmm, well I will make custard pudding. Madison got up from the table, walked over to the freezer and took out some chicken, enough for everyone, she placed it into the sink and added cold water to thaw it out. As it was thawing she started preparing the custard pudding. She knew it would take then longest time to make so she started on the pudding first. About thirty minutes later the chicken in the sink had thawed out completely so she started cutting the chicken up into long strips, and coasted them with a flour and seasoning mixture then placed them in the frying pan. She turned the heat on low, then she decided which vegetable she wanted so she washed, and cut up the vegetables and placed them into a pot and turned the heat on for them to start cooking. Now I just have the rice to start, so went about preparing the rice. Everything was cooking along nicely she thought, even the custard pudding was in the refrigerator keeping cool for dessert. Madison also thought she would put together a green salad, so she gathered up the ingredients and made a big bowl of green salad.

Soon supper was almost ready, she opened the back door and called for Ethan, so he brushed off his clothes and came in the back door. Destiny followed closely behind him, saying Hello I'm home and I have done all my shopping mother. What is for supper she asked as she went past her mother and into her room? Chicken dear, just chicken Madison replied. Ok call me when it is ready she told her. Soon the salad was made so Madison placed the bowl on the table, then she placed a platter of chicken on the table, and then a bowl of steaming vegetables. Destiny supper is being served come and get it please. Destiny came running out of her room and sat down at the table. Ethan had been the first one to arrive waiting for his food. Everyone sat down to the table to eat their meal. And as usual the gossip started. Ethan first started, have you not heard from your friend, what's her name....Agatha yet he asked Madison looking right at her? No, but I still believe she will call me today, maybe after supper she replied. Oh ok he replied, and Destiny what did you buy down town today and how much money have you spent, he gazed at her until she answered him? Well, Destiny replied, I got two very nice dresses and they not very expensive either, and I also got a few skirts which were very cheap. I think I spend about one hundred dollars, that is all she told him. Oh ok, and what did you buy for your mother, she did ask you to get her something, he smiled at Destiny this time? Well, I will get it for after supper mother, I know it will look just great on you, but if you don't like it we can return it, I have the receipt.

Soon the family had finished their meal, and Madison got up to get the dessert. She walked over to the refrigerator turned around and asked, anyone for dessert? Oh why please Destiny replied, followed by Ethan yes please. Madison took three nice size dessert dishes from one of the cupboards, and placed some custard into each bowl then top it with some slices of banana's, turn placed some whipped cream on top of that. She turned and walked over to the table placing a bowl in front of each of them. Wow mom this looks really good. It is Madison replied, it is.Soon the dessert had vanished also, and that's when Ethan got up from the table and said, I am going to watch some television before bed time and off he went. Ethan walked into the living room and turned the television on and sat down, while the girls cleaned up after supper.

When they had finished Destiny told her mother that supper was really good today and thanked her, by giving her a kiss upon the cheek, going to my room now to get your gift, I'll be right back she said and off she went. Destiny returned five minutes later carrying a bag. Here you are mother I hope you like it. Madison opened the bag to find a new dress and a pair of pants inside the bag. Oh my, you did not have to buy me so much Destiny but thank you so much, I will try it on later, thank you again. Oh you are welcome mother you deserve it and off she went back to room closing the door behind. Madison was about to go to her room to try on the dress when the telephone rang. She walked over to the telephone and picked up the receive,Hello she said. Hello my friend it is Agatha, sorry it took me so long to call you but we have been busy talking things over. Oh it is so good to hear from Agatha, so good. How is your friend, got here ok did she Madison asked? Why yes, and thank you for asking. We were going to come over to your place tomorrow but it is a Sunday, so we will wait until Monday if you don't mind, as Miranda does not like to work on the Sabbath day of Sunday. Oh, well that is fine dear that 's just fine, well ok then Agatha said good bye for now my dear friend, I shall call you on Monday and let you know what time we will be there ,ok? Good bye for now Madison replied and hung up the telephone.

Soon Madison went into the living room to join Ethan and she told him what Agatha had told her . Oh ok yea I guess Monday will be ok, just not soon enough for me though he replied, yes I know Madison replied. About thirty minutes later Ethan stood up and said, it's bed time for me dear are you coming he asked? Yes you go ahead and lock up the house and I will go first to the bathroom she told him and off she went while Ethan went about the house locking up all the doors. Madison had finished in the bathroom so she went into her bedroom and tried on the dress while waiting for Ethan. To her amazement the dress fit just fine, then she tried on the pants and they fit just right as well, I will have to tell Destiny she did a good job today. She really knows my size that's for sure she told herself.

Madison got into her pajamas and underneath the bed covers, and waited for Ethan, about five minutes later he walked into their bedroom, put his pj's on and slid under the bed covers as well. He rolled over and kissed his wife saying good night Madison, sleep well tonight ok. Oh yes I will knowing Agatha is coming she told him. Soon Ethan fell off to sleep and so did Madison. That night Madison had another dream, nothing no noise or voices woke her but she was in a deep dream. She was dreaming it was winter time and there was at least four feet of snow outside. As she stood at the kitchen window looking outside, she saw that tall dark figure floating out besides the garden which is now covered with a good layer of snow. She stood there for a long time just gazing at it, she did not know what to make of it but she was sure it was not a good sign.

A few hours had past, or at least that is what it seemed like to her, all of a sudden she felt this hand upon her right shoulder

The Possession Of Uriel

and this harsh male voice telling her to follow him, follow me he kept saying over and over, this time the voice was in English, one Madison understood. She did not know what to make of it, nor did she want to turn around and have a look. Madison stood there, then all of a sudden she was standing outside in her bare feet standing beside this dark figure, she was also floating above the ground. Somehow she got turned around and behind her were four marked graves. As she got on her knees to have a better look she saw the names, marked on each grave...Ethan Blackthorn, born 1940 died 2005, next one read....Madison Blackthorn born 1941 died 2006... next one read Destiny Blackthorn born 1983 died 2006 and the last one read. Our Beloved Uriel Blackthorn born 1981 died 2006... Madison was to say the least beside herself, wondering what in heaven's name was going on?? She stood up very quickly and was about to turn around, when she found herself back in her own bed, laying beside Ethan like she never left the room.Her feet felt very very uncomfortable so she threw the bed covers off and seen her feet were turning the colour purple, like they had frost bite or something. Madison got out of bed went and got a pair of wool socks from out of one the drawers and put them on, and got back into bed.

She lay there for a while thinking, what, what just happened?? My feet are just frozen like I was outside, but yet I have not left this room. And, I heard that if someone dreams about snow, that someone in their family will die soon, oh my I hope that is NOT true she told herself, shivering. I will have to ask Agatha about that question for sure. Finally Madison fell off to sleep, when the alarm clock went off and woke her up.

CHAPTER TWELVE

Madison got up out of bed and slid into her slippers that were laying on the floor beside her bed, and slowly walked around the bed, past Ethan who was still sleeping very soundly, she walked slowly and as quietly as she could, open the bedroom door, closed it quietly behind her and walked down the hall and into the bathroom where she washed her face and combed her hair. Upon looking into the bathroom mirror, she asked herself…I must have had this awful dream last night, but for the likes of me, I can not remember what it is about. All I remember is that there was snow everywhere, that is a bad sign I think, she told herself looking into the mirror like she was expecting an answer!! After she had dried her face, she left the bathroom with Destiny knocking on the door, hey mother I need to come in please. Madison opened the bathroom door and said well, good morning to you to Missy, as she headed towards the kitchen to make the morning coffee. As the coffee was brewing she could hear Ethan get up out of bed and come towards the kitchen, noticing that the bathroom was occupied. Good morning, and how are you this morning he asked? Well, I guess I am fine but had this very strange dream last night she told him. Oh Ethan replied, what did you dream about my dear he asked as he sat down at the table waiting for his morning coffee. Madison poured him a cup and a cup for herself, then sat down at the table.

Well I was dreaming about snow. One minute I was here inside the house in my bed and the next thing I was standing outside in the backyard, in my bare feet, and that is about all I can remember she told him. Mmm he replied that is strange, then what happened? I woke up, the alarm clock woke me, but I found my feet were ice cold like I had been outside, so I put these nice warm socks on to warm my feet. Ethan looked down at her feet, smiling. Well, that is very strange, anyways that is but a dream. What is for breakfast this morning he asked her? Well, what would you like she asked? Ethan thought about it for a moment then said, boiled eggs and toast, please. He smiled at Madison as she replied ok. She got up from the table and walked over to the refrigerator where she took out a dozen eggs and a loaf of bread from the cupboard, and started to prepare them. In the mean time Destiny came into the kitchen, All cleaned up and her hair was dripping wet. Well aren't you a terrible sight this morning Ethan told her. What, or yes I still have not dried my hair yet she replied, as she took up a cup of coffee for herself and sat down at the table. Good morning mother, how are you? I know this is Sunday so I am taking my time this morning, hope that is ok with you? Madison turned around to look at her, yes dear that is fine. Boiled eggs this morning, would you like some Madison asked her with a smile on her face? Oh yes please Destiny replied, that will be great, thank you. Soon the eggs were cooked Madison and had a lot of toast piled on a small plate and placed it on the table. Here you go everyone she said. Ethan took three eggs and some toast, while Destiny took two eggs and one slice of toast. Madison sat down at the table to join them, looking at Destiny's plate she said, well I guess you are not very hungry this morning hey? No, not really Destiny replied, but this is just fine she told her. What is everyone going to do today Madison asked looking around a them? Ethan replied, well not too much today just finishing off a few things I have started. Destiny replied, I am just going to rest and read a book in my room she told her. Oh wow, what a exciting day this will be Madison told them, Soon they were all finished their breakfast,then Ethan stood up and went out the back door, saying, I'll be out back if you need me smiling as he left through the back door. Destiny soon followed, she got up and went into her room. Once again Madison was left alone in the kitchen to clean up after breakfast. She finished her breakfast, got up and started to clean up. Since this is a Sunday she told herself, I think I will just go in the "Library room" and catch up on my reading of Latin and such. Madison finished up in the kitchen and went into her Library room and sat down with the book she opened at the pages of Latin text. She tried her best to pronounce each and every word, but she just could not quite grasp it. Madison wrote down on a piece of paper some words she thought she might be able to use if and when Agatha and her friend got here. Words like ….who are you …. quis es ?? what do you want from us ….Quid ergo vis a nobis?? please leave us alone and go away, leave this place ……. libet tantum nos abire hinc …….

Madison sat there for the longest time trying her best to read and translate some of the words. One hour went by and she decided to get up and go and make some lunch as she was getting pretty hungry. Madison closed the book up, but book marking the page she was on, left the room and walked into the kitchen. Looking up at the clock on the wall she noticed it was 1:00pm, yes time for lunch she thought. What should I make today she thought?? Madison decided on soup and sandwiches for everyone. She took a can of cream of potato soup out of the cupboard, a big can, opened it into a pot and turned the heat on below it. She walked over to the refrigerator and took out some ham and some cheese, walked over to the cupboard and took out a loaf of bread. As the soup was heating up she made four sandwiches, three was ham and cheese and the fourth one was just ham, just for her, she did not want cheese today. Madison also toasted the bread so it was nice and crunchy, and added some cream cheese. Then she made a sandwich for herself. Standing back looking at the sandwiches she had made, she decided to make a fresh pot of coffee to drink.

Soon the soup was very hot and the sandwiches were on the table so she called for Ethan out the back door, to come in and Destiny, if she wanted some lunch come and get it. Soon they were all sitting at the table having their lunch. All of a sudden they ALL heard this loud bang, then the whole house shook again, like there was a earthquake or something, and this time there was still terrible bad smell without the whole house. To Madison it smelt like someone had died, it was not very nice. Ethan stood up and walked over to Uriel's room, knocking on the door. Uriel, Uriel are you in there, what in the hell are you doing, come out here right now young man, right now he screamed at the door. But no answer, and no reply. The shaking of the house stopped, there was no banging going on now and that terrible odor stopped. Ethan stood at Uriel's door for a while, thinking what is going on in there I would love to know. He scratched his head and went back to the kitchen table where the two ladies sat just staring in his direction. He looked up at them and said, what? What? I don't know what that was but I am going to find out and soon. He sat back down at the table to finish his lunch, then he asked Madison again. Have you heard from your friend Agatha yet? Why yes I did Ethan, she will bring her friend by here tomorrow,. then we'll see what will happen she told him.

Well I really hope so, this has to end and end NOW he shouted. Oh it will Madison replied, it will. Ethan then stood up from the table and went back outside to finish his work and Destiny went back to her room to read. Madison was left to clean up after lunch as she normally does. As she stood at the kitchen sink washing the dishes, she looked outside and seen Ethan busy working away in the garden, she did not however, see the dark tall figure, at least not today. When she was finished cleaning up after lunch she went back to her Library room to do some more reading and research. Madison sat in the big comfy chair while she read and re-read the pages trying to make sense of any of this. She could not, but she read on anyways, thinking maybe I could learn something here, she smiled at herself.

After a few hours went by, she decided to go into the kitchen and make herself a nice hot cup of tea. When the kettle had boiled she make herself a cup of hot green tea and sat down at the kitchen table, thinking about the words she just read. Looking up at the clock on the wall again, she noticed it was getting to be supper time. My how time flies when you're busy doing something she told herself with a grin on her face. What should I make for supper today, and why is it always my job to figure that out. Well, let me see. She sat there for a while thinking it over and she decided on chicken. That was a quick and easy meal to prepare and cook she thought. Madison walked over to the freezer and took out enough chicken for everyone then placed it in the sink with some cold water to thaw out for later. Then she decided on some vegetables to have with it and some rice, this time though, she thought I will cook some brown rice, it is much better for us. Soon the chicken had thawed out, so she covered them in flour mixture, added the seasoning then placed the chicken into the frying pan to cook on low heat. She then washed and peeled some vegetables, and put them into a pot and on the stove to cook. Then she started on the brown rice. She knew thew rice would take longer to cook so she started the rice first, then the vegetables.

About thirty minutes later, as the chicken was cooking slowly, so was the rice, she then started cooking the vegetables. Soon supper for ready, but before she called anyone she decided to make a bowl of green salad to go with the supper so she went about making the salad and placed it on the table, along with three settings. Madison soon discovered not to put out a placing for Uriel as he never got to supper table again, that was just a waste of time. Soon the meal was ready, then she called for Ethan who was still out in the garden, and then Destiny who came running. Wow, mother you make supper so delicious every day. Maybe one day I will try to attempt to make us supper. She smiled at Madison and sat down at the table. Oh really Madison replied, smiling at her I did not know you could cook she said. You'd be surprised at what I can do Destiny told her, just wait one day I will surprise you.. Soon Ethan came in and went into the bathroom to wash up and comeback to table and sit down. Everyone was enjoying their meal when the telephone rang. Madison got up to answer the telephone and said Hello. Hello there my dear friend it is Agatha I am just calling to tell you Miranda and I will be at your house tomorrow afternoon about 3:30pm, will this be ok with you she asked? Oh my, yes that will do just fine, we will see you tomorrow then Madison told her and said, good bye for now and hung up the telephone. Madison walked back to the table where Ethan asked, who was that? That was Agatha telling me that they will be here tomorrow about 3:30pm, and I told that would be perfect. Yes replied Ethan and not any too soon either. Soon the family was finished their meal. Ethan stood up and walked into the living room to turn on the television to watch before to bed, while Destiny stayed in the kitchen this time to help her mother clean up after the nice meal she had cooked. Soon the two ladies were finished in the kitchen and Destiny told her mother she was off to her room to do some more reading. I have to be up early tomorrow mother so I might not have time for breakfast, but will let you know for sure in the morning, ok she told her? Ok Madison replied, and when she had finished up in the kitchen Madison went and sat down beside her husband in the living room to watch some television before going to bed. About forty five minutes later Ethan told Madison that he was tired and that he was off to bed. Ok replied Madison right behind you she told him. Madison went into the bathroom first as usual, washed up and went into their bedroom, got into her pajamas and got under the bed covers, waiting for Ethan. About twenty minutes later Ethan entered their bedroom, got into his pj's and got under the bed covers, he rolled over and kissed his wife on the cheek saying good night dear sleep well, please. Ethan rolled back over and just as quickly fell off to sleep. Madison lay there for a while longer and soon she fell of to sleep.

Once again Madison was awaken, looking at the clock on the night stand it said 3:00am. She could voices, faint but she could still hear them. She lay there for a while..all of a sudden this loud crash, like someone had throw a glass or mirror to the floor and it had broken into a zillion pieces this startled her out of bed. Cautiously she got out of bed, forgetting about her slippers, quietly walked around the bed to the door and opened it . Looking down the hallway, she noticed the door to Uriel's room was open. The room seemed to be full of heavy smoke or a heavy fog, every once in a while she would see a dark figure floating about the room, or at least some of it. Madison decided to get a little closer and see what was going on. She got about three feet from the door when this figure of a man made an appearance. Madison looked a little harder and seen it was Uriel's face looking back at her, but somehow it had changed. It looked like Uriel but yet the face was very old and wrinkly, with open sores about his face. He wore this black robe that hung to the floor and looking down, she noticed his feet were not touching then floor. All of a sudden this figure got down on his hands and knees, and took one giant leap to the ceiling where he seemed to crawl across the ceiling of the hallway towards her, turned around and started climbing across the walls like a spider, but very very fast, heading straight for his room, slamming the door behind him. Madison stood there for a few seconds not knowing what to do. All the time this figure seemed to be yelling at her again in a different language,Latin sounding words Madison did not understand, and it frightened her, almost to the point where she felt faint and weak.

She slowly walked backwards towards her bedroom, and closing the door behind her, walked around the bed and back into bed, getting under the bed covers, just shivering, she was not cold but frightened. Madison lay there for quite some time thinking....was that our son Uriel or was that something else, it looked like him, yet it did not, I am very confused and frightened she thought. After what seemed to be a long time she fell off to sleep only to be awaken again by the alarm clock that was on the night stand beside her.

Madison sat up in bed after turning the alarm clock off and rubbing her eyes to help waken herself but that did not help. She got up out of bed, slid into her slippers and walking around the bed, opened the door, and went down the hallway into the bathroom. This time she looked up at the ceiling and along the walls as she walked,but saw nothing. Soon she found herself in the bathroom, washed her face and combed her hair. Never gave that experience from last night another thought. She walked into the kitchen were she put on the coffee pot, making a nice big pot of coffee. A few minutes later she could heard Destiny get up and go into the bathroom then she heard the showering running Oh she will be in here shortly she thought. The coffee was ready for consumption so Madison poured herself out a nice big cup, went and sat down at the table, waiting for Ethan and/or Destiny to arrive in the kitchen asking for breakfast. Sure enough about twenty minutes later Ethan came into the kitchen and walked right over to the coffee pot pouring himself a cup, then sat down at the table Looking up at Madison he said, good morning dear how are you this morning, he smiled at her sipping his coffee? I am fine Ethan and you? How did you sleep? Quietly or not she asked him with this surprised look upon her face? Yes I slept fine, why do you ask? You did not hear any noises last night, or loud voices she asked him? Mmm, no I did not, you must be hearing things again he told her with a giggle.

Madison just sat there with a grin on her face. Soon Destiny came into the kitchen and poured herself a cup of coffee, as she got to the table she asked, mother what is for breakfast this morning? What would everyone like to have this morning she asked looking at Ethan then back at Destiny? After a few seconds went by, Ethan replies well I am in no hurry this morning so how about some scrambled eggs, sausage with some hash browns and toast? Wow that is a tall order, Destiny what about you? She thought for a minute then replied, yes I will have the same please she replied with a smile on her face. Ok Madison replied and she got to her feet, walked over to the refrigerator took out some eggs, sausage, and the hash brown's. She placed the sausages and hash browns into the frying to cook, while she scrambled up some eggs, enough for everyone, then walked over to one of the cupboards and took out a loaf of bread, placing four slices into the toaster. Soon the sausages and has browns were cooked, she took them out of the frying pan and placed them onto a small platter, then she dropped in the frying pan a bowl of scrambled up eggs, and pushed the toaster down to toast the bread.

Soon breakfast was cooked and she brought a plate of some sausage, hash browns and a scoop of scrambled eggs on each plate, and put a plate down in front of Ethan and then one down in front of Destiny, then she returned to the stove and placed some sausage, hash browns and eggs on a plate for herself, and she grabbed the plate of toast from the counter and took it to the table, placing it down in the middle of the table for everyone, as she sat down to eat also. Soon everyone was talking about their day. Ethan was going into town to get some supplies and chat with a buddy of his, while Destiny said she was off to work and will be late in coming home, very busy day she added with a smile. Oh ok Madison replied. Ethan asked, is your friend coming by today, you said something about that yesterday he asked? Yes Agatha will be bringing her friend Miranda by, I hope they find a cure for this she told him with a smile on her face. Me too replied Ethan. I am off to town now, is there anything I can get for you while I am there he asked her? Oh, just a few groceries. I have made a list over there on the counter, if you'd please pick them up, that would be great she said. Ok, Ethan headed for the back door, picking up the list Madison had left on the counter. See you later he told her and off he went. Soon Destiny was ready, and picking up her coat and keys, she was going out the back door as well, she kissed her mother on the cheek and said, good bye, hopefully you will have a very good day, and have a nice visit with your friends ok she told her, and waved good bye as she went out the door closing it behind her. Madison was once again, left alone in the kitchen to clean up after breakfast.

After cleaning up from breakfast Madison decided to clean up a little before the ladies got there. I must have a clean house for them to come into she told herself. Madison finished cleaning up after breakfast, then she got out all the other cleaning supplies. She started at then front door, dusting down everything, and sweeping the floors, then she went back and washed them all with a good smelling Pinesol cleaner. When she had reached the kitchen area, she knew that at least the front entrance and hallway were very clean and smelling clean as well. Then she headed for her room even though she knew the ladies would not be in there but she cleaned her room anyways, and washed then floor leaving them clean and smelling like Pinesol. Then she headed for Destiny's room where she did the same cleaning job and washed the floor with the Pinesol solution. Then there was the bathroom, that was always a big mess and Madison knew it. She went inside and found the mess left behind after Destiny's shower with dirty clothes lying all over the bathroom floor. Oh, we can't have this mess she thought to herself, so she cleaned up the whole bathroom, and when she was done washed the floor with then Pinesol, leaving it smelling an nice clean smelling.

Madison decided to leave Uriel's room, not really wanting to go in there, so she washed the floors in the hallway until she got to the kitchen. She dusted down everything and swept and washed the floors leaving this room smelling clean and fresh as well. When she was done, she looked up at the clock on the wall, and had seen it was getting to be near 3:00pm, oh those ladies should be here in about half an hour, so I will bake some cookies for them. Madison went about the kitchen, taking out of the cupboard what she needed, mixing the dough and made a tray of some nice looking cookies, placing them into the oven to bake. There they will still be warm when the ladies arrive, then I shall over tea or coffee. Just as

The Possession Of Uriel

the cookies were out on the counter top cooling down there came a knock to the front door. Oh Madison said to herself, brushing off her apron as she walked down the hallway, that must be them. Madison got o the front door and upon opening it, found Agatha and her friend Miranda standing there. Agatha had worn just a pair of jeans today, and a odd looking blouse and jacket, they were dark blue on colour with bright yellow strips going up and down, and carrying a large black bag, while her friend Miranda was a rather tall lady must have been at least six feet tall, she has long blonde hair, dyed by the way as Madison noticed, with a rather large over coat also carrying a large black bag. Madison said, well Hello ladies, please come in. She lead them down the hall to the cloths closet, and said, you can hang your coats up in here and she handed each of them a coat hanger, then placed their coats into the closet, closing the door. Please come into the kitchen and have some coffee or tea, whichever you prefer she told them with a smile on her face. All three ladies walked down the hall to the kitchen area.

Please have a seat. As the ladies got closer to the table Agatha sat down and said I'll have coffee please, ok coming up Madison told. When Madison turned around to give Agatha her coffee she noticed Miranda was still standing. She laid her bags on the floor and with out stretched arms, and her eyes closed, she walked about the kitchen, and heading towards Uriel's room, suddenly stopped, turned around and headed back to the kitchen. Agatha looked at Madison and said, that is how she starts, she will need to have a good look around the house before we start. Oh ok that is fine, please tell her that is ok Madison replied. Agatha told Miranda that was fine for her to go and have a good look around the house. Miranda just nodded her headed in a yes motion. Turned around again and headed down the hall to Madison's room, then

Destiny's room, then the bathroom, but she stopped when she got to Uriel's door. She gazed at the symbols painted on the door, and ran her hands over the door, like it was on fire or something, then she suddenly fell backwards landing on the backside on the floor. Both Madison and Agatha ran over to help her up and take her into the kitchen and sat her down. Oh my what was that all about Agatha asked her?

I am not sure Miranda replied, but I know there is a very bad spirit in that particular room. She stopped and just sat there pondering over something. She did not drink and eat anything then all of a sudden she asked for water, which Madison got for her from the refrigerator. Sitting there staring at her Madison asked, well, what is it? What is wrong with my son she asked? It took Miranda a short time before she replied. When was the last time you saw your son as a normal person she asked Madison? Oh, it has to be at least four to five weeks now or more, why do you ask? Miranda replied, I don't believe he is himself now. I feel a very strong spirit in there and it is not in the room but in a body. Miranda looked at Agatha and said. We must go consult a good catholic priest she told her, this will be a very long, bad job there is a lot to prepare for before we even try. Miranda and Agatha talked for a while then Agatha told Madison that they will have to go and return with a priest that could perform a exorcism along with their help. We can not do this alone she told her. Ok Madison replied. Looking straight at Madison Agatha told her that they would have to return , but did not know when and bring with them a good catholic priest who knew how to perform this ritual. Agatha told Madison that she would have to prepare the house and how and what she would need.

Ok Madison replied. Both Miranda and Agatha got up from the table, and headed for the front hallway to the closet where they got into their coats, and went out the front door. When they reached their car, Agatha turned around and waved good bye to Madison who was standing in her front door way. Madison waved back then turned around and went back into her house. When she reached the kitchen she did not know what to make of all of this. She got herself a cup of coffee as there was a lot left over, and went and sat down at the kitchen table. I wonder what it is I will have to do now. I hope the ladies return fairly soon, sooner than later is good for us. She sat there for a long time, then, looking up at the clock noticed it was getting near supper time. Oh my the ladies were here long than I thought, but that is ok. What should I make for supper, since it is getting pretty late now, guess I will have to cook some chicken, a quick meal today and then tomorrow I will cook a roast beef dinner to make up for today.

Madison went into the freezer and took out some chicken for the family and placed it into the sink with some cold water to thaw. Then she took out some vegetables to have with the chicken and some rice, just regular rice today as she did not feel much like cooking the brown rice, it would take way too long she thought. As she went about the kitchen preparing supper the back door opened and there stood Ethan with two arms full of stuff including the groceries Madison asked him to get. Well, how did things go with your friends today Ethan asked her putting the groceries on the counter top, and everything else on the floor beside him? Well, I am not sure, they seem to think we have a very bad spirit here and that they will have to prepare and return with a catholic priest to clean it out and prepare for a exorcism on Uriel, that is all they told me. Oh no replied Ethan, not all that crap again, do we have to he asked staring at Madison? Well yes I think so Ethan, other wise we do not know what to do and as each day goes by it seems to be getting worse and worse, we have to do something. Well, what is all this going to cost me Ethan asked with a worried look on his face? I don't know, but I will find out before they all start, like I said, we MUST do something and dop it right now Madison said.

With that said Ethan just picked up his bag off the floor and went into the bedroom. Let me know when supper will be ready please he asked? Ok I will Madison replied. Soon after that Destiny came in through the back door. Madison was still putting the groceries away and trying to cook supper when Destiny asked about her friends. Well it sounds bad and it just might be, but we have to do something Destiny, we can not let this go on any longer Madison told her. Yes, mother I know. Maybe it is the same apparition that was in our house before Destiny replied. Madison looked at her and said, well, honey I don't think so, Miranda and Agatha told me that there is something really evil in this house, and it will take a lot of work to get rid of this time. Oh, wow mother that does not sound good to me either, when can they do this she asked? I don't know yet, Agatha told me when they have everything ready and get a good catholic priest here, it might take some time, did not know how much time or how long it will take, but they will do the job, I am sure of it Madison replied. Well ok mother, and hey, let me know when supper is ready I am starved today, she told her mother as she went past her and into her room closing the door behind her.

About thirty minutes later supper was ready. Madison had set the table, and placed all the food out on plates, and put them on the table, then called everyone. Ethan came into the kitchen and sat down at his usual place and Destiny came into the kitchen right behind him. Soon everyone was at the table having their supper. No one said one word all during supper. When Ethan had finished he asked, what is for dessert? Well I did some baking today and we can have some cinnamon buns, ok? Yes that will be fine he replied. Madison looked at Destiny and she did the same thing, yes mother that is fine, I will help you. Ethan got up from the table and said I'll be in the living room, please bring it in to me once you are done here he asked? He walked into the living room and turned on the television, sat down and watched some TV until Madison brought him the cinnamon buns. Destiny helped her mother cut the buns up, placing two or three on each plate,and Destiny took a plate in to Ethan. As she laid the plate down she said, now father please bring the plate back to the kitchen when done, and she smiled at him. Ok deary I will. Destiny went back to the kitchen where Madison and she sat at the table eating their buns, and once finished they both got up and cleaned up the kitchen. These are good mother, you will have to make some more one day, and smiled at her. Destiny got up and went into her room, I will say good night mother as I am very tired today, ok? Yes good night dear, sleep well. The Madison went into the living room to join Ethan who was almost falling asleep then, with the plate almost on the floor. Madison grabbed it and placed it on the coffee table. They sat there for about thirty minutes when Ethan said, well I am going to bed I am tired. Ok dear you go and lock up. Madison turned the television off and walked into the bathroom to get ready for bed, combing her hair and brushing her teeth, she then headed for their bedroom. She opened the door and turned on the small lamp beside the bed, and got into her pajama's then got under the bed covers waiting for Ethan. About twenty minutes later Ethan came into their room and change into his pj's and slid under the bed covers. He rolled over, kissed his wife and said good night my dear, there are better days to come I just know it he smiled at her and rolled back and fell off to sleep.

The Possession Of Uriel

Madison just lay there for the longest time before she fell off to sleep. That night Madison, slept like a baby. No noises or voices wakening her, no shaking of the house. She rolled over and looked at the clock on the night stand. It was only 4:00am still too early to get up, She lay there in a daze. All of a sudden there came this big streak of lightening, then the sound of thunder, again and again. The thunder got louder and louder, and the lightening lit up the whole sky. Madison lay there not afraid of the storm, but listened to the sounds it made. Suddenly the rain started as it beat against the window of their bedroom it almost sounded like the rain was going to break through the glass, it was raining that hard. Madison was wide awake at this point so she decided to get up out of bed, slide into her slippers and go stand in the window and watch the storm. Everything was very very dark, Madison stood there just waiting for another streak of lightening and thunder. Then all of a sudden it came, and as it lit up the night sky Madison thought she could actually see the face of her son Uriel in the center of the storm. There was an area of gray and white clouds and Uriel seemed to stand right in the middle of it, but only his head and face appeared to her. His eyes were bright red almost like Satan himself she thought, but there was only dark holes where his eyes should have been with the glowing red color to it, His face was white as clouds and his skin seemed to be gray and wrinkles, like an old man. To Madison as she stood and stared he almost looked like God himself, with very long white hair to boot. She knew that this could not be HER son, but the face of someone evil, not of this earth. Madison stood there until she heard yet another loud crack of thunder and a huge bolt of lightening. The rain kept pouring down harder and harder, the lightening and thunder kept up until Madison heard the sound of the alarm clock go off on the night stand. She walked over to shut the alarm clock off, and went

The Possession Of Uriel

back to the window to look outside. The storm was still there with a strong force of its own, not letting up at all, or at least that is what Madison thought.

She decided to go into the bathroom and wash up, oh my she thought with this storm Ethan is not going to go outside at all today, he will be inside bothering me all day. With that she giggled to herself, after drying her face off and combing her hair she left the bathroom and headed for the kitchen where she started the coffee pot. When the aroma of coffee filled the air Destiny came into the kitchen first. Oh good morning mother and how are you this morning? I see there is a bad storm outside today. Yes there is Madison replied, is was the storm that woke me early this morning. The coffee was ready so Madison poured herself a cup and a cup of Destiny. She walked over to the table and laid a cup down for Destiny and she sat down on her chair. Guess you'll just have to go outside in the rain and get wet, Destiny giggled to her mother. Oh no I won't, I am not going out today, I have to stay in and wait for a telephone call from Agatha and I do hope she calls me very soon. As the two sat there Ethan came into the kitchen, good morning ladies and how is everyone this morning he asked with a smile? Oh we are just fine except for that storm outside, it will be a very wet nasty day unless it stops soon Destiny replied. Yes I noticed Ethan replied, but I have a lot of work I can do indoors, don't have to go outside today unless it brightens up out there.

After breakfast, Ethan went downstairs to the basement as he was going to do some work down there, and Destiny walked down the hallway to the closet and took out her rain coat, went back to the kitchen, took up her purse and car keys walked past her mother and said, well mother I am off to work, hopefully the weather will improve, I will see you later. Ok replied Madison, have a good day at work. Madison was still sitting at the table sipping her coffee when Ethan came up from the basement. He walked over to one of the drawers by the back door, and looking inside, turned to Madison and asked, do you know where my purple screw driver is, I can't seem to find it he asked with a curious look on his face? Why no dear, I don't know where you keep your things, just keep looking you will find she told him. He scurried into every drawer in the kitchen, even looked in then pantry. No no he said, not in here, maybe it's outside in the old shed, I will go have a look. He put his rain coat on and went out the back door and into the shed out back. Madison now was cleaning up the kitchen from breakfast, and as she stood at the kitchen sink doing the dishes Ethan came in the back door and he had his screw driver with him. Haha I found it he told her smiling at Madison as he walked past her and back downstairs.

Good replied Madison, even though she knew he could not hear her reply. As she stood at the sink finishing up with the dishes, she looked outside into the dark sky. Mesmerizing her thoughts, Madison stood there for a while watching the lightening and thunder roll over head, and the rain, it has been a sold down pour since last night, well at, at least I won't have to water the garden, she chuckled to herself. While staring out into the storm, Madison saw the tall dark figure again, only this time it appeared to be white in colour, instead of black. His face appeared to be the same face she thought she saw last night come out of the center of the clouds!! His face seemed awesomely terrifying, she started shaking as with fear though she did not know why. She opened her mouth ready to shout out to Ethan but no sound came out of her mouth, she tried harder and harder but still, no sound. She looked down at the dishes she was washing and discovered she was not doing anything at all, and that all the dishes had been done and put in the strainer to dry. When she looked up again the tall figure had disappeared, just as fast as it came. There must be a meaning for me seeing this figure most of the time, she told herself there just has to be.

Madison finished cleaning up the dishes and decided to go into her "Library room" to do some reading. Madison took her apron off laid it on the counter and went into the library room. She took up the same book she was reading before on Latin and sat down to read some more. Madison came across some prayers that she soon discovered were used to get rid of evil spirits in people, they were used by catholic priests who knew what they were doing in such cases as told by some prominent people around then world. Madison tried to read out loud one of them, to her it went something like this...... crucem sancti eritis mihi in lucem, ut non quod draco sit mihi dux.. Recede satana recede. Non vana vestra temptare. Quid mihi es malum venenum. Meaning .. the Holy cross be my light. May the dragon never be my guide. Get away Satan, get away. Never tempt me with your vanities. What you offer me is evil, drink the poison yourself. Madison sat there for a while just thinking about this statement, maybe I should learn this prayer, so she read it over and over again until she got it correct writing it down too, just in case she forget.

Madison sat there reading for a good three hours and found her stomach was making noises, oh my guess I am hungry for lunch. I wonder what time it is getting to be she asked herself? Madison stood up and walked into the kitchen, looking up at the clock on the wall. Oh my it is lunch time, it is a wonder Ethan is not here yelling at me for his lunch. With that Madison giggled a little and went about the kitchen preparing some nice hot soup, with cheese sandwiches. Shortly afterwards and sure enough Ethan came up from the basement, hey what is for lunch I am very hungry he told her? Oh lunch is just about ready, wash up and go st down at the table, I will put it out for you when you return. Ok he replied and off he went into the bathroom to wash up, and soon came back sitting down in his chair at the table. In front of him Madison had placed a bowl of nice hot steaming cream of broccoli soup, along with a cheese sandwich. Eat up she told him, then get back to work at whatever it is you were doing she told him. Yes my Love he told her. They both sat there having their lunch, not one word was said between them. Madison turned her face to the kitchen window and looking outside said, hey, it looks like the storm is dying down, I don't hear any more thunder out there, do you she asked Ethan. He turned and looked out the window also, and said, I guess it is finally stopping. That is good at least I don't have to wash the car or water the flower bed he told her smiling away. Soon both of them had finished their lunch, Ethan got up from the table and went back downstairs to the basement to finish up. Madison sat there for a while thinking about what Agatha and her friend might have to say and or do when they come back. I will clean up here after lunch and go back and do some more reading, I am going to master this language if I have to try for the rest of my life she told herself. Madison went about the kitchen cleaning up after their lunch and put away the dishes. She then walked down the hallway to the "Library room" as she calls it and sat down in her chair and started reading from where she had left off.

She read for a few hours, trying to pronounce everything she saw and read but she could not. I might have to get a teacher to teach me how to pronounce these words she thought. She studies some drawings she had found in the book as well. She tried drawing them on a piece of paper and writing down beside it what it stood for or what it meant. Oh my she told herself, I am not very good at drawing either, but I will give it a good try. Madison soon got a headache after reading so much, so she put the book down and walked into the kitchen. She put the kettle on for a nice hot cup of tea, and sat down at the table for a while just sipping on it. Madison found her headache to be going away now, boy I am surely not used to do all the reading, at least, not all at one time. I don't know how I ever got through High School, she giggled at herself. Just then Ethan came upstairs looking for something, and what are you laughing at he asked her? Well I just discovered, that I can not read for so long without stopping every once in awhile. I read for so long in the Library room, that I got myself a headache, so I came into the kitchen to get a cup of tea, now it is subsiding. Oh, there you go, see, you are getting old and can't do what you used to do, right Ethan told her? Yes, you are right she replied. Ethan stood looking out into the backyard. Hey, will you look at that, the storm is over my dear, the storm is over. Oh that is good, maybe the sun will come out for a while, what do you think she asked Ethan? Mmm not sure about that, it is getting to be late afternoon now, so maybe not he said. He sat down at the table with her and asked, when is your friends coming back? I don't know for sure Ethan. Agatha told me she would call me and let me know, hopefully very soon, they have to get some people and a lot of things put together first then they will come. Oh ok Ethan replied. Well, then what are we having form supper today he asked. Oh Madison replied, I am going to put on a nice roast, how about that she asked him with a smile on her face? Oh that sounds delightful he replied. I think I go into the living room and watch some television for a while. Ok Madison replied, while I go and get out a nice roast of beef for supper.

Ethan headed for the living room where hen turned on the television set and sat down. While Madison headed for the freezer and looked around inside for a nice roast for supper. She finally found one she liked, took it out and started thawing it out for

The Possession Of Uriel

supper in the sink. About sixty minutes later it was finally thawed, so Madison browned it good in the frying pan then it turned it out into the large roasting pan, seasoned it and added some onions, closed the lid to the stove and turned the heat on to three hundred and fifty degrees. Ok she told herself, brushing off her apron, that will take at least three hours. She put the kettle on to make herself a nice hot cup of green tea. Madison sat down at the table to sip on her tea while the roast in the oven was cooking away. All of a sudden the telephone rang. Madison got up from the table to answer it. Hello she said. Hello dear friend this is Agatha, and how are things going over there she asked? Well guess I have to say, not too bad right now, and how are you? Do you have everything you need yet to come over here and help us Madison asked? Well replied Agatha, we do but we have to wait on a catholic priest, they are going to send us one, all the way from the Vatican in Italy. There is no one here that can do this type of job and do it correctly she said. Oh replied Madison, do you have any idea as to when this might happen? No, replied Agatha I am sorry but I do not know, but as soon as find him and he gets here, In shall definitely let you know, ok. Well ok replied Madison. She told Agatha about this tall dark figure she keeps seeing floating about her house, what do you think it wants from me, or has it something to do with what's going on here with Uriel? I am not sure Agatha replied, but whatever or whoever it is, we will definitely find out what it wants, ok. So be patient and don't do anything until you hear back from us, ok Agatha told her? Ok replied Madison Well I will say good bye for now and I will call you as soon as we get more information and as to when this priest will arrive to help us ok replied Agatha. Ok good bye for now my dear friend, you take care, and please call us again soon, and with that Madison hung up the telephone.

The Possession Of Uriel

Madison sat back down at the kitchen table for a while waiting for the roast to cook for supper. Soon it was time to get the vegetables cooking, and decide on what to have for a dessert today. Oh, Madison thought to herself, I believe we have a pie in the freezer, blueberry I think, I shall get that out and thaw it, we can have pie today. So Madison got up from the table and went over to the freezer and looked around for the pie, sure enough, there it was at the very bottom of the freezer. Madison took it out and said to herself, I guess I shall have to cook a few more pies, I can freeze them here in the freezer. Madison thought that this pie would be quite thawed out for today's supper, so she placed it out on the counter top. She decided on a few vegetables to go with the roast, some potatoes, carrots, peas and green beans. As the roast was finishing up in the oven Madison started the vegetables, She washed them, cut them up and threw them into a pot of boiling water on the stove top. Then she started to make the sauce for the gravy. Soon the roast for done, she took it out of the oven and placed it on a big platter on the counter top, ready for Ethan to carve up for them. She took the roast out of the pan, and started making the gravy,and as she did so the vegetables were almost cooked as well. Soon everything for ready so Madison called Ethan to come and carve the roast for supper. Ethan came into the kitchen, walked over to the roast, and started carving it up. While he did that Madison, spooned out the vegetables onto another plate, and placed it on the table. She also put out a plate of bread, and the bowl of gravy she had made. Everything was ready to eat, so they sat down at the table, when Madison said, I wonder where Destiny is, she is really late today isn't she she told Ethan. Yes she is, but remember she did tell us she would be a little late, I guess they are real busy at work. Just as they said that in the door she came. Oh Hello everyone, sorry I am late, had to work. I'm going to wash up then I'll be right back she told them. Ok Madison replied as both Ethan and herself started eating their meal. Soon Destiny came into the kitchen sat down at her spot, and dished out what she wanted. Wow mom, this looks really good, I know it smells just great, you are such a good cook, thank you mother. Madison replied, you are welcome dear. Everyone was eating their meal in silence.

When the meal was almost finished Madison asked if anyone wanted dessert today? Ethan was the first to speak up, well, what is for dessert today dear, Madison replied, blueberry pie. Oh yes please I'll have some thank you Ethan said. Oh yes, me too please Destiny replied, I love blueberry pie. Madison got up from the table and walked over to the pie, cutting three slices and placed them onto plates. Ethan do you want anything on your pie, like ice cream or whipped cream she asked him? No, just plain is good, ok Madison replied, Destiny how about you, do you want anything on yours? Yes, I'll have a scoop of ice cream please she replied. Madison got out the ice cream and scooped one scoop onto Destiny's pie, and took it over to her. Here you go, eat up. Thank you mom she replied. After everyone had their dessert, Ethan said oh my I am full now, really he said rubbing his stomach. Oh yea, me too Destiny replied, guess I'll have to help clean up after supper to push all that food down she giggled at her mother who was smiling back at her. Ok I suppose you can help Madison replied. Ethan stood up from the table and went into the living room to once again watch some television. While Destiny helped her mother in the kitchen clean up after supper and put away the dishes. Soon the two ladies were finished and Destiny told her mother she was going to room to rest and relax. Think I will go to bed early today as I am really bushed she told her mother. Ok dear, good night then, see you in the morning Madison replied.

Destiny went off to her room, while Madison went and joined Ethan in the living room to watch some television for a while. About one hour later Ethan said, I am tired so am going to bed now, are you coming dear he asked Madison? Yes she replied, you go ahead first and lock up,I will meet you in the bedroom. Ethan went around the house making sure all was secure for the night, while Madison went into the bathroom to wash and brush her teeth, then she headed for the bedroom, where she got into her pajamas, turned on the small lamp on the night stand, got under the bed covers and waited for Ethan. Ethan came into the bedroom about thirty minutes later, got into his pj's and got under the bed covers beside his wife. He rolled over kissed his wife and said good night, please sleep well he told her, then rolled back and fell off to sleep. Well good night to you dear, you sleep well too she replied. Madison lay there for quite some time before she fell off to sleep.

CHAPTER THIRTEEN

Once again Madison was awoken by a horrific thunder storm. Looking at the clock on the night stand beside her she saw it was 3:45 am. This is the second night in a row that we have had a storm like this, what is going on with the weather would it have anything to do with our situation she asked herself?? Madison lay there for a while just listening to the storm outside. It went silent for a while then all of a sudden there came a big flash of lightening, followed by a crack of thunder so loud it startled her right out of bed. Madison got up out of bed and walked over to the window to look outside. As she stood there looking out into the night sky, there came this face of someone she did not recognize. It was huge, there was no body to it just the head and face, with these great big red eyes glowing at her they seem to be talking to her yet Madison could not hear anything. She stood there for a while just mesmerized like she was under a spell or something, then there was this jolt of lightening and it seemed to have pushed her back into her bedroom a few feet just sliding across the floor like there was no floor beneath her feet. Madison found herself standing in the doorway to their room, and turned around facing down the hallway to Uriel's room, what happened she asked herself in silence? Did that face looking at me want me to go somewhere? Looking down the hall she saw a bright blue light coming from under Uriel's door again. She wondered if she should go have a closer look, not able to stop, she found herself slowly "floating" towards Uriel's door, looking down she saw her feet were not touching the floor, oh my maybe I am dreaming all this, yes, that is it I am dreaming. Madison closed her eyes very tightly thinking she will wake up in her own bed, but no suddenly someone or something laid a hand on her right shoulder. To Madison it felt very cold she still had her eyes shut very tightly, not wanting to open them. She stood there frozen for a while, then all of a sudden the hand on her shoulder pulled her back, the long thin fingers dug into her shoulder with a pinch.

Then like it never happened, she found herself back in her own bed, laying there watching the storm outside. Madison was very concerned about all this. She thought to herself, why is this only happening to me? What did I do to deserve this punishment, why me?? I will have to ask Agatha when she returns and hopefully that will be very soon. She rolled over and looking at the clock noticed it was almost time to get up the clock red 6:15 am. Madison just laid there until the alarm went off, then she got up, slid into her slippers and went into the bathroom to wash up. She then headed into the kitchen where she put the coffee on for breakfast. Soon the aroma of coffee filled the air, she could hear someone getting up and go into the bathroom but she did not know who, yet. Then she heard the shower going, oh that must be Destiny getting ready for work. Madison poured herself out a cup of coffee and sat down at the table waiting for someone else to come into the kitchen. Soon Destiny came into view and poured herself a cup of coffee and sat down at the table. Good morning mother, how are you this morning she asked with a smile on her face? Oh, I am fine and how are you, did you sleep well Madison asked Destiny? Yes mother I did, what is for breakfast this morning she asked? Well, what would you like Madison asked? I think some scrambled eggs and toast, that is fast and easy she told her. Oh ok think I can manage that Madison told her. A few minutes later, Ethan came into the kitchen rubbing his eyes he went over to the coffee pot and poured himself a cup then sat down at the table. Good morning sunshine Madison told him, how are you this morning? Well had a good sleep until that storm woke me up, but then I fell back to sleep, really fast, how many more storms are we going to get this week he asked, looking around at both Madison and Destiny thinking they would know the answer? Destiny shrugged her shoulders, oh don't look at me I don't know she told him. Madison looked at him and said, well don't ask me either, do I look like a weather man to you, she asked giggling to herself. Mm was all he said. Madison got up from the table and said I am going to make breakfast now, we are just having scrambled eggs and toast she told Ethan who was looking in her direction. Oh that will be fine he replied. Madison walked over to the refrigerator and took out a dozen eggs, put some in a big bowl and started scrambling them up. As they sat in the bowl she walked over to one of the cupboards and took out a loaf of bread, then she placed four slices into the toaster and pushed it down to toast. Then she poured the eggs into a large frying pan, and started cooking them up, until they were nice and fluffy, scrambling them as they went along. Soon the toast had popped up and she walked over to the toaster, took the slices out, placed them on a plate and buttered them, then she added four more slices and pushed them down to toast. Soon the eggs were cooked so she divided them out into three plates, and on each plate she had sliced up some tomatoes and place two slices of tomato on each plate took them over to the table and placed one down in front of Destiny then one down in front of Ethan, the toast will be forth coming she told them and walked back to the toaster where the remaining toast had popped up so she buttered them placed them on the plate as well, and took it over to the table placing it down in front of Ethan.

Soon the three family members were eating their breakfast, non one said one word this morning, then Destiny looked outside, from the table where they sat they could see outside into the backyard, well it is still raining, but it looks like it will not last long this time she told them with a smile. She stood up and said, well, I am off to work. Have a nice day every one, she kissed her mother goodbye and went out the back door waving her arm as she put on her rain coat. Madison looked at Ethan and said, well what are you going to do today she asked him? I am still working downstairs in the basement but I am almost finished, so I hope by then, that the storm has cleared and I can go outside to the garden he told her. Oh ok she replied. Ethan stood up and went downstairs to the basement closing the basement door behind, as to not make too much noise for Madison. Madison sat there for a while thinking about what her day will bring and what she should do. Well I think I will do some baking today, yes I will maybe bake a chocolate cake and some cookies to have with our tea.

She walked over to the pantry door, opened it and looked around for her baking ingredients and took out what she needed. She then cleared off one of the counter tops, and placed out all the tools she would need, a big mixing bowl, cooking pans, and cookie sheet, along with the utensils she needed. She got out her recipe book and looked for chocolate cake and some kind of cookies that she knew everyone would like. She found a good chocolate cake recipe, and some cookies, that she knew everyone would like. She started making the chocolate cake first, then turned the oven on to the temperature she needed. After all the ingredients were mixed she placed the mixture into two cake pans, this recipe was a layer cake so she needed two round cake pans, which she had buttered and greased, she poured the mixture out evenly into the two pans, shook them a little then placed them into the over, closing the door she said well, that will take about thirty five minutes, and while that is baking I shall start on the cookies she told herself. She started mixing the cookie dough and when it was thouoghly mixed she took the cookie sheet, lightly floured it and pressed the cookies out onto it making a fancy dent into each one. I will add something colorful later she told herself. Soon the bake was baked, so she carefully took the cake pans out of the oven and placed them on a cooling rack on the counter top, then placed the cookie sheet of cookies into the oven and closed the door. The temperature was the same for both the cake and the cookies she thought.

Soon the kitchen filled with the smell of freshly baked goods, as the cookies were also baked now, so Madison took them out of the oven, turned the oven off and closed oven door, placing the cookie sheets on the counter top as well on a cooling rack. She made herself a nice hot cup of tea, so she sat down at the table and waited for the baked goods to cool down enough so she could decorate them. Next thing she knew Ethan came up from the basement and said, wow what is that delicious smell? Oh it looks like you did some baking, that looks really good too, can I have something he asked her? Madison quickly replied no, not yet they are still very hot, you'll just have to wait she told him smiling at him. Well what is for lunch then he asked her looking at the clock on the wall, it is lunch time? How about some soup and a sandwich she told him. What kind of sandwiches are you making he asked her? What kind would you like dear and I will check see if I have it for you? Ethan thought for a moment then said,corned beef please, do you have that he asked her? I will go and look she told him walking over to the refrigerator she looked inside, looking around she found some corned beef, yes we do, I will make sandwiches for you dear she told him. Ok he replied and waited at the table. Madison put on some chicken noodle soup and while it heated up she prepared the sandwiches. Soon the sandwiches were made and the soup was nice and hot, she poured some soup into a bowl for Ethan and placed it in front of him along with the sandwich. There you go Mr. She told him smiling at him, she then turned and walked back to the counter top where she took up her bowl of soup and sandwich plate and walked back to the table where she sat down to eat. The two were quietly enjoying their lunch. Madison just happened to glance up and looking outside said, hey Ethan look the rain has stopped and the sun is out, you can go outside now she told him with a smile. Ethan looked up from his lunch plate and replied, oh yes I see. I will do just that after lunch he told her. Soon they both had finished their lunch, and sitting back in his chair Ethan said, thank you for lunch my dear, I will go finish up downstairs then head outside, and off he went. Madison was left sitting alone at the table as usual. She finally got up and walked over to her baked goods and lightly touches the cake pans and cookies and knew they were cool enough for decorating. Madison started making the icing sugar for the chocolate cake, sense it was a chocolate cake she will make white frosting with a cream butter flavor. She placed a layer of frosting on top of one of the cake later, then put the other cake layer on top of that, then she placed frosting over the whole cake. When she had finished she placed candy sparkles all over the top, to make it look good enough to eat and she placed it on a cake plate, which she had on the counter top and it had a lid to it, so she covered the cake with the lid. Since she had frosting left over, she decided to decorate the cookies, she coloured the frosting orange and red in colour and placed a small amount of frosting on each cookie, along with some sprinkles. She had finished she stood back to look at her creation, thinking ,yes, they look very edible, with that smiled.

She placed the cookies into a cookie tin and cleared away all the mess the decorating had caused, then she went about washing all the dishes even the ones from lunch. When she had finished cleaning up all the mess, she made herself a nice hot cup of tea and sat down at the table to sip on it. As Madison was sitting there having her tea the telephone rang she went over to answer the telephone. Hello!Hello Madison, this is your friend Agatha calling, how are you doing she asked her? Well fine I guess Madison replied, except I have been having some very weird dreams, so I am hoping you are calling with some good news for us Madison replied. Well, I think so, we finally got someone to come help us. He is Archbishop Father Timothy from somewhere in Italy, he will be arriving day after tomorrow. I am told he has performed this ritual many times and he is about eighty percent reliable at getting the job done. I am sure he will be the one to help us. As soon as he arrives I shall call you back and let you know what you need to do when he comes to your house, ok she told her. Well ok she replied. So I will say goodbye for now and I will call you as soon as he arrives. Ok goodbye for now Madison replied and hung up the telephone.

Madison thought for a moment then said to herself, that will be a Thursday hopefully he arrives, I shall have to clean the house again before that day. Madison went back to the table and sat down and continued sipping on her tea. She sat there deep in thought, oh I wonder what I will dream about tonight, if anything, I am getting really worried she said to herself. We still have not seen or heard from Uriel in all this time, I wonder he is he still alive in there and I am very tempted to go in there and find out for myself, but, then she stopped. Madison looked up at the clock on the wall and it told her it was getting near supper time, oh my what to cook today for supper, there is not enough of the roast beef left over, what shall I cook she told herself. She sat there for a while thinking. Well, I guess some chicken with vegetables and rice, it seems we are always eating the same foods over and over, I will have to cook something different one of these days she said to herself. Madison stood up from the table and walked over to the freezer and took out some chicken, enough for the whole family. Walked over to the kitchen sink and placed the chicken in the sink and ran some cold water over it. She then walked over to the refrigerator and had a look around for vegetables. Oh my, guess I will have to go to market soon as we are running out of vegetables, but she took out enough vegetables for today's meal. She also walked over to one of the cupboards and took out the box of rice, which they will have with it the meal. Soon the chicken was thawed out, so she coated the chicken with flour and seasoning, and placed it into the frying pan turning the heat on below it on medium to cook the chicken through. She then washed and cut up some vegetables, and started cooking the rice first as it usually takes the longest time to cook. Standing at the window looking out into the backyard she saw Ethan working away in the garden, even though he was getting very muddy, he looked so cute she thought to herself. Madison was supposedly looking for that strange face she saw in her dreams but it did not show up today, she never seen it again after that. The chicken was almost cooked now so she started cooking the vegetables, as the rice was almost cooked as well. Madison also decided to make a big green salad to go with supper, so she went to the refrigerator and took out what she needed to make the salad and started cutting the greens, cucumber and tomatoes for it, and tossed it up in a big bowl and set it out on the table. She then went over and set the table for supper. By this time the chicken and vegetables were almost cooked, so she put the chicken on a platter and the vegetables in another bowl setting them on the table.

Just as she turned around to go outside and call Ethan in for supper Destiny came through the door, Hello mother I am home, she said. Oh good, just in time for supper, go and wash up she told her. Destiny shook her head and went into the bathroom to wash up then she came back to the table sitting down in her usual spot. Ethan had come in from the back yard he also headed for the bathroom to wash up, but he left a trail of muddy feet prints on the floor.Madison noticed it and shouted, Ethan take your shoes off you are leaving mud everywhere please. She could hear him say back, yes dear I will. Soon he came out of the bathroom all washed up carrying his shoes in his hands, see I did he told her giving her a kiss on the cheek as he went past her to his chair at the table and sat down. By now Madison had placed all the food out on the table, she sat down, and said, ok everyone go ahead before it gets cold. Soon everyone was filling their faces with all the delicious food Madison had prepared. As they sat eating Destiny pipped up and said. What is that nice smell, it is not supper, what else did you cook today she asked Madison with a smile on her face? Madison replied, well, I did some baking and made us a chocolate cake for dessert. Oh yummy Destiny replied, good I love chocolate cake, so does father, don't you daddy Destiny said looking straight at him with a smile? He smiled back at her and replied, yes Destiny I also like chocolate cake. Soon everyone had finished their meal,and Madison stood up and walked over to the counter, and taking the lid from the cake plate, started cutting up three nice size pieces of cake and placing them on a small plate and took them over to the table, placing one in front of Ethan and one in front of Destiny and one for herself. Soon they all dug into the cake finishing it

The Possession Of Uriel

off really fast. Oh my I guess everyone liked my cake she said looking at each of them with a smile. Yes mother we did, thank you for baking. I will help you clean up after this delicious meal, so Destiny got up from the table as did Ethan who walked into the living room to turn on the television as he normally does and sat down in his chair while the two women started cleaning up after supper. Soon they had finished and Destiny went off to her room to read and go to bed, while Madison went into the living room to sit with Ethan for a while before they went off to bed. About two hours later Ethan yawned and said, well, its off to bed for me mother are you coming he asked her? Why yes dear, you go ahead and lock us up for the night and I will go ahead of you. Ethan went off towards the kitchen area to lock up first, while Madison went into the bathroom to wash and comb her hair, then she went into their bedroom where she got into her pajamas, and walked over to the night stand turning on the small lamp, getting into bed waited for Ethan. About twenty minutes later Ethan came into their room closing the door behind him, he also got into his pj's and got under the bed covers, rolling over he kissed his wife and said, good night dear sleep well. Yes Ethan you sleep well too, then he rolled back over and fell off to sleep as Madison could hear him snoring right away. She lay there for quite some time before she dropped to sleep.

 Once again Madison awoke to this strange noise, it was so loud it startled her to sit up in her bed and listen. Looking over at the clock on the night stand it told her it was 3:05 am. She sat there for a while just listening, it sounded like those male voices speaking Latin again. This time she recognized the Latin words, or at least some of them. They seemed to be getting louder and louder and instinct told her to get up out of bed and follow the voices. She slid into her slippers this time, and walked slowly and quietly around their bed, and towards the door which she opened as quietly as she could. Peering out and down the hallway she noticed there was this bright light coming from under neath Uriel's door but this time it was a bright white light. Madison thought about it for a while then decided to go and have a look leaving er bedroom door ajar, just a little. She walked quietly down the hallway and when she approached the door to Uriel's room, with a shaking hand she slowly opened the door, which had this eerie sound, like it was very old and squeaked, liked it needed some oil. Upon entering his room, Madison saw nothing but a white cloud of smoke soon to disappear, there in front of her was this long metal table, and it appeared to have a human body laid out on the top of it, but it was covered with a big white sheet. She looked around and saw nothing else in the room, nothing. Madison nervously approached the table, and when she got within one foot, one skinny gray looking arm fell from under the cover, Madison jumped back, gathered her nerves and very carefully pulled back the cover from the head of the body. It revealed the face of her son Uriel, quit dead, but also he had three marks tattooed on his chest they looked like Z's one a little lower than the previous one, three in total Madison dropped the sheet cover from her hand and put her other hand to her mouth hoping not to make any noise. She stared at the body very intensely thinking to herself, what is going on here Uriel is not dead, he can't be dead, she kept repeating this over and over again.

Madison must have stood there for what seemed to her to be a hour. With a shaking hand she was about to try and touch the face of the body which lay before her, and just before she felt the touch, the body and table disappeared, poof, up in smoke, and the whole room took on the appearance of a grave yard, in which she found herself walking in bare feet on this very wet grass. Walking where she did not know, she was still in her pajamas, but instead of the regular pajamas, she was wearing this long white silky dress, looked like it came from the early 1800's, it was not her's at all. She touched the dress with your left hand, like it was a sheet of satin, and it was made of gold. Looking around at her whereabouts she discovered she was now in a much older grave yard as the tomb stones were crumbling down, the names of the stones were barely readable, she stopped and tried to read one stone which read…here lies Ralph Grabson born 1799 died 1866. She stood up straight and said to herself, where am? How did I get here?

She found herself starting to float away from this place, "floating" because she could not feel the ground beneath her feet. Looking down she saw nothing, no ground, no dirt no grass, just a heavy mist. Wow I MUST be dreaming this, it, it can't be real it just can't be. She closed her eyes thinking maybe this will all go away and she will be back in her own bed. About, what seemed to her to be about five minutes later. Sure enough she found herself back in her own bedroom, not laying in bed but gazing outside into the darkness standing at the bedroom window. She looked down at her feet and they were all dirty, muddy and wet. Again she put a hand to her mouth not wanting to make any sound to awaken Ethan. Oh my she told herself, I must go and wash before going back to bed, my feet are all dirty and very muddy, but I don't remember walking in such mud. She slowly walked towards their bedroom door, which was closed by the way. She thought that to be very odd, as she did not remember being outside in the first place, maybe I was outside and maybe I closed the door when I returned, I can't remember anything she told herself in silence. Madison slowly walked down the hall and into the bathroom, where, trying to be as quiet as she knew how began washing her feet off in the bathroom sink. I shall have to tell Agatha about this dream, or is it a dream she asked herself looking into the bathroom mirror, and noticing her hair was in such a state it would scare even a ghost she thought. Madison quickly ran a comb through her hair, and upon leaving the bathroom turned off the light, closing the door behind her, went back to her room where she got under the bed covers, and fell off tom sleep.

It was two hours later that the alarm on the night stand went off telling her it was time to get up. Madison rolled over and turned the clock off and rubbing her eyes sat up in bed. Thinking wow, what a dream I had last night, or at least I think it was a dream. She got up out of bed, and was about to slide into her slippers that were on the floor beside her, when she looked down at the slippers they were all covered in mud and very wet to the touch. Oh my she thought what is this all about, then she remembered her dream from the night before. Well, I guess I will have to go find another pair to wear for today, as she got out of bed she headed for their closet, where she knew she had another pair of slippers, then she slid into a dry pair, turned around and went down the hallway to the bathroom where she washed her face, combed her hair and went into the kitchen to put the morning coffee on for breakfast. She sat down at the kitchen table to wait for the coffee, thinking about her dream from last night. Is someone trying to tell me something I wonder she said to herself or was that just a dream? She could not answer that. Soon the coffee was ready and as she walked over to the coffee machine to pour herself a cup she seen Destiny come into the kitchen. Good morning mother how are you this morning she asked as she poured herself a cup. Madison sitting at the table now replied, well, I had this very strange dream but otherwise I slept fine, thank you, and yourself how did you sleep she asked Destiny who was getting to the table to sit down. Just fine mother I slept well, thank you, is father not up yet she asked with a surprised look upon her face? Mm no, I don't see him yet, but don't worry he will be along. Before Madison could finish her sentence Ethan appeared in the kitchen doorway. Good morning everyone, and how is everybody this morning he asked as he walked past the table and straight to the coffee pot, where he poured himself a cup, came back and sat down at the table. We are just fine Ethan, Madison replied.

Ethan pipped up, and said where did you go last night he asked Madison with this uncertain look in his face? Oh, why what do you mean, where did I go Madison asked him with a surprised look upon her face? You know what I mean, I saw you get up out of bed last night and walk down the hallway, then you disappeared he told her. What? Madison asked that sounds absurd, I did nothing of the kind she replied. Oh yes you did, you woke me up getting out of bed he told her. Madison sat there for a while and replied, well I don't remember doing that, I don't usually sleep walk if that is what I did, I really don't remember doing that she told him. Mm he replied, what is this family coming to, now my wife is sleep walking and doesn't recall doing it, he just smiled and said, well, ok but if that keeps up we will have to find a Doctor for you and see what's wrong with you he told her. Oh, oh yes she replied I will go see a Doctor if need be she said.

Well, now that that's over, what is for breakfast, we do eat around here he told her smiling at her. Well what would you like to have she asked him? I am famished this morning, so how about some bacon and eggs with toast he replied? Destiny Madison asked, how about you? Oh yes mother that will be just fine, thank you she replied. Madison got up from the table, walked over top the refrigerator and took out some bacon and a dozen eggs. Then she walked over to one of the cupboards and took out a loaf of bread. She then placed some bacon into the frying pan and turned the heat on below it to cook, while the bacon was sizzling away, she put four slices of bread into the toast and pushed it down. Then she added four eggs to one smaller frying pan and started cooking the eggs, sunny side up as everyone likes them. Soon the bacon was cooked and she took it out of the frying pan and placed it on a sheet of paper to take some of the grease off, then the eggs were cooked so she placed two eggs on one plate for Destiny and the rest of Ethan on another plate, along with some bacon, then she walked over to the refrigerator and took out a nice ripened tomato washed it and sliced it up, and laid two slices of tomatoes on each plate. The toast had popped up so she buttered the toast, and placed them on a smaller plate which she took over to the table along with a plate for Ethan and one for Destiny. As the two started eating their breakfast Madison went back to stove and cooked herself two eggs, and pushed down two slices of toast for herself. When it was ready she placed bacon and eggs on a plate and buttered the toast, placing that also on her same plate, as she would have plenty of dirty dishes to wash up after breakfast, she thought. Then she went and sat down at the table to have her breakfast. Well, what is everyone doing for today Destiny asked around the table? Ethan pipped and replied, I must go into town and get a few things, Madison is there anything that we need from the grocery store he asked her? Why yes dear, I will make a list for you soon as I am finished breakfast she replied. Oh ok he told her. As Madison sat having her breakfast she wrote down a list of groceries that they needed for a while and gave the list to Ethan, there you go please get everything on that list as we are right out of almost everything she told him with a smile.

    Ok dear I will get everything on your list, and with that he stood up fro the table and went into the bedroom and got dressed. Soon Destiny got up from the table and said, well I must go to work now mother you have a good day ok and I will see you later she told her mother, as she picked up her purse, keys and went out the back door. Waving goodbye as she left. Madison stood at the counter waving back at her daughter. Ethan came into the kitchen and walked over to his wife, kissed her on the cheek and said well, I am off to town I have to pick up a few things for the garden and the car, I will also pickup the groceries he told her and I won't forget anything. He picked up his keys and went out the back door, closing it behind him leaving Madison standing in the kitchen alone once again. Madison stood there for a while and looking outside into the backyard noticing it was going to be a very nice day the sun is shining and everything she told herself. Madison started cleaning up after breakfast, washing the dishes and putting everything away. When she was finished she put the kettle on and made herself a nice hot cup of green tea, and sat down at the table to sip on it.

What should I do today she asked herself? I think since my friends are supposedly coming tomorrow I will leave the cleaning until tomorrow so the whole house will look and smell very clean and fresh, so today I will do some laundry, yes that is my day. Madison finished off her tea, got up from the table, put her tea cup in the kitchen sink turned around and went down the hallway to their bedroom. She walked over to their clothes closet and took out the laundry basket, which to her surprise was almost full again, as a matter of fact it was over flowing. She picked up all the dirty clothes there laid on the floor, turned around and pulled the sheets from the bed, today I shall wash these and put clean ones on she told herself, whistling as she went along. She picked up the laundry basket and headed down the hallway to Destiny's room, and upon opening the door she found again that Destiny had just thrown her clothes all over the place, not one inch of flooring could be seen. I hope one day this child will find a good man and get married and out of my house, then we will see how her new husband will put up with this mess. Madison just shook her head as she picked up all the dirty clothes and she also pulled the sheets from the bed and laid them into the laundry basket. She then turned went down the hall to the bathroom, and upon opening this door she found a whole bunch of dirty towels thrown all over the floor, along with some clothes to boot she thought. She gathered up all the the dirty towels and face cloths, along with the clothes, and left the bathroom closing the door behind her. Madison then headed for the kitchen, passing by Uriel's room, not wanting to go in there at all. In the kitchen area, she gathered up the dirty tea towels, hand towels anything she thought was dirty and needed a wash she grabbed. She then headed to the basement, and when she opened the door to the basement she turned on the lights that lit up the stairs so she would not trip and fall. She went down the stairs and walked over to the laundry area, put down then laundry basket and pulled the string to turn the above light on that hung over the laundry machines. She sorted out the clothes, and opened the lid to the washing machine and put in all the white clothes and linens. She then added some bleach for whitening, and some laundry detergent. She closed down the lid and turned the washing machine on. She then sorted out the rest of the laundry into two piles, she laid one pile on top of the washing machine saying to herself, there that is the next load, and the last load would be the darks, so she put them back into the laundry basket to do them last. Madison then turned around and headed back upstairs to wait on the washing. She turned the light off at the top of the stairs to the basement. Madison headed to the kitchen where she put the kettle on to make herself a nice hot cup of tea, then she sat down at the table to sip on it while she waited for the laundry.

Looking up at the clock on the wall she noticed it was lunch time. Oh my Ethan is not back yet, wonder where he can be, maybe he is having lunch with his buddy's in town, so I will just make myself a sandwich, so she did. Madison walked over to the refrigerator and took out some lunch meat and some bread. She toasted the bread, and put some butter on it when it popped up from the toaster. She then placed a few slices of cold meat she found in the refrigerator, into the toasted bread and added some mustard. She walked back to the table and finding her tea was cold now put the kettle on to make herself another cup to have with the sandwich she made. Soon the kettle had boiled and she made herself a cup of hot tea, and sat down at the table to have her lunch. One hour plus had gone by so Madison headed back downstairs on the laundry room. She walked over to the laundry machine and took the wet clothes out of the machine and placed them into the dryer along with a dryer sheet, she now uses the dryer sheets because she would always forget to come back at the rinse cycle, she found the sheets to be more efficient. She closed the door and pushed the button to on while she returned to the washing machine and placed the next load of clothes into the machine adding some detergent, she then closed down the lid, and turned the machine on. She then stood up straight and brushing off her apron said to herself there, that will take at least forty five minutes, then I will return. She then turned around and went back upstairs to the kitchen, and sat down at the table to continue her tea.

Madison must have sat there for about one and one half hours reading over her notes she had made from the Latin words in her book. Boy I wish I had taken Latin language in school when I was younger then I would not have to do this, I would know ow to speak it as well, she appeared to be frustrated with herself, but kept on going. All of a sudden she looked up at the clock, and decided it was time to go back downstairs to see to the laundry, so she did. When she reached the laundry room, she found that both machines had finished their cycle and had stopped. Oh, just in time she said to herself giggling away. She took the dried clothes out of the dryer and placed them into the laundry basket, folding everything as she went along, then she took the wet clothes out of the washing machine and placed them into the dryer along with a dryer sheet,and turned the machine on. She then placed the last load of laundry into the washing machine,added some laundry detergent and closed the lid down, turning the machine on. I will return within the hour this time she told herself, as she turned and went back upstairs to the kitchen. As she checked out the time on the clock, she found it to be getting pretty close to supper time, well, what should I cook today she asked herself? Maybe some pork chops in a sauce for a change, yes that is it. Madison walked over to the freezer and took out enough pork chops for everyone, and walked over to the kitchen sink and ran some cold water into the sink enough to cover the pork chops to thaw them out. Madison then decided to have some vegetables and mashed potatoes today, we have not had that for along time she told herself. She went about washing and cleaning up the vegetables and a whole lot of potatoes as she needed to mash these up. Soon the pork chops had thawed,so she started heating up the frying pan on low heat at first, she did not coat these chops, as she was going to make a nice sauce to cover them later. She started cooking the pork chops on low heat, then started making the nice white sauce, which she would lay on top of the pork chops when they were cooked through. As the pork chops were cooking she also started cooking the vegetables. Noticing the time, she went back downstairs to gather up the laundry which she figured by this time would be finished. Yes, sure enough everything was finished its cycle, she took the dried clothes out of the dryer and placed them into the laundry basket and took the wet clothes out of the washing machine and put them into the dryer and turned it on. Almost finished here she told herself, almost. With that done she headed back upstairs to the kitchen to check on the supper meal which as cooking on the stove top, all was well so far, so she sat down at the table waiting for things to be completed.

About ten minutes later Madison noticed Ethan had come home carrying all the groceries Madison wanted him to buy and placed them on the counter top. Here you are dear, groceries are here he told her, I am going to wash up for supper had a long day in town he told her with a smile on his face. Oh ok, thank you Madison replied, as she turned around to start putting the groceries away where they all belonged. Soon their supper was almost cooked,and just as she was going to set the table Destiny came home in through the back door. Hi mother how was your day she asked? Oh just fine Destiny, and how was your day she replied? Just fine, I am going to wash up for supper she told her mother and off she went to the bathroom. Madison had the table all set, and the meal was cooked so she placed the pork chops out in a shallow dish and poured the white sauce on top of them and placed the dish on the table. Then she took the vegetables and placed them into a bowl and set them out on the table, along with a smaller plate of bread. Madison called out, supper is ready come and get it please. With that said, Ethan was the first to arrive and sat down at his place at the table, and started to dig out his food onto a plate. Destiny also arrived and did the same thing, soon everyone was sitting at the table having their meal. Destiny, Madison said, your bed as no linens on it I took them off to wash, can you put some cleans ones back on please? Yes mother I think I can do that much and she giggled looking at her mother. When everyone had finished their meal, Ethan of course retired to the living room and turned the television on to watch some TV before going to bed while the women stayed in the kitchen to clean up. They talked for a while Madison telling Destiny that the ladies and their friend will be here tomorrow to help us clear our home, I don't know what time, ok? Oh why yes mother that is fine I want this matter cleared up right away she said. Ok Madison replied looking right at her. Soon they had finished and Destiny went off to her room to read then go to bed, while Madison walked into the living room to join Ethan and she told Ethan that the ladies would come by tomorrow. Oh good I certainly hope they can clear this matter up,I really do he said. Me too replied Madison. Madison had forgotten about the laundry so she got up from the couch and went down to the basement to collect the rest of the laundry. She walked back upstairs and went into their room and laid the laundry basket down on the floor, telling herself that she would put the clothes away tomorrow she was way too tired today, so she left it there and went back to find Ethan still sitting on the couch so she sat down beside him. They must have sat there for about forty minutes, when Ethan told her he was tired and that he was going to bed. Oh ok replied Madison, you go ahead and lock us up and I will head to the bathroom first she told him. Ethan went into the kitchen where he normally starts and went about the house making sure all the doors and windows were locked up tight and by the time he got to the bathroom Madison had finished and had gone off to bed. She had turned on the small night lamp that was on the night stand and was under the bed covers, when Ethan came into the room. He got into his pj's and got under the bed covers beside his wife, he rolled over kissed her on the cheek and said, good night Madison, sleep well please, then he rolled back onto his back and went off to sleep. Madison lay for the longest time before she fell off of sleep.

That night, again it was 3:00 am when something woke Madison. She heard loud cries coming from somewhere she did not know really where. She sat up in bed and listened, finally getting out of bed she slid into her slippers and slowly walked around the bed to open their bedroom door Looking down the hallway in the samedirecti9on as Uriel's room she could these loud cries again, only they seemed to get louder and louder. And also in Latin or at least that is what she thought. As she got closer to Uriel's room, once again the door just flung open, and to Madison's surprise, she seen this terrible sight. In the middle of the room, there was no other people or furniture around, or it seemed that way,that Madison seen this human body. He appeared to be tied up with bob wire.His arms were out stretched,and his wrists were tied with bob wire, on the left hand side of the room and then the other on the right hand side of the room. His legs were also tied with bob wire, out stretched, from one side of the room until they reached the other side of the room, like he was about to be pulled apart. Madison noticed also that he was only wearing a pair of very dirty looking shorts, and no other clothing, his head hung, as if looking towards the floor, and there was blood dripping from his mouth. All over his body were cut marks like someone had got at him with a sharp knife, slashing him from side side, he just hung there seemed to be waiting for something. Madison got up enough nerve to walk over to this body and take a closer look. She very gently and with a shaking hand, lifted the head up so she could get a better look at its face. Madison let out this very loud scream, and ran from the room. Ethan quickly got out of bed and ran towards her, what is it Madison what is wrong he asked her? As soon as Ethan held her in is arms she seemed to settle down a bit and said. Go have a look in Uriel's room and tell me what you see she told him with a quivering sound to her voice, go and have a look please. Ethan let go of her and turned around walking slowly towards Uriel's room, and upon opening the door, which had closed tightly behind Madison as she turned around and ran out of there. He opened the door, and found nothing wrong, he slowly went inside and saw Uriel just laying on his bed sleeping like a baby, though he could not see his face, he slowly crept backwards out of this room closing the door gently behind him, turned and walked back to Madison who was still standing in the same spot as when he left her. He walked up to her and said, what is wrong with you Madison, I saw nothing wrong, Uriel seemed fine, though I could not see his face, he was facing the wall, apparently sleeping so I left the room. You saw nothing she screamed at him?? No, come on lets settle down and go back to bed, I swear I saw nothing wrong, he tried to calm her down but as they walked back to their room he could feel her still shivering with fear. He held her tightly and put her back into bed, pulling the covers up to her neck and tucking her in like a child, kissed her on the cheek and went back to his side of the bed, got in and fell off to sleep again, like nothing happened. Madison lay there for quite some time thinking what in God's name just happened??? What, she lay there long enough to fall back to sleep.

CHAPTER FOURTEEN

Six thirty the next morning, Madison was waken by the sound of the alarm clock. She rolled over and turned the clock off, then got up out of bed sliding into her slippers that lay at her feet. She walked around their bed,opened the door and walked down the hallway to the bathroom were she went inside, to wash her face and comb her hair. Then she headed out of the bathroom and into the kitchen where she put the coffee pot on for the morning coffee. She stood at the kitchen sink just gazing out the window, was there anything out there this morning she asked herself? A few seconds had past when she heard someone come into the kitchen.Good morning mother how are you this morning, it was Destiny and she walked right over to the coffee pot, and looking at it asked, is coffee ready? Madison turned to her and said, yes dear I will pour us a cup. As shed so Destiny walked over to the table and sat down. Madison soon followed with the two cups of coffee in her hand, and setting them down on the table said here you go, enjoy and she smiled at Destiny. The two women sat at the table when about ten minutes later Ethan entered the kitchen, and passing by the table said, good morning everyone, I hope there is coffee left for me, he turned looking at Madison with a smile on his face? He poured himself a cup and walked over to the table sitting down at his usual spot. What is for breakfast he asked? How about some scrambled eggs with toast Madison told him? Oh ok, yes that will be fine he replied.

Madison walked over to the refrigerator ad took out a dozen eggs, and walked over to one of the cupboards and took out a loaf of bread. She started scrambling up the eggs and placing them into the frying pan that she had heating on the stove top. Then she walked over to the toaster and placed four slices of bread into it, the pushed the button down to toast. Soon the eggs were cooked and the toast had popped up, so she buttered the toast and serving out some eggs on a plate along with some of the toast, she loaded two plates and walked them over to the table and set them down, one in front of Ethan and the other in front of Destiny. She then walked back to the stove and put some more eggs on for herself, along with some toast, which she put into the toast and pushed down. When her meal was cooked she walked over to the table and sat down. As the family ate their breakfast, Ethan was the first to speak up, well, what is everyone up to today he asked, looking at Destiny first then Madison? Destiny replied, well, I am off to work soon got another busy day on our hands she told them, as a matter of fact, I have to leave soon. Destiny swallowed down her coffee, stood up and said, well I am off, you guys have a good safe day. She kissed her mother on the cheek as she walked past her and went out the back door. Madison spoke up and said, today Agatha and her friends are coming by to help us out, hoping they can settle this matter today, but I don't know what time, I am guessing Agatha will call and let me know. Oh ok well, that is good news I hope, when they get here I will go into town and keep busy until they are finished and leave, ok he told her? Yes, that will be fine, I am sure they don't want too many of us in the house when they are working, Madison replied. Ethan told her he was going outside to work in the garden until Madison heard from her friends,

The Possession Of Uriel

then he will head into town. Ok Madison replied Ethan stood up and went out the back door leaving Madison sitting alone in the kitchen. Madison sat there for a while just thinking about what will happen today if anything, she told herself that if this did not work she would move away from here. Madison slowly got up from the table and started to clean up after breakfast. Maybe I should start cleaning a little before they arrive, so she went about cleaning. She started in the front hallway where she knew they would enter their house first and then she worked back to the kitchen. She washed all the floors leaving them smell clean and fresh. She made herself a nice hot cup of tea and sat down at the table waiting for a phone call or something.

About one hour later the telephone rang. Madison got up and walked over to the phone and picked up the receiver, and said, Hello. Hello my friend this is Agatha calling, how are you doing she asked? Madison replied, well we're not doing well, I hope you are calling with some good news she told her. As a matter of fact I am Agatha told. Early this morning Archbishop Timothy O'Brien from Milan, showed up at my door. He told me who they were and introduced me to Sister Kathleen, also from Milan. We had a nice long chat about you, and with everything ready we will come over to your house about 2:00 pm this afternoon, if that is ok with you Agatha told her. Oh yes, definitely I shall have the coffee on for everyone Madison told her. Is there anything that I need to do before you come she asked Agatha? Archbishop Timothy only asks that there be only you and Uriel at home, he does not really know what is going to happen so to be safe he just wants the two of you at home. Oh ok, yes that is fine, everyone else is out and they won't be home for a while Madison told her. Ok then I will say good bye for Madison and we will see you at 2:00 pm this afternoon. Good bye Madison replied and hung up the receiver.

The Possession Of Uriel

At exactly 2:00 pm there came a knock to the front door. Madison was very nervous about what was going to happen so she walked very quickly to the front door. Upon opening the door she seen Agatha standing there, and there was this very nicely dressed in a nun's uniform, a young lady, whom Agatha introduced as Sister Kathleen, she was very short as Madison had noticed, she looked upon her and said Hello welcome to my home. Then behind the two ladies walking very slowly, hesitating once in a while, then he stopped, waited, then continued but slowly, came this gentleman, he did not appear to be dressed as a priest, but Agatha introduced him to me as Archbishop Timothy O'Brien. Madison welcomed he in and told them to all please come in. They all walked down the hallway and into the kitchen except for Archbishop Timothy, he seemed to hesitate in the doorway to her home, like he wasn't wanted, or something was holding him back by force. Eventually he came into the kitchen to join the others, but he did not sit down he stood there turning his head only towards Uriel's room, turning his head back bowed his head and started praying, kissing the cross he held in his hands.

Please sit down, and tell me what will happen because as you can tell I am very nervous she told them. Archbishop Timothy was the first to speak out. You have a very lovely home, but I feel there is some very wrong here. How long have you been going through this matter he asked her? Well, Madison told him, it all started a few years back. She started telling him what was going on from the very beginning, then we thought it had gone disappeared, and we were so happy for a few years until recently. She then went on to tell them all the things that had happened in their house until today, then she stopped. Archbishop Timothy just stood there looking at her then said, do you mind if I take a walk throughout your home? Oh my no, please, please go ahead Madison told him.

The Possession Of Uriel

He walked from the table and slowly walked towards Uriel's room with Sister Kathleen following close behind him. They stopped before they reached the door to Uriel's room, and hesitating Archbishop Timothy re-sighted something from the bible. Then he motioned a cross then walked back into the kitchen. Madison noticed that Sister Kathleen was shaking as she returned.

Archbishop Timothy told Agatha and Sister Kathleen what they must do, then told Madison to stay in the kitchen, do not come near Uriel's room, even if you heard screaming or yelling going on, ok? Oh my yes I will surely just stay right here she told him.

Archbishop Timothy, Sister Kathleen and Agatha slowly walked towards Uriel's room. Sister Kathleen turned the door knob to his room and slowly opened the door. To their surprise Sister Kathleen did not see anything out of the normal as she slowly walked over to Uriel's bed where they all thought he lay sleeping. Archbishop Timothy slowly put on his long purple sash, and with a rather large size cross in his hand, slowly walked towards Uriel's bed side, chanting a verse from the bible. When he got within two feet from Uriel's bed side, all of a sudden Uriel sat upright and not turning his body just turning his head stared at Archbishop Timothy. He started speaking in foreign tongue, which Agatha understood as some form of Latin. He started yelling at Archbishop Timothy, and his voice got louder and louder repeating over and over again the same words. All of a sudden this gust of wind came up from nowhere, and it was strong enough to throw Sister Kathleen and Agatha from the room, slamming the door behind them. Madison looked over and saw the two women laying the floor, with this look of surprise on their faces. Madison quickly ran over to them and asked are you all right, are you ok she repeated until Agatha finally stood up and helping Sister Kathleen with a lending hand up from the floor, replied they were both ok and they walked into the kitchen where they both sat down on a chair to catch their breathe.

What is going on in there she asked them? We do not know, all of a sudden we were thrown from the room, leaving Archbishop Timothy alone in there Agatha told her. Do you ladies need a cup of tea or something Madison asked? Oh yes, yes please Agatha told her. So Madison went over to the stove to put the kettle on and when it had come to a boil she made three cups of nice hot green tea for the ladies, and placed it down in front of them while they all waited for Archbishop Timothy to return. Here Madison told them, maybe this will help. All three ladies sat at the kitchen table, sipping the hot tea and all the while listening and waiting. Every once in a while they would hear a loud crash like something falling hard to the floor, some yelling and screaming going on, then silence. This went on for about one hour, when finally Archbishop Timothy came out and into the kitchen. His appearance surprised all three ladies, his robe and purple sash was tossed about his body like he was in a fight or something. His hair was a complete mess. The look on his face told the ladies that this was not over yet. He sat down at the table and Madison quickly made him a cup of hot tea. Here you go Archbishop, maybe this will help she told with a smile on her face. Archbishop Timothy tried sipping on the tea with a very shaky hand, eventually he settled down and once again started praying.

As they all sat at the table waiting they could still hear strange crashes and loud bangs coming from Uriel's room, and a shaking of the whole house. Everyone held onto the table with shaking hands. Archbishop Timothy looked up at Madison and said, oh don't be alarmed, this shall be over soon, he assured her with a smile. They sat there for some time before Archbishop Timothy stood up and shaking himself off and fixing his appearance said well I am going back in there everyone please stay out here for now. He walked slowly and nervously back to Uriel's room, closing the door behind him as he entered. The ladies could not hear anything going for along time, then all of a sudden they could yelling and screaming going on. Madison stood up and said, I want to know what is going on there I must know she screamed looking at Agatha. Agatha told her, please sit down and be patient, Archbishop Timothy knows what he is doing, he has performed this ceremony many times, please Madison sit down and wait, that is all we ask.

Madison sat back down looking very impatient and nervous. It seemed like hours had past,while they sat there. All of a sudden the whole house went dark, it turned very dark outside too, yet it was only late afternoon. All was very silent for about ten minutes, then came this argument from Uriel's room, like Archbishop Timothy was arguing with Uriel. They seemed to argue back and forth in a Latin tongue, which none of the ladies knew or could make out what was being said. This went on for what seemed like hours. All that could be heard coming from Uriel's room was... praefecti mili'tia caele'stis sub alis tuis precibus circu'mdas materia gloriae, qui cadens fidelius seruaret invocaverint te.Eripiet vos de cunctis principibus et potestatibus in excelsis ....over and over again.

There came silence again, not one sound coming from his room. All of a sudden there came this huge flash of what seemed like lightening. But yet, how could it be as they were inside the house not outside, it was a very very strange sighting to say the least Madison thought to herself. This was followed by yet another loud bang an the shaking of the house. Then all that could be heard out loud was ......Sancti eritis mihi crux lucis. Quod ad Nunquam draco sit mihi dux. Apage, Satana scandalum away.

The Possession Of Uriel

Never me temptatis vanitatum tuam. Quid mihi malum venenum ipsum. Spoken over and over again.

About forty minutes later, Archbishop Timothy came out of Uriel's room with his head looking downwards at the floor.He was again re sighting a prayer.. Sancti eritis mihi crux lucis. Quod ad Nunquam draco sit mihi dux. Apage, Satana scandalum away. Never me temptatis vanitatum tuam. Quid mihi malum venenum ipsum. Over and over he was repeating this prayer.

He walked over to Madison and in a very low voice said, I am very sorry Madison but we have lost your son Uriel for he is gone. What, what repeated Madison are you telling me she asked, kneeling down on the floor beside her chair, kissing the Archbishop's hand.

Your son Uriel has past away, he could not get through the recitual, his body signs were too weak, I could not save him, so I prayed for his soul over and over. I am sorry for your loss but there was nothing else I could do. Archbishop Timothy walked away with his head held low and gazing towards the floor, repeating his prayer over and over. Sister Kathleen and Agatha followed closely behind him, praying as they walked towards the front door. He reached the front door to Madison's house and turned around to say goodbye my friend, all the evil spirits in your house are now gone, we have cleaned them away, they will not bother you ever again, but truly again, I am very sorry for the loss of your son. You may go in his room now, but please, don't be alarmed at what you see. Your son Uriel is now sleeping in peace, please visit your nearest priest and have a decent funeral for him for he really does deserve one. I will send a letter from the Archbishop John Tallient in Italy with our condolences. Archbishop, Sister Kathleen and Agatha turned around before leaving and seen Madison crying her eyes out, and trying to pray with her head looking downwards. Before they left Archbishop Timothy once again blessed their home.

Madison finally waved goodbye to them, turned around and went back into the kitchen. She stopped in the doorway then decided to walk into Uriel's room. Slowly she turned the door knob to his room and opened the door. Looking inside she saw the body of her son laying on his bed, motionless. Everything else in the room was thrown about like a hurricane had hit it, yet it did not. Madison slowly walked over to her son and kneeling down on the floor beside Uriel's bed, she lowered her head and started once again to pray for him, the only prayer she knew... Our Father who Art in Heaven, Hollowed be thy name, by Kingdom thy will be done on Earth as it is in Heaven. Give us our daily bread as we forgive those who trespass against us. But lead us not into temptation for thy is the kingdom, the power and glory forever and forever. Omen

Madison stayed there for quite some time, repeating her prayer over and over again until her knees started hurting, then she stood up and pulled the bed covers over the head of her son. She turned around and slowly left the room, closing the door behind her.

Soon she saw Ethan come in through the back door. She stood up from her chair and ran over to him hugging him very hard. Madison said to him, we have lost Uriel for he is gone. She looked up at Ethan with tears in her eyes. Ethan replied..What what has happened he asked? Madison pulled away from him and said. Come and sit at the table I will explain everything that happened today she told him. They both walked over to the table and sat down. Madison told Ethan everything that happened that day, and that Archbishop Timothy did all he could to save Uriel. We shall have to make funeral arrangements she told him, crying so much she could barely get the words out. They both sat there for quite some time holding each other. All of a sudden Destiny came in through the back door. Looking at both of her parents asked. What is going on ? Come and sit down Destiny, we have something to tell you. Destiny joined them at the kitchen table,and Madison told her what had happened. Now even Destiny started crying, all three family members just sat there for a while with their heads bowed.

Even though it was supper time no one was very hungry. Instead, Destiny pipped up and said, can I go in and see him mother can I she begged her? Ok if you want to, but please, don't take to long. Destiny walked off in the direction of Uriel's room, opened the door and slowly walked inside. She walked over to his bed, and uncovering his head saw him laying there, like nothing had happened. She stood there for a moment, returned the sheet covering his head, turned and left the room closing the door behind her, went inside her own room closing the door behind her. Ethan and Madison, finally stood up from the table, and went into their own room. Passing at Uriel's door Madison asked him if he wanted to go inside, Ethan replied no not at this time and kept walking.

The next day Ethan and Madison arranged funeral for Uriel and they had the ceremony their son two days later. Madison decided to cremate Uriel, not to bury him, as cremation in her mind would rid him of any bad spirits that were still inside him. After the arrangements were all finished, everyone got into their cars, there were a lot of people there that day, one day Madison will never forget, and left the church. Madison picked up the ashes of her son and carried him, back to their car and everyone got in as Ethan drove them home. After that day, there was no more happenings in their house. Madison referred to them as happenings, for she did not know what else to call it. Their house was silent once again, but all three family members where not quit themselves for a very long time after that. Five years later Ethan had become very ill and past away leaving Madison and Destiny to live alone in their house. Once again Madison had Ethan cremated not buried. There was a mantle piece in their living room, where Madison set the two Urns with the ashes of Uriel and Ethan, they sat there reminding her of their memories.

www.ingramcontent.com/pod-product-compliance
Lightning Source LLC
LaVergne TN
LVHW091535060526
838200LV00036B/614